Praise for The Amoveo Legend series

"Spellbinding… This fast-paced, jam-packed thrill ride will delight paranormal romance fans."

—*Publishers Weekly*

"Humphreys's skillful storytelling is so intriguing, you'll have a hard time putting this book down."

—*RT Book Reviews* Top Pick of the Month, 4.5 Stars

"Compelling… Searing lovemaking, interesting world-building—lions and tigers and bears, oh my!"

—*Booklist*

"Plenty of action, paranormal influences, and romance to satisfy your appetite. Being sated but greedy, I am waiting patiently right now for the next Amoveo adventure."

—*Night Owl Reviews* Reviewer Top Pick, 5 Stars

"A fast-paced, gripping story that starts out with a bang and continues straight to the explosive ending."

—*Fresh Fiction*

"Sexy and unique… a must-read for any paranormal fan!"

—*Booked and Loaded*

"Sara Humphreys knows how to keep a reader turning the pages."

—*Book Lovin' Mamas*

"Humphreys takes a chance and it works, completely and totally."

—*Tea and Book*

"Strong, admirable characters, a sizzling love story, and a seat-of-the-pants action plot."

—*Star-Crossed Romance*

"Amazing world-building, a great plot full of suspense and mystery, great characters, and, of course, a fated romance…"

—*The Romance Reviews* Top Pick

"Fast-paced mystery, twist and turns, lots of passion and romance. The last two chapters of this book will have you in awe!"

—NetGalley Reader Review

"Another sizzling, passion-filled book that will keep you engrossed."

—*RomFan Reviews*

"Outstanding… Red-hot love scenes punctuate a well-plotted suspense story that will keep readers turning pages as fast as they can."

—*Publishers Weekly* Starred Review

"A fresh and original take on shapeshifting… Humphreys takes on the challenge of creating a whole new world and mythology for the shapeshifting Amoveo clan."

—*Debbie's Book Bag*

"Sizzling sexual chemistry that is sure to please... I really can't wait to see where we go to next."

—*Yankee Romance Reviewers*

"A moving tale that captures both the sweetness and passion of romance."

—*Romance Junkies*, 5 Blue Ribbons

"*Unleashed* earned its Best Book rating in spades... The characters haunted my dreams and I thought about this book constantly."

—*The Long and Short of It Reviews*

"Spectacular... A stunning new shifter series will thrill paranormal fans who love the genre. A fascinating world."

—*Bookaholics Romance Book Club*

"A blend of intriguing urban fantasy with rich romantic overtures."

—*That's What I'm Talking About*

"Sweet and passionate. An enthralling story... Ms. Humphreys has created a fantastic world [that] will leave you wanting more."

—*Anna's Book Blog*

"The characters are very strong and warm... There is enough action and danger to keep it interesting and the romance is sexy."

—*Book Reviews by Martha's Bookshelf*

Also by Sara Humphreys

Unleashed
Untouched
Undenied (novella)
Untamed
Undone

SARA HUMPHREYS

sourcebooks
casablanca

Cover design by Jamie Warren
Cover image © Jon Feingersh Photography/SuperStock/Corbis
Cover image © Image Source/Getty Images
Cover image © John Foxx/Getty Images

Published by Sourcebooks Casablanca, an imprint of Sourcebooks, Inc.
P.O. Box 4410, Naperville, Illinois 60567-4410
(630) 961-3900
FAX: (630) 961-2168
www.sourcebooks.com

Printed and bound in the United States of America
VP 10 9 8 7 6 5 4 3 2 1

"You'll meet more angels on a winding path than on a straight one."

—Terri Guillemets

For my street team, Sara's Angels.

Thank you for your unwavering dedication and limitless enthusiasm. I am honored to be a part of your lives, and I thank you for joining me on this winding path.

Chapter 1

THE TANTALIZING SCENT FILLED HER HEAD THE MOMENT SHE slipped the key into the front door of her club.

Blood.

The sweet, cinnamon flavor titillated her heightened senses. Olivia's head snapped up sharply as fangs burst in her mouth. She closed her emerald green eyes and stilled as she breathed deeply and listened to the comforting noises of the night that blanketed her. The chatter of humans passing her on the city streets, cars idling, and horns honking filled her head.

Olivia sharpened her focus on the sounds within her club—her home. What the hell was going on in there? She remained motionless as the sound of light, feminine giggling came from deep within the building.

Her fangs retracted, and she swore with frustration. "Maya, you incredible asshole," she hissed.

Olivia threw the lock and pushed open the enormous mahogany doors, slamming them shut behind her with ease as she threw the main house lights on. She stood in the cavernous foyer of the old church with her hands on her hips, while she delivered a withering stare to the young vampire. Instead of looking contrite for being caught, Maya looked rather pleased with herself. As a human, Maya had been a giggling fool who delighted in toying with men, and now, as a vampire, she was in her glory.

She sat demurely on top of a human male, who was currently on all fours, acting as her makeshift throne. Maya's long blond hair washed over creamy, bare shoulders as her hands remained folded in her lap and her legs crossed sweetly at the ankles. The innocent pose was a stark contrast to the black leather bustier and miniskirt she wore.

She blinked her large blue eyes and laughed again, while the human grunted helplessly beneath her. Based on the look of him, if he weren't under her spell, he would never submit like this for a woman—ever. He was an enormous muscle-head who likely spent most of his waking hours at a gym in a desperate attempt to be the next Arnold Schwarzenegger.

At the moment, he was doing a great impersonation of a bench.

"How many times have I told you? Never play with your food in the club." She let out a sigh and softened her tone, reminding herself that Maya was still young. "It's not safe to do things like this, Maya. We don't want to draw unnecessary attention to ourselves, remember?"

Olivia pushed her thick, curly red hair out of her face and shrugged her long black coat off her slim shoulders. She knew that reprimanding Maya was useless, but felt the need to remind her of the rules. She'd only been turned a few years ago and was still in the defiant adolescent phase. Since Olivia was her sire, Maya was her responsibility for the first century of her immortality, but at the rate she was going—it was going to be longer than that.

"Maya?" Olivia folded her arms as her green eyes flashed with impatience at her uncooperative offspring. "Please get him out, and don't leave any loose ends."

"Oh, you're such a poop." Maya waved dismissively and looked at the pathetic fool beneath her. "We were just having a little fun," she said, stroking his head the way one would pet a dog. "Weren't we, baby?"

Maya smacked him on the ass, and he whimpered, a sound that hung somewhere between pleasure and pain. She straddled him like a horse and leaned in, slowly licking the blood that still dripped from the wound she'd made in his neck. Maya looked like a cat playing with a mouse. The poor bastard had probably been toyed with like this all day long, which meant Maya had not slept.

Great.

The smell of blood grew stronger, and Olivia watched Maya lick a trickle of red from his neck as she writhed seductively on his back. He closed his eyes, grunted, and shuddered as the orgasm ripped through him.

Olivia's fangs erupted, but she quickly willed them away, disgusted by her lack of self-control. It was no wonder this mess aroused her. Between the blood, the sexual energy, and her abstinence, it was bound to happen. Her maker, Vincent, never understood her self-imposed celibacy, although that wasn't terribly surprising—he'd never been in love. If he had watched the love of his life die in his arms, then he might have a better grasp of why Olivia was unwilling to open her heart again. Most vampires could separate sex and love, but that was one little piece of the vampire world she never adjusted to.

Olivia. She jumped as Vincent's sharp voice cut into her mind. *Just because you haven't had sex in centuries, that is no reason to start salivating over this childish nonsense*.

Speak of the devil. Olivia had not seen hide nor hair

of her maker in over fifty years, but given his emotional eavesdropping, he must be back in the city. If he had been more than fifty miles away, he would not have been able to sense her feelings so easily. *What can I do for you, Vincent?*

Do for me? Nothing, my dear. Can't a maker check in on his favorite offspring? Olivia tore her gaze away from Maya and swiftly walked behind the bar, creating busywork for herself in an effort to quell the bloodlust and the plain old lust. *I'm fine, Vincent.* She looked at Maya again briefly, before tending to the stock again. *I take it that you're back in the States? Does this mean that we can expect a visit from you this evening?*

Still celibate, Olivia? It's obviously not doing you any favors. I can smell your sexual frustration from miles away, and it's really quite unattractive.

Are you coming by the club or not? Olivia shielded the telepathic conversation between them because the last thing she needed was Maya, a youngling vampire, butting into it. Vampires could telepath with their sire, progeny, or siblings, and though Maya was her progeny, this conversation was definitely not for her.

Perhaps. His voice faded as the connection was broken.

Great. She shoved a stray curl from her face and swore under her breath. Maya decided to act up just when her own maker comes to town. What shitty timing.

"Maya," she said more firmly. "Your boy toy has to get going, and you've got to get to work."

This was her place of business, and she refused to encourage behavior that could jeopardize it, especially by a member of her own coven. She hated to admit it, but Vincent was right. The fact that she had been celibate for almost three centuries was really starting to grate on her.

At least she had sex dreams.

Her lips curved at the memories. She might've gone bonkers if it weren't for her dream lover and his talented hands. Three hundred years ago, he'd been her human lover and the only man she'd ever loved, but he was long dead and now only existed in her dreams. The dreamscape was the one place she could find pleasure after all these years.

There was just one problem. Vampires did not dream.

Aside from the lack of sunlight, the absence of dreams was one of the hardest losses for new vamps to adjust to. After over two centuries of enduring the leaden dreamless sleep of a vampire, Olivia had practically forgotten what it was like to dream, to fall through the mystical dreamscape and revel in fantasy.

Then, almost twenty years ago, out of nowhere, she began to dream again.

The first one freaked her out. It was a sudden burst of color and light after years of slumbering in utter darkness. Her dream lover looked just as he had when she first met him, a young boy entering manhood. Over the years, he aged in her dreams, just as he had when she knew him as a human.

As fascinated as she was by the dreams, as curious as she was to decipher their meaning, she did not dare mention them to anyone.

Olivia had heard of only one instance when vampires could dream—the bloodmate legend. Vincent told her the story soon after he turned her, and it gave her hope that her life would not be forever shrouded in the night.

However, when she tried to get him to tell her more, he dismissed her harshly and said he knew nothing. He scolded her for being a foolish child and told her the entire story was made up to placate new vampires while they got used to their new lives.

No one else had ever spoken of it, and the whole legend remained shrouded in secrecy and possessed an air of danger.

When the ghostly visits first began, she did some research online but found little information, and any references to the bloodmate legend were few and far between. According to the tale, when a vampire found a bloodmate and performed a blood exchange, then both became daywalkers.

She rubbed at the tattoo on the back of her neck absently. When Douglas's ghost began visiting her, she had the symbol of eternity inked on her neck, a private reminder of her lost love and her promise to love him, *and only him*, for eternity.

Olivia shook her head at her foolishness. Even if there were truth to the whole legend, it was a moot point, since Douglas was long dead. However, dead or not, she kept her pledge of devotion. Maybe the young, innocent girl she used to be lingered inside, because as far as Olivia was concerned, being devoted to someone meant that you did not diddle with anyone else.

Celibacy was a ridiculous notion for many humans, and positively insane for most vampires, at least the ones she encountered.

She sighed as she wiped the bar down and glanced at Maya with her flesh-and-blood plaything. Sympathy for the man tugged at what was left of her heart. Olivia didn't hate humans, quite the opposite in fact, but she did hate the idea of them being feasted on inside her club.

"Come on, Maya." She kept her voice even and her eyes trained on the bar stock, noting what needed to be refilled. "You've had enough fun for one day. Now, get him out, and don't forget to glamour him again before you leave him. Why don't you give him a pleasant memory? He was kind enough to provide you with life-giving blood, so the least you can do is give him a memory that will make him smile."

"Oh fine," she pouted. "He'll think we fucked like rabbits all day long and that he rocked my world."

Maya leaned in and licked his wound closed, leaving no evidence behind. She whispered to her prey, erasing all memory of their day together and replacing it with something palatable. He stood slowly and adjusted his crotch, while looking around the empty club somewhat bewildered.

"You better be back here in an hour ready to work," Olivia shouted. "I don't want to hear any complaining. You *chose* not to sleep, so don't make that *choice* a problem for the rest of us."

"My goodness, Olivia," Maya sang. "Getting cranky in our old age?"

Her singsong tone made Olivia want to smack her, but she could not prevent the smile that played at her lips. Maya was right. She was a little cranky, but three centuries of no sex or intimacy would do that to anyone.

"Cut the chatter, and get him out of here," she said more sharply than intended. She did not want Maya to know that she had been rattled by the situation, because she would never live it down. Olivia glanced at the human who stood there looking confused and found herself feeling sorry for him. "Seriously, let the poor guy off the hook."

"Hey… I gotta get going. I'm really tired. I think I should go." The big oaf babbled absently. "Man, my knees are killing me," he mumbled.

"Poor baby," Maya purred in a velvety soft voice as she glamoured the boy, giving him false memories in place of the real ones. "We should probably get going. Come on, kitten. I'll walk you out, but didn't we have fun at the park today? You're such a sweetheart for walking me to work this evening and for giving me multiple orgasms last night. You big stud."

Maya winked a long-lashed eye over her shoulder at Olivia, as they disappeared into the crisp winter night. Olivia shook her head and smiled in spite of how irritated she was. Maya absolutely loved being a vamp—she genuinely loved it, and there was something refreshing in her enthusiasm. Olivia never found that kind of passion for what she had become, and part of her was a tad jealous of Maya's love for her vampire life.

At first, Olivia had been disgusted and frightened, but Vincent had been a patient teacher, and eventually she accepted it.

But she never loved it.

Even when she served as a sentry for the Presidium, the vampire government, she did it out of duty, loyalty, and respect. She served her one hundred years as a soldier but retired as soon as her term was up and never looked back. Olivia enjoyed the quiet life of a private citizen, even though she never expected that to include a coven of her own.

As she readied the club for that evening's patrons, her

mind wandered to the night she sired Maya, and her smile quickly faded. She found her in the alley behind the club just before dawn, raped and beaten to within an inch of her life. The dirtbag who had done it dumped her there like garbage, and raw anger still flared at the memory.

Olivia sensed it the moment he dropped her broken body next to the dumpster. Maya would have died if she hadn't been turned; there was no time for ambulances or hospitals, and even though it had been almost five years since that night, she remembered it like it was yesterday. It was the last time she killed a human.

The memory both sickened and frightened her because when she drained that piece of shit dry—she loved every fucking minute. Olivia relished watching the fear in his eyes as she pinned him against the wall of his bedroom and savored his whimpering pleas for his life as he struggled uselessly. She took pure pleasure in feeling his heart slow, beat by beat, as the life faded from his eyes.

The red haze of rage consumed her, took her over, and blinded her.

Olivia swallowed the bile that rose in her throat, disgusted with her basest instincts and the primal pleasure she took from eviscerating him. She was a monster. A killer. No different from the vicious, pathetic excuse for a man she killed.

But there was a price to pay for her vengeance—there's always a price.

His blood memories would remain with her for eternity, and that was her penance. The horror and fear of all the women he raped lingered in her memories now, including Maya's last conscious, horrifying hours as a human.

Monsters don't go unpunished, and Olivia knew she was no different.

⁂

The music pounded loudly through the club as it reverberated through Olivia's body. She walked the dance floor, taking note of the various humans writhing with one another amid the pulsating lights. She stuck out like a sore thumb, since she was the only one wearing a black Armani suit, not the leather or spikes of her faithful patrons.

Olivia waved at the regular customers peppered throughout the club and allowed herself a moment of pride. The Coven had become one of the most popular dance clubs for the Goth set in NYC, and she had worked her ass off to make it happen.

She paced the floor more than usual tonight because she had been on edge ever since walking in on Maya. She could not afford any mistakes that would draw human attention or piss off the Presidium. Humans were easy enough to deal with, but she was less than pleased at the idea of vampire officials butting their noses into her life.

She liked it here and had no desire to leave, but the drawback of immortality was that moving on eventually was an annoying necessity—can't stay somewhere for thirty years if you don't age. Although, the prevalent use of Botox among humans certainly helped explain her lack of facial wrinkles.

Olivia scoped out the club and marveled at how far society had come—and yet not.

Humans who loved to dress like vampires, or what they thought vampires looked like, flocked to this place every night as the sun went down. Except Sunday—she closed the joint on Sunday, since the place used to be a church. She figured it was the least she could do. Olivia grinned and shook her head as she watched the humans wooing one another in their *vampire* garb.

Ironically, most vampires did not dress like horror-movie rejects; many adopted the fashion of the era they lived in, but not all did. Vincent, for example, liked the Victorian era so much that sometimes he still adorned himself in a top hat and ascot, although she thought it looked ridiculous. Vampires retained their individuality at least.

Imagine if they knew this club was owned and operated by an actual vampire who preferred silk and cashmere to leather and spikes. Olivia had to wear the leather sentry uniform every day for a century and loathed the idea of wrapping herself in it again.

I'd be a sad disappointment to them.

She glanced to the bar as she made her way to the DJ platform. Maya was playing up her charms with various drooling idiots who were only too happy to give her enormous tips in exchange for the smallest bit of her attention.

Trixie, her other bartender, was Maya's opposite but worked her charms with equal fervor. Her short pink-spiked hair and black eyeliner were a stark contrast to Maya's blond, innocent look. Both vamps were great at bringing in the crowd and keeping them happy. They gave a quick wave to Olivia as she passed, and Maya stuck her tongue out in her usual flippant, childish manner.

Olivia climbed onto the DJ's platform and gave Sadie a pat on the back. Sadie was one of the best spinners out there, living or undead, and Olivia's oldest, most trusted friend. She was dressed much like the patrons of the club, except Sadie actually *was* a vamp, and the girl had a serious passion for leather and lace.

"Hey, boss. Feels like a lively crowd tonight." Sadie winked and smiled. "No pun intended."

"Did you hear what Maya did?" Olivia kept her eyes focused on the crowd, her senses alert for anything out of the ordinary. A sense of impending doom flickered up her spine. Trouble was coming. "She's a pain in my ass."

"Sure did, and she sure is." Sadie put her headphones around her neck. "Think that girl will ever listen?" she asked with a nod toward the bar, as she laughed and pushed her long brown hair out of her eyes. "'Cause I don't."

"Maya's still young." Olivia gave Sadie a friendly nudge with her elbow. "It took you a little while to get the hang of it, if I'm not mistaken?"

Sadie was the first vamp she had ever turned. Olivia and Vincent were traveling through a largely unsettled part of Arizona and picked up the distinctly potent scent of blood. The Apache Indians had been attacking settlers at that time, not that Olivia could blame them, and Sadie's family had been among their victims.

Sadie was barely alive when she found her. The faint beat of her heart called to Olivia, and before she even knew what she was doing, she turned her. It was an instinctive need to save her, to help this poor girl who had lost everything, left seemingly alone in the world.

Vincent, of course, was less than pleased, and that was the beginning of the end for them.

Olivia looked fondly at her friend and smiled. "You

have been around a couple hundred years longer than she has."

"Truth." Sadie winked and adjusted the headphones around her neck. "You're just a sucker for hard-luck cases. Face it. You would rescue the world if you could."

"Not the *whole* world," Olivia said dramatically. "Just the ones who really need it."

"I sure needed it," Sadie said with a warm smile.

Olivia swallowed the surprising lump in her throat before looking back at the crowd. Sadie had tried to thank her on several occasions, but Olivia never let her get the words out. Deep down inside she felt as though she hadn't saved Sadie or the others. Perhaps the vampire hunters of the world were right. What if vamps really were damned to burn in hell for eternity? Would anyone thank her then?

"I should get back down there before Maya finds another boy toy."

Sadie grabbed the microphone and Olivia's arm before she could escape.

"Everyone having fun?" Sadie bellowed into the silver microphone. The crowd responded with insanely loud screaming and whistling. "Then I think we should all give it up for Olivia Hollingsworth, the owner and proprietor of The Coven."

Olivia waved to the screaming crowd and shot her friend a narrow-eyed look as she made her way down from the altar. She hated being the center of attention, and Sadie knew it but delighted in razzing her on occasion.

Another loud, bass-driven song tumbled over the crowd as Sadie's voice floated into her head. *Hey, boss.*

I see our VIP table is full again tonight with your boyfriend and his crew.

Olivia threw an irritated glance over her shoulder at Sadie and shot back. *He's not my boyfriend. He just wishes he was. What a termite.* She could hear Sadie stifle a giggle as she navigated the crowd and made her way to Michael's table.

How long has it been since you got laid? I forget. Olivia did her best to ignore that last jab from her friend. Other than Vincent, Sadie was the only one who knew that Olivia had been celibate since becoming a vampire. *Don't you think you've tortured yourself long enough? I never knew this Douglas guy, but if he really loved you the way you say he did, would he want you to spend eternity alone?*

I'm not alone. Olivia threw a wink over her shoulder. *I've got all of you, and sex is overrated anyway.*

Damn. Sadie's laugh jingled through Olivia's mind. *Now you're just talking crazy.*

Olivia shook her head and smiled. Her heart had been stolen long before Vincent made it stop beating, and besides, even if she did have her heart to give, Moriarty certainly would not be a candidate.

Michael was a greasy little worm who used his family's reputation to get what he wanted. He came to The Coven every Saturday night with his gaggle of dirtbags, and Olivia could smell his fear and feelings of inadequacy a mile away. He'd been trying to get into her pants for months now, and apparently was still trying, even after a multitude of rejections.

She felt his eyes on her all night and had managed to ignore him, but now it was time to play the game.

She had to placate the little weasel. Jerk or not, he was a customer—a customer who spent a lot of money in her club.

Olivia flashed the most charming grin she could muster as she approached Michael and his motley crew.

"Hey there, hot stuff." He leered at her and his lips curved into a lascivious grin. "I was wondering how long it was gonna take you to get your sweet ass over here."

She wanted to bite his face off. What an asshole.

"Hello, Mr. Moriarty," she said through a strained smile. "Are you gentlemen finding everything satisfactory this evening?"

"We're just fine, aren't we, boys?"

He took a long sip of his martini as he ran his hand up the leg of some young girl who was draped all over him, probably believing he'd make her rich and famous. She definitely didn't fit in with the other clubgoers. This blond was more mainstream and never would have stepped foot into The Coven if it weren't for Moriarty. Many humans were easily swayed by money and power. Moriarty had both.

"I'd be doin' a lot better if you'd come here and sit with me."

The girl next to him made a noise of disgust, shoved his hand away, grabbed her purse, and stomped off. He shrugged and snickered as she stalked through the crowd toward the door.

"It seems you've upset your date, Mr. Moriarty." Olivia watched the foolish girl run from the club. She probably expected him to chase her. Not likely. "Looks like she's leaving."

"She's not my date," he spat. "Just some bimbo

hanger-on—you know how it is. She should know better than to do that." His lip curled in disgust as he watched her leave, and the smile faded. Olivia felt the anger roll off him as he stared after her. "I don't give second chances. One and done. Know what I mean?"

"Yes, of course." Olivia smiled tightly and looked at him like the black-haired little bug he was. "Well, *gentlemen*, I hope you'll let me buy the final round here. It's almost last call."

She motioned to the waitress who covered the three VIP tables opposite the bar. Suzie, one of only two humans who worked at The Coven, came over quickly, but Olivia sensed her anxiety long before she arrived at the table.

"Sure, baby." He leered. "You can buy me a drink."

Olivia wanted nothing more than to glamour this guy into dancing naked in the middle of the club with only his socks on, but the image alone would have to be enough.

"Suzie. Please get our guests their last round." She flicked her gaze back to Moriarty. "On the house, of course."

"Yes, ma'am." She looked like a skittish lamb surrounded by wolves. She almost hadn't hired Suzie due to her naive nature, but Olivia was a sucker for hard-luck cases. Suzie was straight from the farm and as green as the fields. By hiring her, she figured she could at least keep an eye on her.

Olivia nodded and said a brief good-bye before working her way to the front door. The place was starting to thin out, since it was just about last call. The tension in her shoulders eased as soon as she set eyes on the only other human who worked at the club—their bouncer Damien.

Damien, unlike Suzie, knew what Olivia and the others were. He was what some referred to as a *familiar*, but Olivia hated that term. It seemed like a dirty word, laced with innuendo and ill intent. Most humans who worked with vampires did it out of love and friendship.

However, Damien wasn't just a friend—he was more like family. He was the only human who knew what Olivia was and kept her secret, and not because he had to, but because he genuinely cared for her. She'd met him when he was a boy, spending most of his time on the streets and clearly heading down a bad path.

She'd heard his cries one night, and even though it was against Presidium rules to interfere with humans and their problems, she couldn't help it. That cry of a young boy in the dark overrode any rules she was supposed to follow, and before she knew it, she was plucking him from what was sure to be a deadly situation.

She planned to rescue him from the local drug dealer and send him on his way. Yet the second she looked into those soulful, brown eyes, she was hooked. At first, she told herself that she would only check on him for a few nights to be sure he was safe, but those few nights turned into weeks, and then years. Since vampires couldn't have children, Damien was the closest she'd ever have to a child, and she loved him as if he was her own.

"Hey there, handsome," Olivia said. She walked through the vestibule crowded with folks leaving for the night. "How's it going out here?"

"Hey there, boss," Damien said in his deep baritone.

He gave her his trademark toothy, white smile, the

one that completely changed the perception of who he was. He was a wall of solid muscle, stood over six feet tall, and had lovely olive skin. One look from this hulking fellow would send most people running, but in reality, Damien was a giant teddy bear.

"So is everything okay on your end tonight? Nothing, um, out of the ordinary?" Olivia asked as she scanned the exiting crowd warily. Damien raised one eyebrow at her skeptically. "You know, out of the ordinary for us?" she clarified.

"Just the usual fare and a few drunken idiots. I did have one crier though, just a little while ago," he said as he pulled the velvet ropes in for the night. "She looked pretty upset. I tried to stop her, but she ran away, down toward Sixth Ave."

"Mmm." Olivia rolled her eyes. "That was Moriarty's date."

"Moriarty's still here?" Damien had barely finished the question, when Michael appeared in the vestibule with his posse.

"We were just leaving, big guy." Michael gave him a smack on the back as he walked to the enormous stretch limo waiting at the curb. Olivia put her hand on Damien to keep him at bay. She couldn't blame him for wanting to go after him, because she wanted to punch the little bastard's lights out too.

"You know, Olivia, one day that guy is gonna get what's coming to him," Damien said quietly as the limo pulled away. "I just hope I get to see it."

"You know what they say, babe," she said quietly. "Be careful what you wish for. Besides, his money is as green as anyone's."

"I realize you're not into live feeds like most of your *crowd*, but boy, does that guy deserve to be dinner or what? I know you can handle yourself, but I don't like the way he speaks to Suzie or any other woman for that matter."

"I know." Olivia smiled and rubbed his arm reassuringly. She knew he had a crush on Suzie but would never admit it. "Suzie is tougher than you think, and you know I've always got her back. Besides," she said in a weary voice, "Moriarty's not worth the trouble."

"Hey, you okay?" He looked at her worriedly with his arms folded across his massive chest. "Did you feed today?"

"Yeah, well, not a live feed, obviously," she quickly added. "Just from my microwaveable stock, which reminds me, we need to place another order with the Presidium's blood bank."

She rubbed her temples absently as various patrons pushed past as they left. Live feeds were always best, but Olivia tried to avoid them. While the live feed was most rejuvenating, it was also the most dangerous. Live feeds were like a drug. The more she did it, the more she wanted it, and each time it got harder and harder to stop. Besides, blood memories came with it, and she wasn't interested in anyone else's baggage. She had quite enough of her own shit to deal with.

"This incident with Maya earlier really rattled me. She's got to learn not to feed in or near the club," she said with frustration. "I don't want any trouble. I mean, it's not just my place of business. We live here too."

"What happened exactly?" Damien asked quietly. He leaned down and looked around to make sure no one would overhear. "I saw her leave with him last night after closing, so how'd she end up back here? I got some of the dirt from Trixie, but then Suzie came around, and well, you know." He shrugged and smiled sheepishly.

He knew Olivia wanted to keep Suzie in the dark about the vamps because it was bad enough she'd let Damien in on their world. It took years for the Presidium to accept him, and *accept* would be a generous description of their feelings on humans in the know. *Tolerate* was a more appropriate word.

"I saw her leave with that meathead last night after closing. I figured she'd ditch him before sunrise, so I locked up and went downstairs to sleep. Then tonight, right after sundown, I go run an errand, and when I come back, I find her in the middle of the club with her boy toy." Olivia looked past him and through the door at Maya, who was cleaning up the bar. "She obviously brought him back here just before sunrise and messed with him all day long. I'm not sure why she'd do that," she murmured.

"My guess is that she wanted to get a rise out of you. Want me to talk to her?"

"No." She shook her head. "I'll speak to her again before she leaves tonight. She's my…"

"Responsibility," Damien finished for her. He sighed and shook his head. "Not everyone is your responsibility, you know."

"No, but *she* is." Olivia patted his shoulder wearily. "I hear the last song of the night." Sadie always played The Strike Nineteens's "Forever in Darkness" as the final tune, and the irony was never lost on Olivia. "Time to go inside and clear out the stragglers."

As she turned to go back inside, an oddly familiar voice floated over, and the scent of the ocean filled her head.

"Excuse me. Can you tell me where I can find Ms. Olivia Hollingsworth?"

Olivia stopped dead in her tracks, and the tattoo on the nape of her neck burned. Her fangs erupted, and little licks of fire skittered up her spine, as one note of that smooth, velvety voice banished all self-control. She closed her eyes and willed her quaking body to settle.

It can't be.

Terrified and hopeful, Olivia steeled herself with courage she'd forgotten she had. She turned around, excruciatingly slowly, and found herself face-to-face with the man of her dreams and the love of her life.

The problem was he'd been dead for almost three hundred years.

Chapter 2

DOUG GAPED AT HER LIKE AN IDIOT. A WOMAN HE NEVER expected to see in the flesh stood in front of him, larger than life, staring with the most intense green eyes he'd ever seen—the same green eyes that had haunted his sleep since he could remember. Her curly red hair flowed over slim shoulders and glinted brightly like flickering firelight in the glow of the New York City night. The fire framed creamy ivory skin, which he had the sudden urge to nibble, as he had so many times in his dreams.

The tattoo of the dagger on his back burned, and one word flickered through his mind—the same word he heard when he slept. *Eternity*. Doug blinked but didn't take his eyes off hers.

He'd gotten the damn tattoo as a way to make the redheaded goddess from his dreams more tangible, but here she was, looking all kinds of tangible. He dreamt of her ever since he could remember, but now she—or someone who looked just fucking like her—was standing here in the flesh.

She was dressed impeccably in a jet-black suit that hugged her long, well-formed figure. Doug's mouth went dry, and for a second he forgot how to speak. The most breathtakingly beautiful woman he had ever seen was here, and he stood there staring like a mindless boob.

She looked at him as though he was from Mars, and for a second he thought she was going to laugh right in his face. *Speak. For Christ sake, say something, you moron!* Doug straightened to his full six feet, two inches and cleared his throat, hoping neither she, nor the giant bodyguard, noticed how she'd thrown him off balance. It was never good for a cop to lose his bearings, especially when investigating a murder and speaking with a possible suspect.

Thankfully, his partner spoke up and saved him from his own stupidity.

"You'll have to forgive my partner. He's so used to dealing with the scum of society that he's forgotten how to speak to a beautiful woman." Tom quickly flashed a charming smile and his badge to the stunner and the bodyguard. "I'm Detective Tom Daly, homicide. This massive mute next to me is—"

"Doug Paxton, ma'am," he finally managed to croak out. Doug reached into his jacket pocket and quickly flashed his badge as well.

"I'm Olivia Hollingsworth. How can I help you, officers?" she asked coolly, her arms crossed tightly across her chest. Doug cocked his head and eyed her more carefully. Even though her voice remained calm, her body language screamed how uncomfortable she was. She rubbed the back of her neck briefly with one graceful hand, before folding her arms over her chest again.

Now his radar was on full tilt.

Something was up here. He had a knack for sniffing out trouble, and this woman—no matter how gorgeous she was and how much she might look like the siren from his dreams—had it written all over her.

"We're investigating the death of one Ronald Davis," Tom said as he perused the small notepad in his hand.

"I'm sorry. I don't know anyone by that name." She turned her head slightly toward the bouncer but never took her bright green eyes off Doug. "Do you, Damien?"

His attention was now drawn to the enormous bouncer who looked more like a mountain than a man, and the muscles in his arms that were barely contained by the leather jacket. He hadn't taken his glare off Doug for a second and had positioned himself in a protective posture near the Hollingsworth woman.

When he opened his mouth, the voice matched the body.

"Nope," he uttered in a deep baritone. "Can't say that I do."

Doug took the picture out of his pocket and held it up for the odd couple to have a look at. He kept his attention focused on the woman, looking for any sign of recognition, but she didn't flinch.

"Don't recognize him?" Doug asked quietly as he kept his gaze fixed on her oval face. She reminded him of a porcelain doll with smooth, delicate skin, and he'd bet his entire shitty salary that it tasted like snow.

Concentrate, Paxton. Jesus. What the hell is wrong with me?

He cleared his throat, hoping that his partner didn't notice how off balance this woman made him. "Could he have been here in the club last night?"

"I have hundreds of people in and out of here six nights a week, officer. Could he have been here? Sure," she added with a casual shrug.

"Well, ma'am," Tom began, "we hate to be pests, but

according to his friends, he was here last night real late. Until closing. We were told he was buzzing around one of your bartenders. A pretty, little blond… by the name of…" Tom looked at his notes.

"Maya," Doug finished.

He locked eyes with the Hollingsworth woman, and a shock went straight to his dick. His gaze slid to her full lips. Damn. He bet they were soft and sweet, like plums in the summertime. It was all he could do to keep from reaching out to touch her and see if he was right. He glanced into those glittering pools of green, and he could swear she smirked. If he didn't know better, he'd think she knew exactly what was going through his dirty mind.

Heat crept up his neck at his lack of professionalism. He'd never flirted with anyone while on an investigation, but this woman had him forgetting himself on every level. Doug cleared his throat and focused on the notes he was making in a useless attempt to stop ogling her. That lasted about three seconds, before he found himself looking into those bright green eyes once again.

"Maya is one of our bartenders," she said, with a polite smile. She turned to Damien. "Go get Maya please, so we can straighten this out."

Damien nodded and went inside to get the girl.

"Ms. Hollingsworth," Doug began in an attempt to regain some semblance of professionalism.

"Olivia. Please call me Olivia." Her voice softened a bit. "Would you gentleman like to come inside? The club is just closing up."

"No. Thank you, ma'am—I mean, Olivia." Doug felt foolish, like some adolescent schoolboy.

"So how was he killed, Detective Daly?" Her attention shifted immediately to Tom, and the icy tone had returned as quickly as it had left. Doug sighed. He would never understand women.

"Well, you see, ma'am, they found him inside a dumpster over on Second Ave. Someone cut him up pretty good." Tom stopped suddenly, slapped Doug in the chest, and nodded past Olivia.

Doug saw the bouncer approaching with a sexy blond, and the moment he set eyes on her, he knew she wasn't the doer. She was far too small to have put Ronald in the dumpster—at least without help.

He glanced at his partner. Tom had a weakness for sweet, young things like this one, which was why he was no longer married. The petite bartender looked innocent, but Doug had enough time on the street to know that she was *anything* but that, and the image of a black widow spider came to mind.

She wasn't the kind to kill a man dead and leave him a dumpster. No. She was the kind to rip out your heart and laugh all the way to the bank.

A different kind of deadly, but deadly nonetheless.

Olivia turned to see Damien on his way out of the club with Maya. She looked back in time to see the two cops smile and exchange a knowing look. *Typical*. Olivia struggled to keep from rolling her eyes. Detective Daly may have been old enough to be Maya's father, but that didn't stop him from wanting to bang her. Most men wanted to bang Maya, along with plenty of women for that matter.

"So, I hear you two handsome officers want to speak to little old me?" Maya's singsong voice made Olivia want to puke.

Olivia pulled Maya close and put an arm around her. "Maya, these two detectives are investigating the death of a young man. Do you know him? Perhaps you served him last night at the bar?" *If you know what's good for you, you will act like you barely recognize him. You are in such deep shit with me, Maya, it's not even funny.*

Doug held up the picture, and Maya looked sweetly at it, with all the innocence she could muster. She shook her head and tossed her long blond locks over her bare shoulders with one hand. It was moments like this that Olivia wished like hell she could telepath with Damien.

"He's awful cute." Maya smiled. "Yes, sir. I saw him here last night. He put away plenty of beers, and when that happens, well, you know how flirty boys can be," she said, batting her huge blue eyes. "But I didn't really pay much attention to him after I served his drinks. After we closed up for the night, I hit the sack." She giggled. "A girl just can't get enough beauty sleep. Sorry I can't be of more help, officers."

Olivia was surprised by the violent and uncharacteristic surge of jealousy that flared inside of her. She had the ridiculous urge to beat the crap out of Maya for looking at Doug the way she did. Flustered, she straightened up and dropped her arm from Maya's shoulders, hoping that her jealousy wasn't visible to anyone but herself.

Doug put the picture back in his notebook and smiled at Maya. Olivia's jealousy subsided when she saw he looked at Maya the way one would look at a silly child. *At least he's smart,* she thought.

"Maya lives here in one of the apartments in my building, and I can assure you that she was at the club working until well past closing. Thank you, Maya," Olivia said a bit too quickly. "Why don't you go back and help the girls clean up?"

Maya locked her big blue eyes on Detective Daly and winked. "Be sure to come and have a drink with us some time, detective." Giggling, she flounced back inside the club.

Olivia noticed that the older man couldn't take his eyes off her ass, which wasn't surprising. Men fell all over themselves to get her attention when she was human, and now that she was a vampire—all bets were off.

Doug, however, kept his attention on Olivia, which she found surprisingly unsettling. It had been centuries since anyone made her so on edge and uncertain of herself. Hell, she was a retired sentry and had spent the better part of a century kicking all kinds of supernatural ass, so feeling like some kind of lovesick teenager was bizarre.

"Well, if you do remember anything, please don't hesitate to call." Doug handed his business card to Olivia and delivered the most knee-buckling, dimpled smile she'd seen in centuries. "Anytime. Day or night."

Her lips curved, and it was all she could do to keep her fangs at bay.

When Olivia took the card, her fingertips brushed his, and every coherent thought flew out of her head as the tattoo on her neck tingled warmly. His intense blue eyes captured hers, and if her heart still beat, it would've stopped.

She studied his handsome and painfully familiar face

with genuine awe. The chiseled cheekbones, square jaw, perfect nose, and full lips added up to the man she used to know and the lover from her dreams.

She wasn't crazy—he looked and sounded exactly like Douglas. For shit's sake, they had the same first name.

Bloodmate.

The word ran through her mind over and over, like a broken record.

His dark blond hair looked as thick as she remembered and probably felt just as good. However, it was those sharp, turquoise blue eyes that set her on fire and ignited something far more than bloodlust. His gaze remained locked with hers, and the exquisite pang of desire flared brightly, warming her normally chilly body.

In that brief moment, she remembered what it felt like to be alive.

Doug started to leave with his partner but stopped and turned to face Olivia. "By the way, Ms. Hollingsworth, if we need to speak with you again, is this the best place to reach you?"

Olivia smiled before she could stop herself. "Yes, detective. I live in an apartment within the building." She reached into the pocket of her slacks and retrieved her black and silver business card. "You showed me yours, so it's only fair that I show you mine."

Doug gave her a knowing smile and took the card from her fingers without looking away.

"My personal cell number is listed on the back." She arched one eyebrow. "Feel free to call me if you *require* anything at all."

"Good to know," he said softly, before looking at the card. "Thank you, Olivia."

"Yo, Paxton," Tom called from the corner. "We gotta go, man."

"Duty calls." Before he disappeared around the corner, Doug looked back and flashed that disarming smile one more time. She caressed his business card between her fingers and rubbed her tongue along the tip of her fangs. The combination of anger, lust, and longing had sent her body into overdrive.

A customer had been murdered, and the love of her life was back from the grave.

Fate was one cruel bitch.

Unnerved, and off her game, Olivia turned and swept through the almost-empty club with her sights set on Maya. *As soon as this place clears out, I want the entire coven at the bar for a meeting. No excuses, Maya.* Her voice touched their collective minds with all the force she'd intended, and the concerned looks exchanged between them weren't lost on her.

She was annoyed with the mess Maya had made and totally off balance by the appearance of Doug. However, at that particular moment, she didn't give a crap how uncomfortable it made the rest of them. Maya had brought this shit-show to their doorstep, and it was about time she learned to take responsibility for her actions.

Olivia strode past without sparing a glance at anyone, went directly to her office with the Authorized Personnel Only sign, and shut the door quickly behind her. She closed her eyes and leaned against the door, struggling to gather control over her hot-wired body. Her head spun as that word continued to thunder through her mind—*bloodmate*.

"Douglas is back from the dead, Maya might've

killed a guy, and both events happen when Vincent is in town." Olivia pressed the heels of her hands against her eyes. "Awesome."

A warm, furry body rubbed against her legs, and a familiar whine filled the room. Olivia looked down and smiled wearily at the loyal German shepherd. He barked his welcome and sat on his haunches, waiting for her to give him a proper greeting.

"What?" Olivia shook her head, squatted next to the enormous dog, and rubbed his brown and black coat. "I know, I know. I should've seen the Maya thing coming. She's still a youngling and has a hearty appetite for screwing around with the boys. Maybe I'm showing my age, or maybe I just don't give a shit anymore? Either way, it's sloppy, and when the Presidium gets wind of this, there's going to be hell to pay. Not to mention Vincent's impending visit. Shit."

Van Helsing licked her face and put his large paw on her knee in his own version of a hug.

"Hey!" Olivia laughed. "I just got this suit."

Van Helsing growled and dropped his paw.

"But I appreciate the gesture."

She scratched his ears before making her way to her desk. Olivia sat in the large leather chair, and Van immediately lay at her feet, as he was prone to do.

"If Maya killed that kid and made this mess, then we're in some deep shit, my friend. You know how the Presidium feels about messy and public human killings."

Van Helsing lifted his head and watched her intently. She spoke to him as if he could actually understand her, and sometimes she was convinced he did.

She didn't want to scare Maya or the others, but the

severity of the crime was not one to take lightly. The only disruption the vampire government hated more than messy human killings were unregistered new vampires—that was *the* biggest indiscretion as far as the elders were concerned. All seasoned vampires were limited to two vampires per year, and they had to be registered with the Presidium records keeper in their district immediately.

Olivia held up the white business card and read his name over and over.

Doug Paxton.

Her lips lifted as she switched on the computer. Not only did he look and sound exactly like her young lover from her human life, but he also had the same first name. Even though it had been close to three centuries since she'd laid eyes on him in the flesh, she'd never forget that silky smooth voice or those piercing blue eyes.

Douglas was killed the same night she was turned, and the memory of it still stung.

Shaking off the unpleasant memories, she did a quick search online and found a considerable amount of information on the detective. Apparently, he arrested a serial killer who had been hacking up hookers in the city.

He was about thirty years old, had been raised in a series of foster homes, and once on the force, he climbed quickly to the rank of detective. There was no mention of family, and he seemed married to his job.

However, another name in the article captured her attention—Pete Castro.

Pete was a newly turned vampire and currently worked as a sentry for the Presidium. The emperor appointed Pete to the position within a couple of months of being turned, and in true Emperor Zhao fashion, he didn't explain why. He simply did it. Pete now reported to the Czar of New York, Augustus. He and his senators lorded over this district with the kind of decadent laziness that many ancient vampires succumbed to after centuries of existence.

Pete was the last vampire Olivia turned, and she only did it as a favor for her friend, Marianna. She may not have a beating heart, but Olivia wasn't heartless. Marianna had finally found her life mate, and Olivia could not bear the idea of her friend suffering the same lonely existence that she had, so she turned Pete before he died. Marianna was an Amoveo, a shapeshifter, and having a vampire for a mate was a first for the shifters, but Marianna didn't care. The implications their mating might have did not even cross her mind; she simply could not live without Pete.

Olivia let out a sigh and kept her gaze fixed on the black-and-white photo of Doug that glowed brightly on the screen. The serious, brooding eyes looked back with gut-wrenching familiarity.

Marianna *could have* lived without Pete—Olivia knew that better than anyone—but she did not *have to*.

According to this article, Pete was Doug's former partner and helped him crack this case, among others. Olivia smirked at the interesting connection. She knew Pete had been a cop, but what were the odds that he was Doug's former partner? She should be able to get the inside scoop on Doug from her latest progeny, a bright light in a quickly darkening situation.

A knock at her office door ripped her from her thoughts and had her abruptly closing the browser window on her computer. Van Helsing hopped to his feet and trotted to the door with his long tail wagging behind him.

It was Pete. Van loved Pete almost as much as he loved her. She sensed him immediately, as she would with any of her progeny, but Pete's presence was stronger than the others due to his unusual heritage.

"Come in, Pete," Olivia said as she sat back in the leather desk chair.

The door swung open, and to her surprise the entrance was empty, but seconds later, Pete's smiling face peered around the corner. "Is it safe to come in?"

Van barked, which immediately elicited scratches behind the ears from Pete. Satisfied with the greeting, Van returned to his spot by Olivia's feet.

"What are you talking about?" Olivia tried to sound blasé, but her frustration got the better of her.

Pete shook his head and shut the door.

"I heard your meeting *request*."

He leaned against the wall next to the door and removed his leather gloves, before stuffing them into the pockets of his long black leather coat. Dressed in the standard paramilitary sentry uniform, he cut an imposing figure as a human or a vampire. His weapons, an arsenal of guns, silver ninja stars, and knives, were hidden discreetly beneath his coat, yet remained easily accessible.

"I know I don't live here. However, I am part of the coven, so I still heard you loud and clear. One benefit of being your progeny, correct? This special meeting wouldn't have anything to do with that guy who turned up in a dumpster here in the Village, would it?"

"Shit." Her green eyes flicked to Pete's. "The Presidium already got wind of this?"

"Nope." He shrugged. "Old habits die hard. I listen to the police scanner from time to time and keep an eye out for Doug. I saw him here earlier with his partner."

Relief washed over her because she needed to get ahead of this mess. Ideally, she would squash it before they even heard about it, and at the very least, she needed more information in case they called her to task.

Olivia narrowed her eyes and wagged a scolding finger. "I can't imagine that the czar would take kindly to you spending your time and energy looking after human affairs. I'm sure Augustus has far more important jobs for you to do in the district."

"Like I give a crap," Pete scoffed loudly. "They don't own me, and I'll look after whoever I want. If they don't like it, they can kiss my vampire-demon ass. Besides, you're my maker, and my mate's best friend. As far as I'm concerned, your opinion is the only one that matters." He grinned. "Boss lady."

Olivia laughed at his ridiculous nickname for her and smiled with pride. She secretly adored the fact that he was a bit of a rebel because he threw off the Presidium's pomp and circumstance, like she did when she was a sentry. Her maker, Vincent, never had the same appreciation for that kind of rebellious nature; instead, it served as a source of embarrassment for him.

"I knew I liked you." Her brow knitted with concern. "How's it going, by the way? Any other side effects from your demon lineage, or is daywalking the main consequence?"

Pete shifted his feet and looked away. Olivia knew

how uncomfortable he was discussing his demon bloodline. The poor guy had only found out a few days before he was turned into a vampire, but he had adapted surprisingly well. The fact that he was already mated to a shapeshifter likely helped him adjust faster than a human who had no knowledge of the supernatural creatures who lived in their midst. Most vamps had a hard time accepting their new life at first.

"It turns out I don't require sleep, at least not the way most vampires do, and when I do sleep, I don't dream anymore. Is that normal?"

"Yes," she said abruptly. "Sorry, I forgot to warn you about that."

Had she forgotten? Or had she conveniently avoided the subject, since it made her incredibly uncomfortable that she was dreaming again? Until Doug Paxton showed up at her club tonight, she assumed it was a ghost visiting her, but now that she'd met the detective, she had no fucking idea what was going on. Damn it.

Olivia's eyes captured his briefly, and she cleared her throat. "What else?"

"I tolerate sunlight to a point, silver stings but doesn't burn me like most vamps, and I can manipulate heat, but that's it as far as the demon stuff." His serious eyes locked on hers, and his lips set in a tight line. "They hate it, you know. The czar and his senators—they really hate the fact that I can daywalk."

"I know," Olivia sighed and rubbed her eyes. "The daywalking ability really galls them because they all want it, they *desperately* want it, and they'll never have it. I still think that's why the emperor appointed you to the position of sentry so quickly. Well, that, and the fact you're a liaison to the Amoveo." She smirked. "If you work for them then it's easier for them to keep an eye on you."

"What about that bloodmate legend?"

"Bloodmates?" Olivia stilled and leveled a serious look in his direction. She had never told Pete about it. Her voice dropped low. "Who told you about that?"

"You probably shoulda," he teased good-naturedly as he wagged a finger at her. "Marianna told me. If a vampire finds his or her bloodmate and bonds, then both become daywalkers. Right?"

"Please."

Olivia rolled her eyes and put her Louboutin-clad feet on the desk, attempting to seem casual when she was actually freaking out. She wasn't even sure what was happening with Doug, so she certainly did not want to drag Pete into it. They had enough on their plate with the dead guy.

She kept her voice light and a smile in her eyes. "I didn't tell you because it's a silly, made-up story, and that's all it will ever be. Vamps have been chasing after that one since God was a boy."

"Maybe. But rumors usually spawn from a grain of truth," Pete murmured as he studied her intently, but Olivia remained resolute. "Something's up with you."

"Yes." Olivia dropped her feet to the floor and straightened the few items on her desk. "It looks like Maya made a big fat mess for me to clean up, and as if that's not bad enough, Vincent is coming to town for a visit. The timing couldn't be worse."

"Your maker?" Pete smirked. "I can't wait to meet this guy," he said sarcastically. "From what you've told me, he's a barrel of laughs."

"I'm sure he'll likc you as much as you'll like him."

"Mmm-hmm." Pete glanced at the clock on the desk. "When is this big coven pow-wow? I've got a pregnant woman at home who will be looking for pancakes and bacon when she wakes up."

"How's she feeling?" A smile curved her lips. Marianna had gotten pregnant just before Pete was turned, and their twins were due soon.

"They're due in a few months. She's hungry as hell, but I can't figure out if it's because she's pregnant with twins, or because she's a shifter. She's in the Bear Clan, and believe me, she freaking eats like a bear, but if you tell her I said that, I'll deny it," he added quickly.

"Your secret is safe with me." Her smile faded as she picked up Doug's business card. "What can you tell me about Doug Paxton?"

"He was my partner, a great cop, and one of the best men I know—human or otherwise. He's loyal and fiercely protective of the people he cares about, not that there are that many of them. It's been hell keeping my distance from him."

"Why are you keeping your distance?" She cocked her head as curiosity got the better of her. "Do you think he suspects something?"

"He knew something was different when I saw him a couple of months ago but couldn't put his finger on it." Pete folded his arms over his chest. "I've been avoiding him ever since. The man is like a dog with a bone. He won't let go until he figures it out, but that's what makes him such a great cop."

"I see." She glanced at his business card. "You said

he doesn't have many people in his life. So, no wife or girlfriend?"

She tried to make the question sound casual but failed miserably.

"No." Pete crossed to the desk and leaned over with both hands on it as he studied her closely.

Damn it. Olivia kept her expression neutral and flicked her confident gaze back to Pete, hoping she could bluff him.

"Why are you interested in Doug's personal life? Wanting to know about him as a cop, that I get. But questions about his dating life? Now *that* is interesting."

Olivia rose slowly from her chair and kept her eyes fixed firmly on Pete. "My only concern is protecting my coven and my business. Detective Paxton is investigating the murder of a guy whose last living moments were at my club with my bartender, so I want to know who I'm dealing with, and one of my progeny is his main suspect." Her voice dropped low. "And that's it. Got it?"

Van Helsing whined and shifted to a sitting position.

"Whatever you say." A wide grin cracked Pete's face as he pushed himself off her desk and opened the door for her. "After you, boss lady."

Olivia wanted to tell him to shove it, but she grinned in spite of herself. "You're just lucky that I like you and you married my friend," she said as she brushed past him with Van at her heels. "Otherwise, I'd kick your butt for being such a wise-ass."

Olivia strode through the empty club with Pete and Van just a few steps behind her. Sadie, Trixie, Maya, and Damien were seated at the bar waiting for Olivia, and whatever conversation they'd been having abruptly stopped.

"Where's Suzie?" Olivia asked as she stepped behind the bar.

"She split a few minutes ago," Damien responded.

All eyes were on Olivia, except for Maya's. Her weepy gaze was transfixed on her hands, which were folded neatly in her lap as tears rolled down her cheeks. Olivia studied her carefully, looking for any sign that this was more of her manipulative behavior but found none, and in spite of how irritated Olivia was, she actually felt sorry for Maya. Apparently, she was genuinely upset.

"So, Maya," Olivia began quietly. "Are you crying because the young man is dead, or is it because you actually realize what a fucking shit-show you've brought down on your coven? Or both?"

Maya shrugged and wiped the tears away but said nothing. Olivia knew she was being hard on the girl, but she had to impress upon Maya and the rest the serious nature of their situation.

"How could you be so careless?" Olivia asked. "First you bring him back here and toy with him all day long. *Here*. In our *home*."

She inched closer to the bar but kept her hands behind her back, knowing that it would be far too easy to grab her and attempt to shake some sense into her. While lecturing Maya on self-control, it would completely undermine her to the coven if Olivia lost hers.

"Then, as if that's not bad enough, you show even less restraint by draining him dry and tossing him in a dumpster for any *human* to find." Her voice rose higher with every word as anger and fear got the better of her. "Everyone in the club saw you flirt your fangs off with him all night long, and who fucking knows how many people saw you leave here with him after closing? How could you do this? Do you realize what kind of risk you've put all of us in?"

Silence hung in the air, and all eyes were on Maya.

"I—I didn't kill him, Olivia." She turned her large, teary blue eyes to Olivia. "I swear to you, as my maker, I didn't do it." She stuck her arm out to Olivia. "Here. If you don't believe me, check my blood memories."

Everyone looked at Olivia, and the room fell silent.

As the leader of the coven, this was a defining moment. She expected her progeny to trust her at her word, and in exchange, she should do the same for them. If Olivia took Maya up on her offer, it would demean all of them. No. She had to trust Maya if she wanted them to continue to trust her. Her coven was her family, not a police state.

"Not necessary." Olivia glanced at Maya's arm and shook her head curtly. "If you're telling us that you didn't do it, then we, as your family, will take you at your word."

In a blur, Maya flew over the bar and wrapped Olivia in the tightest hug of her life. "Thank you, Olivia." Sobbing, Maya laid her head on her shoulder, like a child seeking forgiveness from a parent. "Thank you so much. I'm so sorry. I won't ever feed on boys in the club again. I promise."

Unaccustomed to public displays of affection, Olivia stood with her arms out at her side and Maya clinging to her like a baby chimpanzee. Sadie shot her a look and nodded. *Jeez, Olivia. Hug the poor girl back before she soaks that expensive suit with all her bawling.*

"You're welcome." Olivia patted Maya on the back and gave her a reassuring hug. After a moment, she took her by the shoulders and pulled back, forcing Maya to look her in the eyes. "I know that you're sorry, and I appreciate the apology, but we still have a problem."

"I know, and I really am sorry for breaking the rules. I shouldn't have fed on him in the club." Maya sniffled and wiped her tears away. "What can I do to fix things and make it right?"

"For starters, you are forbidden from live feeds until further notice, and you aren't to leave the confines of our building for any reason."

Maya opened her mouth to protest but snapped it shut almost as quickly.

"Is that clear?" Olivia asked.

Maya nodded. "So basically, I'm grounded?"

"Grounded?" Trixie laughed loudly and pounded the bar with a ring-studded fist. "That's freaking brilliant. I feel like I'm living in an episode of the Vampire Brady Bunch."

Maya shot her a look and flounced back to her seat at the bar. "Oh, shut up."

"Enough," Olivia said wearily. "Let's not turn into the Bickersons on top of everything else. Maya is still a youngling, and we all make mistakes. Right, Trixie?"

The smile ran from Trixie's face the second Olivia mentioned mistakes. She'd made her fair share as a new vampire too, and it was unlikely she'd want to revisit them now.

"Yeah," Sadie chimed in with a wink. "If memory serves, *someone* tried to fly at sunrise and see if she really was going to get burned." She tapped her chin and pursed her lips. "Who was that again?"

"Okay, okay." Trixie giggled and punched Sadie on the arm. "Point taken. And how can we forget the story about the time you made out with that human guy before you realized he had a sterling silver tongue ring. From what Olivia says, you cried like a baby, and that was only like twenty years ago."

"Tasted like battery acid." Sadie grimaced and shivered. "I only grazed the damn thing with my tongue, and it hurt like a bitch. Silver sucks."

"See? It's all good, Maya." Trixie tugged Maya's long hair playfully. "Olivia's right. Everyone makes mistakes."

Olivia winked at Trixie. *Thanks*. She self-consciously twirled one of her pink spikes of hair and lifted one shoulder as a sheepish grin cracked her face.

"What about you, Pete?" Maya said as she swiped at her tearstained eyes. "What dumb things have you done?"

"Too many to mention, kid."

"Like I was saying," Olivia continued. "We still have a problem. Maya was the last person seen with this guy before he died, which makes her the prime suspect. The humans will be easy enough to deal with—we can glamour them if we need to—but the Presidium is another problem entirely. I've got to get down to the city morgue, so I can have a look at the body and take a DNA sample from the wounds. Czar Augustus will eventually hear about this, and I want to stay a step ahead of the investigation. I'll check the sample against the records at the Presidium, and if it was a vamp killing, it will be easy enough to prove that you didn't do it."

She looked at Maya and softened her tone. Olivia

knew she'd been hard on Maya, maybe too hard on her, but she had to learn somehow. Her behavior put the entire coven at risk.

"If you didn't kill him, then we shouldn't find your DNA in the wounds, and you have nothing to worry about."

"Boss lady," Pete interrupted. "Why don't you let me take care of that stuff?"

"No. I appreciate the offer, but you've got a personal life outside of this shit, and the last thing you need is an angry, pregnant wife, especially one that can turn into a bear," she added with a wry grin.

"At least let me give Millicent a heads-up," he added. "She'll have your back."

Millicent was the records keeper for the New York branch of the Presidium and almost as old as the czar. As a former sentry herself, she had a soft spot for Olivia and would do the DNA test without making a stink.

"Agreed." Olivia nodded and glanced at the clock. "Sunrise is in about an hour. Damn it." She rubbed her eyes and let out an exhausted sigh. "Pete, let Millicent know I'm coming but give her as little information as possible. I don't want to make her complicit in case this goes the wrong way. If the laws have been broken and a human was killed, the Presidium won't take it lying down—especially Augustus," she said under her breath. "He's still got the mind-set of a Roman senator. Arrogant and absolute in his beliefs. If he thinks Maya made this mess, then he'll report her to Emperor Zhao and have her executed."

Maya blanched and nibbled her lip but said nothing.

"I got your back, kid," Pete said with a wink to Maya. "They're not that bad. Just a bunch of old windbags."

Olivia folded her arms across her chest and turned her attention back to the rest of the coven. She knew they would be unhappy with her next request and braced for their resistance. "In the meantime, I'd like the rest of you to refrain from live feeds as well, until this is resolved. Damien has another shipment of blood coming in, so there'll be plenty for everyone."

"No problem," Damien added in his smooth baritone.

"Very funny," Sadie said. "As the only human in the room, it's certainly not a problem for you."

"Like I said"—he shrugged his massive shoulders—"no problem."

Sadie flipped him the bird.

Olivia shook her head and laughed at the banter.

"Damien, do some research online later today, and find out anything you can about Ronald Davis. Maybe his death has more to do with him than it does with us. As of right now, all we know is that he's dead and that Maya didn't do it."

"You got it, boss."

"Oh," Olivia said through a weak laugh. "I should warn you all that Vincent is coming to town for a visit." A collective groan rose from the group, but Olivia held one hand up, which silenced them. "I know he's a stodgy pain in the ass, but he is my maker and an elder, so give a girl a break, and be nice. And I think it goes without saying that we don't need to discuss this whole mess with him. Correct?"

They all nodded in agreement.

"One more thing," Pete interjected. "If it's alright with you, I think we should let Shane in on this."

"The other sentry?" Olivia put her hands on her hips

and let out a long breath. She stared at the vaulted ceiling as she spoke. "I'd really rather keep this between us for now. Besides, I haven't even met him yet." She looked at Pete through narrowed eyes. "Do you trust him?"

"Yes." Pete raised his hands to prevent her from arguing. "Listen. The guy has been a sentry for four hundred years, and he is Mr. By-the-Book. I'm worried that if we don't clue him in, and he gets wind of it some other way, it will only make matters worse."

"Fine." She leaned back against the shelves of booze and looked at the faces of her diverse coven. "Keep it to a minimum. Let him know there was a suspected vamp killing near the club, and that you're looking into it. Leave Maya's name out of it until we get that DNA sample checked out."

"Not a problem." Pete gave Maya a brotherly wink. "Don't worry, kid. We'll get it all straightened out."

"Are you sure?" Maya sniffled and looked at Olivia.

"Absolutely." Olivia mustered a weary smile. "Hey, we don't even know for sure if it's a vamp killing. Let's take it one step at a time."

That was bullshit. She knew deep in her gut that it was a vamp killing. Olivia prayed Maya was telling the truth. If she wasn't, if she did indeed kill Ronald Davis, then there would be no saving her from the Presidium's justice.

Chapter 3

Doug leaned back in the chair at his desk, laced his fingers behind his head, and stared at the computer screen without really seeing it. They had questioned several witnesses, but none yielded solid leads. In true, late-night New York City fashion, no one saw anything, or if they did, they weren't talking. The Hollingsworth woman provided an alibi for the bartender, so for the moment, the little blond was bumped from the top of his list.

They reached a series of dead-end leads far too quickly for his liking.

One thing bothered him more than anything else. He couldn't get his mind off Olivia and the striking resemblance she bore to the woman from his dreams. How in the hell was he supposed to keep his mind on this case when he couldn't keep it off her?

"Shit, you got it bad, kid." Tom's gravelly laugh pulled him from his thoughts.

"I don't know what you're talking about," Doug said with as much disinterest as he could muster.

His chair squeaked in protest as he leaned both elbows on the desk and flipped through pictures of the crime scene and Ronald's mutilated body. He had to get his head back in the game. Running his hands over his face, he turned his attention to the file on his desk, unwilling to look at Tom.

They'd only been partners for about two years, but the guy knew him better than almost anyone on the planet—the only one who knew him better was his former partner, Pete.

He could feel Tom staring at him.

"What?" Doug asked without looking up.

Tom's desk butted up against his, and their computers were back-to-back, which normally worked out great, but right now it felt too close for comfort. Doug never told a soul about the sexy dreams he had of the mysterious redhead, and he would be damned if he was going to start now. If he was going to tell anyone, it would be Tom, but the middle of a murder investigation was not the time to talk about dreams.

He would have told Pete, but he had barely spoken to the guy in months. He had gotten really reclusive ever since he got married, and there was something else different about him too. Doug could not pinpoint what it was, and that nagged at him. He hated not being able to figure it out, but it was more than that. He missed his friend.

Tom leaned closer and lowered his voice, so that none of the other cops in the room would hear him. "You've got a serious hard-on for that tall drink of water from the club, and don't try to deny it."

He glanced over his shoulder at the other cops sitting outside the captain's office playing games on their cell phones. Everyone was trying to stay awake and kill time before the shift change.

"In the two years I've known you, you have never been at a loss for words, and tonight you actually forgot how to speak for a second. I think all the blood rushed to your dick and out of that college-boy brain."

"Me?" Doug responded with a wry grin and peered past the computer at his partner. "You practically drooled all over that Maya chick, and *she's* a potential suspect."

"You know I've always been a sucker for blonds," he said with a wink.

Doug chuckled and shook his head. "Isn't she a little young for you, old man?"

"Age is a state of mind, my friend."

"Then that would make *you* about twelve."

"Probably." Tom laughed loudly and sat back in his chair as he scratched his balding head. "I'm sure my two ex-wives would agree. It's a good thing I never had any kids. They would've ended up outgrowing me."

"I'm pretty sure that's what happened with your last wife."

"Most likely." Tom groaned as he pushed himself out of his chair. "I'll learn from my mistakes one of these days." He shrugged on his jacket. "Come on. Let's get the hell out of here."

"You go ahead." Doug waved and turned his attention back to the folder on his desk. "I want to check out a few more details before I head out."

"Shit," Tom sighed and started to take off his coat. "And here I thought I was going home before the sun came up."

"Get off the cross, Tom," Doug said without looking up. "There's only room for Jesus."

Tom burst out laughing and ran a hand over his head. "You sure, kid?"

"I'm only staying a few more minutes. I just want to see if I can find more information about that bartender he was hanging out with. Maybe she's got a pissed off ex-boyfriend. Go on. Get the hell out of here. I'll see you back here tonight, and we'll hit it again."

Tom waved as he disappeared through the doorway, and Doug heard his boisterous voice as he said good-bye to the various people he passed on his way downstairs. He shook his head and smirked. Tom was anything but stealthy, which was probably why he never did undercover work.

Doug jotted a few more observations in his notebook, mostly notes to himself about going back to the club and interviewing that bartender again. He knew in his gut that she was not the killer, but he also had a hunch she knew more than she was letting on. Getting to see Olivia again would be an added bonus. Doug shut down his computer, snagged his cell phone, and stuck it in his pants pocket.

"Night guys."

The other detectives waved absently and mumbled their good-byes as Doug headed downstairs and passed through the front lobby of the precinct. He pushed open the heavy door and sucked in a deep breath of the late spring morning. Darkness would soon be replaced by gray as the sun crept its way up, but he reveled in the last breath of the fading night.

An array of city smells assaulted his senses. Garbage and exhaust from the passing cars dominated, but the fresh smell of bread baking from Spinelli's Bakery around the corner managed to make it tolerable.

However, the moment his feet hit the sidewalk, his phone buzzed, and he cursed under his breath. A text at this hour was rarely good news.

His brow furrowed as he read the message.

Can you come down here? There's something I want to show you.

It was from one of the coroners in the medical examiner's office, but not just any coroner. Dr. Miranda Kelly was his ex-girlfriend.

Be there in 10. He texted a response quickly and stuffed the phone in his pocket.

Thank God for texting. He hated talking on the phone, and with an ex it was always better to keep communication to a minimum. It helped avoid the awkwardness that inevitably followed after he ended a relationship with a girlfriend.

Well, *girlfriend* was probably a generous description. They slept together a few times, and she wanted more, but he simply was unable go there. He never could, and likely never would. Luckily, they were able to maintain a professional relationship, at least so far.

He felt like a shithead. He did not want to hurt her. Doug knew the more he prolonged any type of physical relationship would only make breaking it off worse. Hell, he didn't relish being alone night after night, but he knew it was better that way. Better to bail out in the beginning before anyone had a chance to really get hurt. No ties. No commitments. That was the way to go and the way he lived his life. At first it was circumstance, and after a while it became the norm.

Commitments.

He wondered if Olivia had any commitments. His jaw set at the idea of her with another man, which was ridiculous. He barely knew the woman, so what right did he have to suffer from caveman-like territorialism? None at all. But that did not squelch the jealousy that bubbled up from the mere idea of her with another man.

His thoughts went to Ronald Davis and the bartender Maya. She was a pretty thing, and he bet that plenty of men wanted to claim her. Maybe Olivia could fill him in on the bartender's private life?

Doug snagged his phone out of his jacket and stopped at the corner as he fished around in his back pocket for Olivia's business card. He found the private number, dialed it, and pressed send before he could talk himself out of it.

She was probably sleeping.

He told himself that he would leave a message, and that was it. As the phone rang in his ear he knew he was full of shit. He just wanted to talk to her, to hear that sweet voice one more time.

Doug squeezed his eyes shut as it rang for the fourth time, and as he was about to chicken out and hit the end button—she answered.

"Hello?" Her honeyed voice drifted into his head, and his body froze as he struggled to remember why he called in the first place. The dagger on his back tingled. "Hello? Is anyone there?"

"Ms. Hollingsworth?" Doug said after clearing his throat. "It's Detective Paxton. I—I hope I didn't wake you."

"No," she said with the hint of a smile in her voice. "I'm wide awake. What can I do for you?"

"I needed to ask one more question about Maya, your bartender." Doug leaned against the brick wall of the building and watched two pigeons fight over a piece of hot dog bun. "Did she have an old boyfriend, the jealous type? Maybe someone who might be bothered by her flirtatious behavior with Ronald Davis?"

Silence hung on the line. Doug butted his head against the wall as he prayed she would not see through his bullshit reason for calling.

"His attack was particularly savage, a crime of passion. If it had been some random attack or mugging, there would be one, or maybe two, wounds, but Davis was hacked up." Doug opened his eyes again and watched as the pigeons hopped out of the path of an oncoming car. "This was like an act of revenge, completely rage-driven."

"I'm sorry, but Maya doesn't ever stick with one guy for long." Olivia laughed softly. "She likes to play the field, so to speak, and rarely goes out with the same guy twice. I wish I had more helpful information for you."

Doug stuck his free hand in his pocket and fiddled with her business card.

"Actually, that is helpful." He started walking again toward Miranda's office. "Looks like we can rule out an old boyfriend, and sometimes ruling things out is the quickest way to get to where we want to be." He paused before continuing, knew asking the next question was a mistake, and asked it anyway. "How about you, Ms. Hollingsworth?"

"Me?" she asked in a low, husky voice.

"It was your club he was hanging out at. Could you have an enemy or an old boyfriend who wants to cause trouble?"

To his surprise, she laughed. It was a smoky, sexy laugh that made him stop dead in his tracks. He fought the urge to turn and go back to the club so he could hear it in person, but he shook his head and kept on his present course.

"No, detective."

"Doug," he interrupted.

"Alright," she said through a chuckle. "No, *Doug*, I don't have any enemies, at least none that would've messed with Ronald Davis, and I definitely don't have any old boyfriends looking to cause trouble."

"Current boyfriend?" he asked quietly as he looked over his shoulder, worried that someone would overhear.

"No," she said slowly. "I'm quite single. Not so much as a dinner date in a long time. You could say that it feels like centuries."

Doug stopped at the corner and looked both ways before jogging across the street.

"How about Mexican?"

"Mexican boyfriends?"

"No." Doug laughed loudly and ran one hand over his head. "Mexican food. Do you like Mexican food?"

Nail-biting silence filled the line as he waited for her to respond. He started to sweat. Doug suspected he overstepped his bounds, and just as he was about to take it back, she answered.

"Are you asking me out on a date?"

"That depends."

"Oh really?" She laughed again. "On what?"

"Would you say yes?"

"Maybe."

Doug tried to suppress the grin that bubbled up. She was flirting with him as much as he was with her.

"Maybe, huh?"

"Is there anything else that I can *do* for you?"

Doug bit his tongue because he thought of about a hundred different things she could do for him, to him, and with him, but instead, he replied, "I'll be sure to let you know. Don't leave town or anything," he said playfully. "I may have a question or two tomorrow."

"I can assure you that I'm not going anywhere, except to bed… alone."

Before he could say another word, she hung up, leaving him with the beginnings of a hard-on and a blanket of guilt. Doug shook his head and stuck the phone in his pocket. He really was going off the deep end. Asking her out in the middle of an investigation? What the hell was wrong with him?

Doug made it the rest of the way to the examiner's office in record time. He was beat and wanted nothing more than to crash in his crappy apartment and sleep for a week, but his curiosity about Miranda's text trumped his exhaustion.

He peered through the small window on the door to the exam room and saw Miranda perched over the body of Ronald Davis. He swung it open and was instantly hit with the stink of death and antiseptic. Doug knew he should be used to the smell by now, but it still made his stomach lurch.

Miranda glanced over her shoulder and waved him closer. "Thanks for coming."

Her brown hair was tied back tightly and went well with her strictly business attitude. She was professional, which made the tension in his shoulders ease, but it flared again when he set eyes on Ronald's mutilated body. Granted, some of the damage was from the autopsy—but not the worst of it.

"Someone did a fucking number on this guy," Doug said without looking at Miranda.

This was definitely a crime of passion. Doug would bet money that if Maya had not pissed off an old boyfriend, perhaps Ronald cock-blocked someone else.

"Someone or something," Miranda said evenly.

"What do you mean?" Doug asked warily.

He turned his attention to Miranda and shifted his weight when her serious brown eyes met his. To his surprise, she removed the protective eyeglasses and burst out laughing.

"Relax, Paxton." She held both gloved hands up in surrender. "I'm not going to jump your bones or stab you with a scalpel."

A smile cracked his face, and he crossed his arms over his chest. "Am I that transparent?"

"Pretty much," she said, dropping her hands. "We had fun. I'm married to my job, and you… well, you're married to not being married."

"Right." He nodded, but a little voice inside said, *nope*.

Not that he had anything against marriage as an institution, but he had a hunch he would suck at it. Besides, in his experience, most people leave. His father split before he was born. His mother died. Foster families were like layovers at random airports. You never stayed for long, and if you did, you wished like hell you didn't.

Miranda shook her head and put the glasses back on as she turned Ronald Davis's head, giving Doug a better view of his neck. "Look at this," she said, pointing at the jagged wounds. "This wasn't done by a knife or any other kind of weapon, at least not one that I can match it to."

Doug squinted and leaned closer. "How the hell can you tell? It looks like chopped meat."

"The edges are jagged." She stepped away from the autopsy table and stripped off her latex gloves before tossing them into a wastebasket. "I thought it might be a dog bite, so I swabbed the wound and had a closer look."

She went to a table on the other side of the room, which was littered with various pieces of lab equipment, and tossed her glasses on the counter. Miranda leaned back on the edge of the counter and nodded toward the microscope next to her.

"Have a look."

Doug sighed. "Give me the short version. I won't even know what I'm looking at."

"Oh, you're no fun." She crossed her arms, and he knew she wanted him to play her game, but he held his ground. "Fine." She sighed. "There was saliva in the wound, but it wasn't from a dog." She grabbed a folder and held it out. "I had a sample from that pit bull attack we had a couple of weeks ago and compared it to the saliva that I found on Ronald. No match. It wasn't a dog."

Dread crawled up his back as he glanced at the data she handed him. "It's not another fucking freak biting people again, is it? The press will have a damn field day. I can see the headline now: *Zombies in New York*."

"No, it's not from a person either."

Doug furrowed his brow and glanced at Ronald's body. "I don't get it. If it wasn't a dog or some doper hopped up on crack, then what was it?"

"I don't know, but he's practically drained of blood. From what the crime scene report said, there wasn't much at the scene."

"I know." Doug nodded. "He was killed somewhere else and dumped where we found him."

Miranda pushed herself off the counter and met his concerned gaze. "I'm sending the sample to the lab for analysis."

"Shit. You mean we could have some psycho out there with a vicious animal that's attacking people?" Doug ran a hand through his hair and gave her back the folder. "How long is that gonna take?"

Miranda let out a short laugh. "A few weeks, if you're lucky."

"Damn." Doug sighed. "Those guys on television have it easy. They get their answers after the first commercial break."

"I'll see if I can get them to move it along, but you know how things work." She gave him a weak smile. "You look exhausted. When was the last time you slept?"

"Don't ask." He lifted one shoulder. "Sleep is overrated."

Silence hung between them. Her pale brown eyes looked at him with the unmistakable twinkle of invitation. He knew she still wanted him. Hell, Miranda was beautiful and smart, and most guys would probably give their left nut to go home with her. Up until a few hours ago, he probably would have asked her to come back to his place, but all he could think about was Olivia Hollingsworth.

He didn't even know the woman. What was his problem?

The sound of the door opening caught his attention and interrupted what was sure to be an awkward exit. Miranda cleared her throat and went back to that strictly business attitude that she wore when he first arrived.

A young guy, probably no more than twenty-two, stood there holding the door open. He pushed his glasses up with his free hand and glanced nervously between the two.

"What is it, Henry?" Miranda asked with mild irritation.

"Sorry to interrupt you, Dr. Kelly, but you asked me to come and get you at five fifteen because you always forget what time it is and don't remember to eat."

He let out a short, nervous laugh and pushed his glasses back up his nose.

"Of course," Miranda said with less bite than before. "Thank you, Henry."

"Um, you also said that you would be willing to have a look at my thesis over coffee." He flicked a glance to Doug, who was doing his best not to laugh at the poor kid. "Would—would that still be a possibility?"

"Absolutely. Why don't you grab a table in the cafeteria, and I'll meet you there in five minutes."

"Thank you so much, Dr. Kelly." The kid tripped and stumbled out the door.

"Looks like you've got a groupie." Doug gave Miranda a sidelong glance. "I never met a medical examiner who had a fan club."

"He's one of my best interns, but I kind of like *groupie* better." Miranda put her hands in the pockets of her long white lab coat and headed to the door. "I'll text you as soon as I get some answers on what attacked Ronald, okay?"

"I'd appreciate that." Doug opened the door for her and took one last look at Ronald's body. This case was getting stranger by the minute, and instead of answers, all he had was more questions.

They walked down the sterile hallway in another awkward silence. Doug squinted against the glare of the fluorescent lighting. As he turned the corner, the familiar squeak of a door swinging open caught his attention, and he glanced back, expecting to see someone, but to his surprise, the hallway was empty. He stopped as a tickle of awareness tripped up his spine and kept his eyes on the door to the autopsy room.

"Paxton," Miranda called to him from the waiting elevator. "Ronald isn't going anywhere, and I need coffee, so come on."

"Coming." Doug went to the elevator but glanced over his shoulder. He couldn't escape the sense that someone was back there. As the elevator doors closed, one image filled his mind—Olivia.

Olivia stood inside the doors of the autopsy room and waited. She glanced at the wall of stainless steel refrigerated compartments, knowing she could take refuge in one, if necessary, and slip into the tunnels. She managed to get in without Doug seeing her, but she could still hear his heartbeat at the other end of the hallway, and it took major willpower not to get closer. She closed her eyes and forced herself not to move, not to fly down that hallway and sink her fangs into the tender flesh just below the jaw.

Her fangs emerged, and her head buzzed with need. His heartbeat, strong, steady, and surprisingly distinct, called to her, but a few moments later, it faded and finally vanished.

Olivia let out a sound of relief and sheathed her fangs.

She picked up his phone call when she was flying over from the club and answered as soon as her feet hit the roof. She recognized the number from his business card, and since curiosity got the better of her, she answered, even though it was against her better judgment. Olivia sat on that roof talking on the phone with him like some silly teenager. She could tell within five seconds that he used the question about Maya as an excuse to call. He wanted her. There was no mistaking it, but getting involved with a human was less than smart—especially one who happened to look exactly like, and quite possibly could be, her long-dead true love reincarnated.

She felt his presence as he moved along the sidewalk far below, and she resisted the urge to fly down there and talk to him in person. Her sense of duty and the looming mess with Ronald's murder drowned out her raging hormones, and she held back. Although, she did peer over the side of the building to get a peek and found him as desirable from six stories above as he was from six inches away.

It would not have been the end of the world if he saw her as she slipped down the hallway and into the room. She could glamour him and the medical examiner, easily erasing any memory, but she didn't want to do that.

Well, at least, not to him. The doctor was another story entirely. Olivia went to Ronald's body and tried not to think about drinking that doctor dry. The woman was intensely attracted to Doug because the room was full of the distinct scent of female arousal. Jealousy reared its ugly head again, but Olivia shook it off. No time for bullshit.

She sensed the sun starting its slow ascent, and if she didn't hustle, then she would have to take the tunnels all the way to the Presidium's New York offices.

No sane woman, living or undead, would want to wear an Armani suit into the tunnels that led to the Presidium's underground network. She wrinkled her nose at the thought.

Olivia snagged two glass specimen tubes from her pocket, removed the long swabs, and ran them along two of the wounds, first from the neck, and then from the wounds on his arm. She shook her head and cursed. This was most definitely a vamp killing and a vicious one at that. It was sloppy and savage, which gave it the clear markings of a youngling attack.

Someone turned a new vampire, let him or her loose with no training, and didn't bother to clean up the mess. Great.

After securing her samples, she snagged the travel-size bottle of bleach from her other pocket and squirted it over the wounds, removing traces of vampire DNA. She smirked as she capped the bottle, knowing what a shit storm this would bring on for the doctor. It was petty to take satisfaction in a human woman's discomfort, but she really didn't care.

Olivia went to the computer, noticed the doctor had neglected to log out, and deleted all of the files related to Ronald's case. She grabbed the folder that the doctor had shown Pete and slipped it beneath her jacket.

Olivia tucked the samples in her pocket and listened at the door. Satisfied the coast was clear, she made her way swiftly and silently down the hallway to the stairwell, up the cement staircase, and seconds later arrived at the door of the roof. Even if someone glanced through one of the windows on the doors, they would not have seen her. The surveillance cameras were more of a nuisance, but as long as she moved swiftly, all they would pick up was a blur.

Most people would see the anomaly and brush it off as the light playing tricks. Humans were quick to dismiss anything outside the norm, and those who didn't would post their videos on YouTube as proof of the existence of ghosts.

The sun was starting to crest. Even if she really hustled, she would never make it back to the Presidium's offices without getting toasted. *Damn it*. Olivia popped the lock on the door and swung it open. She stood for a moment in the cool, late spring evening and watched as the pale golden glow emerged along the edge of the horizon.

She missed watching the sunrise and basking in the warmth of it on her face, however, not enough to take a chance of turning to ash. Olivia strode across the roof and glanced at the empty alley six floors below as a grin cracked her face. An eternity of darkness sucked, but the ability to do Superman-type stunts was pretty freaking cool and balanced out the whole no-daylight thing.

Olivia took off her shoes. While *she* may be unbreakable, the *Louboutins* weren't. She dropped soundlessly to the dark alley below and landed on her feet as sure as an alley cat.

As she slipped her shoes back on, the growing noises of the city streets washed over her, and moments later, a distinctly familiar sound snaked into her mind, surrounding her.

Something strong, steady, and enticing.

It was *him*.

Doug's heartbeat thundered through her mind,

drowning out the rest of the sounds, and captured her full attention. She heard heartbeats of the humans in the surrounding area and had grown so accustomed that over the years it had become white noise.

Not Doug's. His rose above the din, clamoring to be heard.

Why was his heartbeat so clear and enthralling? It called to her like a siren song, willing her closer and taunting her. Confused and aroused, she struggled to keep her fangs at bay. In all her three hundred years, she'd never shown such a lack of self-control or intense reaction to anyone, and she hadn't even tasted him yet.

Was this connection a lingering effect of the dreams she had? Was Doug her bloodmate? Or was it an echo from their human life together? They only made love once, that one fateful night, but in the dreamscape it happened over and over.

Memories of them entangled were burned into her mind, her heart, and her body. Images of them in the dreamscape—Doug falling to his knees, burying his face in her breasts, and teasing her to the edge of oblivion with his nimble fingers. Through it all, neither of them ever spoke, and as the dream faded, one word wafted through her mind on a whisper.

Eternity.

Olivia groaned as the sun rose, along with her driving need to taste him. She had to get out of here. *Now.* Olivia glanced down the alley and spotted the manhole, which was her key to freedom, and promised relief from the taunting, enticing sound of his heart.

She didn't care if anyone saw her.

Already feeling the weakening effects of the

approaching daylight, Olivia ran down the alley as Doug's heartbeat called to her like a beacon. Her head was fogged with desire and desperation, which was probably why she didn't see him as he stepped off the sidewalk and directly into her path.

Olivia swore loudly as she knocked him backward toward the street. In a blur, she snatched him in midair and flew with him back into the alley to safety. She pressed his tall, hard body against the wall of the building, using the shadows and a dumpster for cover. The blow knocked him out, but his heart still beat strong and steady beneath warm flesh.

Olivia glanced at the sky and noted it was getting lighter by the second. The sun was rising, and time was running short. She took his face in her hands and brushed her thumb over the stubble on his cheek. The feel of his sun-kissed flesh beneath her fingers had her aching with—what?

Desire? Love? Loss? Regret?

Her gaze skimmed over his masculine features as she threaded her fingers through his short blond hair. That was the only real difference between her memory of him and the man in front of her. His hair had been long and silky smooth, and she recalled the way it tangled temptingly between her fingers.

Olivia leaned closer and reveled in the way his body melded so perfectly with hers. Her breasts crushed against the hard planes of his chest, and the pounding of his heart reverberated through her, invoking memories of what it felt like to have a heartbeat.

She tilted his head to the right and breathed in his clean, masculine scent. Olivia pressed her cool lips along the smooth, warm skin of his throat that fluttered as his blood pumped through his veins. Her fangs vibrated, begging to be freed, but she clung to her last ounce of self-control.

He smelled like the ocean. Clean, fresh, and wild. She bet a year's worth of blood that he tasted that way too. Just like she remembered.

Doug groaned as he wrapped his large hands easily around her waist. Olivia tensed as he pulled her close and held her against him. She glanced up to find his blue eyes peering down at her fiercely beneath furrowed brows.

"What happened?" he rasped. His fingers dug into her hip as he wavered, letting his weight lean into the wall. "What are you doing here?"

She should glamour him. She should do it and get in the damn tunnels.

But she didn't.

"I—I bumped into you." She blinked and barely noticed that her hands were now resting on his broad shoulders, and he was standing without her assistance. "I have to go, but I wanted to be sure you were okay. You hit your head on the edge of the building when we ran into each other," she lied.

He never touched the building, but the force of her body slamming into his had been enough to knock him out for a minute. She was grateful he didn't break anything.

Olivia stepped back and glanced down at the shadow line, which crept closer every second. With surprisingly fast reflexes, his hands snaked around her waist again and tugged her against his muscular body. She could have eluded him easily, but she didn't want to; all she wanted was to press her cheek against his chest and stay there.

"You did a hell of a lot more than that," Doug murmured as he pulled her tighter against him, while his hands spanned her waist. "Don't go." His voice, edgy and full of need, washed over her, while his thumb brushed the curve of her hip, heightening her desire and testing her strength. "Are you really here with me now, or is this just another dream?"

Heat emanated from him and covered her like a blanket. The truth was it could have been the sun getting ready to fry her, but she didn't care. All she cared about or could think about was the man in her arms and getting one, sweet taste. It had been *so long* since she kissed anyone. But *he* wasn't just anyone.

Olivia moaned, a sound that hung somewhere between lust and warning. She shook her head and meant to lean back, but before she could stop herself, she was leaning into him.

His mouth crashed down on hers with a groan of pleasure. She opened to him and sighed as his tongue tangled with hers, and she fleetingly noted that he did taste like the ocean. Salty, clean, wild, and full of life. Olivia held his head with both hands and angled hers, deepening the kiss. She licked and nibbled at his lips, desperate to get closer, as one strong hand slipped down her hip to cup her ass, and the other tangled in her long hair.

The dam broke.

Lust clawed at her. The rest of the world fell away as she allowed herself to revel in the taste of him on her lips and the feel of his body pressed against hers. She forgot how exquisite it felt to be cradled in the arms of a man and devoured as if she were the most desirable creature on earth. The sweep of his tongue along hers and the brush of his fingers against her scalp as he sipped from her lips, sent licks of fire through her body.

In the swell of lust and swept up in a moment of weakness, her fangs emerged. Holding him against the wall, tangled in his arms, the knifelike points of her fangs scraped his tongue as it explored, and then… the world exploded.

Light. Heat. A heartbeat.

His blood touched her tongue and danced through her body in life-giving electric pulses. It was like getting shocked by a defibrillator, and for the first time in close to three hundred years—her heart actually *beat*. As his blood shot through her veins, she clung to him in shocked desperation, wondering what it meant, and at the same time, not caring.

All she could do was *feel*.

With every beat of their synced pulses came a picture, a memory from his life now, his life with her centuries ago, *and* his dreams with her. As memories of this life and the last collided in a flurry of images, she realized that she was as much a part of him as he was of her. The floodgates had opened, and there was no going back.

Olivia gasped and broke the kiss, abruptly tearing her mouth from his, and she blinked as her heart beat in her chest almost to the point of pain. He looked at her through hooded, lust-filled eyes and tried to pull her in for more. As the sensations faded and reality came roaring back into focus, the sun rudely intruded and demanded an end to their stolen moment.

Breathing heavily, Doug pressed a kiss against her forehead as his heart raced with the clear cry of desire against her now silent chest. She lingered, allowing herself to lean into his embrace and float in the tender feel of his warm lips against her skin for one minute more.

A million thoughts raced through her mind, but one cried louder than the others.

Bloodmate.

His heated gaze was the last image she saw as she slipped from his arms and flew down the alley like the wind. The instant she left the shelter of his embrace, the sun blazed over her, and she waited, expecting to feel and hear the familiar sizzling as it burned her skin. Olivia tore off the manhole cover and dropped silently into the safe darkness of the sewer tunnel before securing the cover tightly behind her.

She stood in the dank space and touched her lips as they curved into a smile. She didn't notice the rats that ran over her feet because she could still taste him on her tongue, and the lingering, brilliant effect of his blood echoed through her body. She held up her unmarred hands and touched the smooth skin on her face with genuine awe. For the first time since she had been turned, the sun had not damaged her. Not even so much as a tan.

In that brief moment, Doug had given her *life*, and as she inspected the undamaged skin, one word escaped her lips on a whisper. "Bloodmate."

She didn't know how or why it could be true, and she didn't care. In fact, after getting that taste, she knew that all bets were off, and the dreams would no longer be enough. Now she craved more than flesh and blood. She craved *him*.

Chapter 4

Olivia moved through the tunnels with the ease of experience, although not as quickly as she hoped. The Presidium's New York office was located directly beneath the Cloisters, a museum full of medieval artifacts, and Fort Tryon Park, which wasn't that far from the medical examiner's office. For a human it would be one hell of a walk to the Cloisters. As a vampire using the underground network, it was less of a trek, but since she hadn't fed in almost twenty-four hours, she was dragging ass a little.

She whipped around the turns effortlessly and with such speed that the stone and cement walls became nothing more than a blur. Even though she was tired, she pushed herself and moved as swiftly as she could. Heightened vampire senses were great, unless you were running through a sewer tunnel. Then it was just an extra dose of gross.

As distasteful as her surroundings were, and regardless of the vermin that scurried through the tunnels to get out of her way, a smile lingered on her lips. Doug didn't just look like the man she loved as a human or strongly resemble the man in her dreams. He was one and the same, reincarnated, and larger than life. She saw his memories from three hundred years ago; memories of their shared dreams flooded her, trimmed with his emotions, his desire.

But if he had these memories, why didn't he know her? Why not recognize her? Were they simply buried so deep in his unconscious mind that he was unable to see what they were?

Her smile faltered as the dank air blew over her face, and the din of human life on the streets above filled her head. She had fed from countless humans over the years, and not one gave her life, albeit briefly, the way a drop or two of Doug's blood had. She had tasted demon blood and Amoveo blood, but neither had that kind of effect.

So what was it about Doug's blood that jump-started her heart? She knew the answer before she even asked herself the question. Doug was her bloodmate. He had to be. It was the only explanation that made sense, and while the thought thrilled her, the reality didn't. The only way he could truly be her bloodmate would be if she turned him, and that was the last thing on earth she wanted to do.

Olivia arrived at the main entrance of the Presidium, in the catacombs beneath the Cloisters, and let out a sigh of relief. She brushed at the droplets of moisture and dirt on her suit that she'd picked up along the way.

"Damn it." Her voice echoed. "I'm going to make Maya pay the dry- cleaning bill."

Olivia pushed in one of the rectangular stones along the top of the wall, and moments later an oblong section of the wall swung inward to reveal the opulent hallways of the Presidium's central office network. She stepped through, and as the door shut silently, she allowed herself a moment to appreciate the pristine environment. Olivia looked down the hall in both directions, but thankfully, found herself alone, at least for the time being.

She adjusted her suit jacket and fluffed her hair in an effort to not *look* like she had been in the tunnels. Olivia shuddered. The pictures on the wall looked like they were watching her. The czar and his senators loved to honor themselves any chance they got, and it started by having their pictures lining the main hall of the central office.

As if they could forget who ruled their society. Memories of executions she had overseen as a sentry came roaring back in living color, and while she remembered all of them, there was one face that would haunt her forever.

The young vampire slaughtered an entire frat house before they caught her, but the damage was done—and so was she. The girl was only twelve. She suffered from a bad turn, and after her maker abandoned her, she went the wrong way fast. The last sound Olivia heard as she dove into the desert tunnels leading back to Las Vegas were the little girl's screams as she turned to dust.

She paused at Czar Augustus's portrait, and her mouth set in a tight line as she studied her former boss. He was the czar in Vegas during Olivia's time as sentry and heartlessly ordered the girl's execution. Augustus was a bastard and took sheer pleasure in executing anyone who broke the precious rules, unless, of course, it was one of his own progeny.

Augustus's son, Brutus, turned the girl and left her to run amok with no guidance or training, fearful with a burning thirst for blood. Brutus should have been executed for his crime because the rules had been broken, but he's Augustus's flesh and blood son. So instead of death, Brutus was banished to hibernation for fifty years.

She heard when he woke up that he split for Europe. Too bad dear old daddy didn't go with him.

Augustus and Brutus were no different from human men who thrived on power.

They were both sick fucks.

She never understood why Emperor Zhao put Augustus in charge of the northeastern territory after his century of service was up in Vegas. He seemed suited to the Eastern Bloc nations. Augustus and the four senators who served with him reveled in the dark side of the city. There were plenty of drunks, drug addicts, and homeless to indulge in continuous live feeds.

Her heels clicked along the blood-red marble floor and echoed around her with irritating clarity as she hurried toward the records room. The ornate crystal chandeliers hung from the curved ceiling and glittered brightly along the yellow halls, giving the illusion of sunlight.

The buzz of the security camera captured her attention as it followed her every move. Olivia waved to the blinking eye and delivered a tight smile as she stopped in front of the arched wooden door. The click of the lock releasing echoed through the empty hallway, and Olivia readied herself for whoever was waiting on the other side.

It could have been Millicent with a few of the pit bulls that watched the Presidium halls during the day. It would be highly unlikely to find Augustus awake during the day, let alone roaming the halls, because he would think that was beneath him. She slipped her hand in the pocket of her jacket and wrapped her fingers around the cool glass tubes as she pulled the door open.

Pete leaned casually against the gray stone wall

with his arms crossed over his chest and winked. "Hey, boss lady."

Olivia narrowed her eyes as the door closed behind her. "I thought I told you not to worry."

"Yeah." He shrugged and pushed himself away from the wall. "You know how much I suck at following orders. Besides, Marianna told me that if I didn't help you, then I wasn't getting laid for a while."

Olivia smothered a laugh and shook her head. "Nice."

"Come on." He headed down the stone hallway. "Millicent is waiting."

Olivia's senses were on high alert as she glanced around the vacant hall. "Where are the dogs?"

"I'll put them out when we're done. Oh, by the way, I filled Shane in on the murder, but not the specifics, like we agreed."

"Good," she said tightly. "I haven't met him, which means I don't trust him. We need to have proof that Maya is innocent before they get more information. Augustus in particular."

"Not a problem." Pete kept his voice down and adjusted one of the weapons beneath his long coat. "They rely on Shane and me to keep them apprised of the happenings out there. We're lucky that poor old Ronald was murdered in my borough. If it had been Queens, Staten Island, or Brooklyn, then Shane would be all over it. He did tell me that if we need his help, he'd be obliged to assist." Pete let out a short laugh. "Those were his exact words, by the way, *obliged to assist*."

"Sounds like a fun guy," Olivia said under her breath.

They strode side by side through the maze of stone hallways, their path lit by the flickering light from wrought iron chandeliers. The halls that led from room to room were medieval in their décor and hadn't changed in centuries. However, when Augustus took over the New York location, he decorated most of the rooms with the same opulence of the main entrance, and all of the floors were laid out with bloodred marble.

After several turns down the passageway, they arrived at the Hall of Records. The heavy wooden door with studded steel bolts and iron hinges swung open before they got within ten feet.

Olivia grinned. Millicent always was dramatic.

Cloaked by a cloud of smoke, she sat behind a massive mahogany desk with a cigarette dangling from her red lips and her feet on the desk. Her white hair was carefully coiffed into her usual bouffant bubble hairdo. Clad in her standard gray skirt suit, she looked like she owned the place.

She may not have owned it, but she sure as hell ran it.

The wall behind her desk was one massive computer with several screens. The large plasma screen along the top currently held the image of a tropical beach at sunrise.

"Well, get your ass in here," she croaked. The older woman dropped her feet to the floor and crushed her cigarette in an ornate crystal ashtray full of a hundred butts. "I'm fucking tired and would like to get some sleep before sundown."

At first glance, she was a harmless old lady, and maybe she had been in her human life, but as a vampire she was deadly. In fact, her unassuming physical appearance made her an extremely effective assassin as a sentry. She served during the Civil War and put down more rogue vampires than any other sentry in history.

Wartime had a funny way of increasing the number of untrained vampires on the loose.

Olivia handed Millicent the specimen tubes and smiled. "Thank you for helping us with this and for being *discreet*."

"Discreet?" Millicent made a snort of derision. "There's something I haven't ever been called." She shot Pete a narrow gaze. "Shut the fuckin' door already."

Pete chuckled and closed the door. "Whatever you say, Millicent."

"Lucky for you, you're so damn cute," Millicent muttered as she took the sample to the massive computer.

Olivia and Pete watched as she put the two swabs into a scanner and pushed several buttons on the touch screen. An iridescent blue light scanned the cotton swabs, and everyone's attention switched to the center console as they waited for results.

"If your girl did it, we should find her DNA." Millicent speared Olivia with a glance. "You took it directly from the wounds, right?"

"Yes."

"Good girl. Still smart as a whip, and you're pissing your time away in a nightclub," she said on a sigh. "Pity."

Millicent held her hands behind her back and kept her sharp eyes glued to the information in front of them. The three watched in tense silence as a series of numbers scrolled over the screen. The computer searched for a match as Olivia prayed it wouldn't find one.

Pete was the first to break the silence. "So, there's a record of every vampire in New York City?"

"You're still thinking like a human." Millicent snorted, snagged another cigarette from the pack in her pocket, and lit it. "Gotta think bigger, boy. We have the DNA of every vampire on the planet. I have the northeastern files here, but I can access the Presidium's worldwide network, like I am right now. All new vamps have to be registered with their local records keeper within the first week of their new life, just like you did."

"How many?" Pete asked casually. "Five hundred, a thousand?"

Millicent burst out laughing, but the laugh quickly turned into a choking cough.

"Why is that funny?" he asked Olivia, who hadn't taken her eyes off the computer screen.

"Try over a hundred thousand."

Pete froze. "What?" he whispered. "I didn't think there were that many of us."

"It's really not that many compared to the millions of humans. The DNA of every vamp is in there, even the dead ones." Olivia flicked her green eyes to him briefly. "Really dead. Y'know, turned to ash. How long is this going to take?" she asked impatiently.

"Don't get your knickers in a twist." The computer beeped loudly, and Millicent went directly to the control panel. "It's done." She punched a few buttons as the cigarette dangled precariously from her weathered lips. "Well, I'll be strapped with silver."

Olivia and Pete stared at the screen and moved closer.

"Your girl didn't kill this kid." Millicent pointed at the screen. "But neither did anyone else in our database."

The screen blinked in bright red letters. *Unregistered vampire*.

Before anyone could say anything, the computer started beeping again.

"Hang on," Millicent rasped. She punched a few more buttons. "We're not quite done."

Dread gnawed at Olivia as she waited for the infernal machine to provide more information. Moments later, her worst fears were realized when Maya's identification card came up on the screen.

"The scanner found trace evidence of Maya's DNA on one of the swabs." Millicent stared at the screen with an unreadable expression. "It's barely anything, and most likely left over from feeding on him. Pete said she drank from the guy all day off and on, so it's not surprising."

She stuck the cigarette in her lips and began tapping away again. Olivia stood still while keeping her eyes locked on the screen, and her mind raced with different ways to get Maya out of town and keep her out of the Presidium's reach.

"Don't go getting any funny ideas," Millicent said as she gestured to the center screen. "According to this data, Maya's DNA is only in trace amounts, and the bulk is from the unregistered rogue vampire. Maya didn't kill him. Not enough of her DNA left behind."

"Something tells me that Augustus will consider that semantics." Olivia swore loudly and ran both hands over her face. "We have to find this rogue so we can match its DNA to the sample, get it to confess to killing Ronald, and then put it down before it causes more damage. Tracking a rogue vampire is a pain in my ass. The scent is crazy hard to pick up."

"I'm gonna get this rogue's DNA sample over to Xavier." Millicent retrieved the swab and put it back in the tube, sealing it. "He's been working on some pretty cool bioweapons, so this may be of use. Who knows, maybe he can come up with something that will help you."

"Good idea, Millicent." Olivia knew if anyone could find a way to use the rogue's DNA, it was Xavier. He ran the Presidium lab and weapons division in New York and was always coming up with new toys for the sentry. He was one of the smartest, most ingenious people Olivia ever knew. Living or undead. "I'm going to need all the help I can get."

"Let me take care of finding the rogue." Pete put his hands on her shoulders in a brotherly gesture. "I'll tell Augustus and the senators about the rogue. Shane and I will take care of it. Hey, you should be happy Maya's off the hook. They'll never know that we found any of Maya's DNA."

"Whoa!" Millicent extinguished her cigarette amid the pile of butts. "This information is instantly put into the worldwide database, so it's not like it's gonna be kept quiet for long. I mean, I'm not taking out an ad in the paper or nothin', but eventually, Augustus could get wind of this."

"What?" Olivia's voice rose to hysterical levels. "Can't you delete it?"

"Sorry, kid." Millicent sat in her chair and put her feet back on the desk. "Records can't be deleted once they're entered. Amended? Yes. Completely deleted? No. I guess it's a good thing you know the sentry who covers Manhattan," she said with a smile and a nod to Pete. "You know full well that he's the one who has to keep Augustus informed, and if you ask me, the best approach is to handle it head on. Tell him about the rogue vampire, and omit the bit about Maya's DNA if you want, but *don't lie*. All he'd have to do is check the database, and if he finds out that you lied, then we're all dead."

"I don't want anyone putting themselves in jeopardy over this," Olivia said firmly. "Maya is confined to the building until we take care of the rogue."

"What's this *we* thing you speak of?" Pete asked in a half-joking manner. "You're not a sentry, remember? Just a private citizen."

"Not anymore." Olivia walked to the screen with Maya's smiling picture staring back, and her voice dropped low. "Looks like I'm out of retirement. Unofficially, of course."

"What are the human cops saying?" Millicent snorted and lit yet another cigarette. "I bet they'll go right to serial killer."

"We already had two detectives come by the club." Olivia pointed at Maya's picture on the screen. "Witnesses saw Maya flirting with him not long before he died, so they came to ask her some questions. We provided her with an alibi, but it's still attention that we don't need."

"Just glamour 'em," Millicent said sharply. "Shit."

Olivia's thoughts immediately went to Doug, and memories of that kiss in the alley came roaring back as heat flickered over her skin. She shut her eyes and attempted to will the feeling away, but it was no use. Her hands balled into tight fists at her side, and her slim frame shook with concentration. The image of his blue eyes filled her mind, and that's when she heard it—or more to the point—heard him.

Eternity.

It was a whisper along the furthest corners of her

mind, but there was no mistaking it. It was Doug, and he was calling to her from the dreamscape. That was new. Her eyes flicked open, and she found Pete and Millicent staring as if she'd clucked like a chicken.

"Pete," Olivia said in the most authoritative tone she could muster. "Why don't you go on home to Marianna and get some rest. Come to the club tonight after sundown, and we'll go hunting for the rogue. We should probably get Shane's help on this too." He opened his mouth to protest, but she cut him off before he could say a word. "Now."

"Okay." Pete looked at her curiously and then to Millicent.

Olivia couldn't even look at him. She rarely spoke to him like that, and never in front of other people, and even though she felt like a shit for doing it, she didn't want him privy to the next conversation.

He bowed with a flourish. "Whatever you say, boss lady."

In a gust of wind, he was gone.

Millicent eyed Olivia warily from behind her desk. "What's going on with you, girl? I mean, aside from this crap."

"You've been around about a thousand years, right?" Olivia folded her arms over her chest and paced the room.

"Yeah," she said slowly. "Why?"

Olivia stopped pacing and turned to face her. "What do you know about the bloodmate legend?"

"Stories—rumors mostly." She flicked her lighter off and on absently. "Most vamps think it's a whole lot of bullshit."

"Do you?"

"Off the record." Millicent gestured to the chair by her desk, and Olivia, even though she felt too wound up to sit still, complied and forced herself to sit. "According to the legend, or at least the rumors I've heard, some vampires have a bloodmate, and if the two bond, then they both become daywalkers." She stared at Olivia over the flame. "As far as the *official records* are concerned, there has never been any proof of bloodmates." Her lips lifted at the corners, and the wrinkles around her eyes deepened.

"What about unofficial?" Olivia leaned both elbows on the massive desk and rested her chin on folded hands. "Would you be privy to any of that information?"

"When I was a sentry, I was ordered to put down two vamps that were supposedly making rogues and letting them run loose. They were accused of being a vampire Bonnie and Clyde. It was during the Civil War, and we had lots of problems with rogue vampires. Made a big damn mess." She lit another cigarette. "Anyway, wasn't unusual to get a contract like that."

"I remember the stories. You used several during my sentry training."

"Yeah, well, I left this one out." She leveled a serious gaze at Olivia. "I went to a house where I heard the two were holing up. It was an abandoned plantation in the south. I'd planned on getting there well before sunrise, but I got sidetracked by a gang of five rogues and had to put them down. At any rate, by the time I got to the plantation, it was almost sunrise. I figured I'd get in there quick and dust them as they were going to ground."

Riveted, Olivia leaned closer and gave Millicent her full attention.

"Didn't exactly happen that way." She let out a short laugh. "The sun was coming up as I flew into the house. I gotta be honest. I was a little antsy and wanted to get my old ass in the ground before I got singed. Couldn't believe it. I found them sitting in the back parlor, right in front of the window, holding hands and watching the sunrise. I was mesmerized." Her voice dropped to a whisper. "They knew I was there, watching them. They knew I was in the hallway, and they simply waved me in."

Olivia nodded and listened intently.

"Crawford, the fella, he said he knew I was there to kill them. Puzzled me, y'know? They didn't try to fight me. There was no aggression. They told me that they were bloodmates, and as a result, both of 'em had turned into daywalkers. They said that they knew the czar in the southeastern territory put a contract out on them because he didn't want word getting out about daywalking."

"Who was the czar down there then?"

"Christian Edwards, but he's dead now." She tossed the lighter on the desk. "Guy was old as dirt and took a walk in the sun one day. I guess eternity is a bit too long for some. Anyway, they said the Presidium made up the story about the two creating rogues so that they'd have an excuse to put them down."

"Why would the Presidium want to kill vamps that can daywalk?"

"Are you serious?" Millicent scoffed loudly. "Vamps that could daywalk would have all the power and easily overthrow the Presidium government if they wanted. All us nightwalkers would be exposed during the day and vulnerable. Hell, we'd be perceived as weaker than daywalkers, and you know what they say. It's all about perception."

Olivia nodded. It was true. If daywalkers were allowed to exist, then the czars, senators, and even the emperor would be lower on the proverbial food chain. The only reason they hadn't killed Pete was because he was a liaison to the Amoveo, the shapeshifting clans his mate was from. If the Presidium killed him, then it would cause a war with the shifters.

"So, what happened?"

"Well, the sun was rising, so I told them to prove it." She waved her arm. "Go walk in the sun, and prove it. Hey, I thought they were full of shit, and if they didn't do it, then I'd dust 'em, *or* they'd go out and burn in the sun. I figured I'd get 'em either way."

Olivia's eyes widened, like a child hanging on the edge of a bedtime story. "They didn't fry, did they?"

"Nope." Millicent folded her hands in her lap. "I hung back in the darkest corner of the front hall and watched as the two walked hand in hand into the sun. Damnedest thing I've ever seen. Anyway, they just stood there, fangs bared, bathing in the sun like they were on a tropical holiday, and then they flew off." She dropped her feet, rose from her chair, and started shutting down her equipment. "I never saw them again. It was the only time I've ever lied to a czar. I told him they were gone before I got there, and the trail was cold."

"Unbelievable," Olivia whispered. "How did the two of them figure out that they were bloodmates? How did they even find each other?"

"Not sure." Millicent snagged another cigarette. "I've heard there's some kind of imprinting that takes place during a blood exchange, and another rumor mentioned something about dream connections. Hell,

I have no idea. Maybe it's both, or maybe it depends on the vamps."

"Dreams?" Olivia's eyes flicked to Millicent's, and her body stilled. "But—but vampires don't dream."

"No," she said, hitting one last button, while staring intently at Olivia. "None do." A smile cracked her wrinkled face. "At least, none that I know of. Why the sudden interest in bloodmates?"

"No reason." Olivia shrugged and rose swiftly from her chair. "Thanks for the bedtime story. I always liked a good fairy tale, but I should get going. I've taken up enough of your time, and I'm sure we could both use some sleep."

"Mmm-hmm." Millicent made a face and shook her head. "Something tells me that your little blond progeny isn't the only one playing with fire." Millicent flew across the room, grabbed Olivia's bicep, and pulled her close, dropping her voice to a barely audible level. "Do us both a favor, and don't go asking anyone else about the bloodmate legend. Some legends are best left as that and nothing more. I've always liked you, and I'd hate to see you end up a pile of dust because you go stirring up trouble."

Olivia said nothing but nodded her understanding and left the room before Millicent could say anything else. She had more questions, a hell of a lot more, but she didn't want to drag her old friend any further into this whole mess.

As she breached the Presidium's barriers and entered the sewer tunnels, all she could think about was getting back to her apartment and falling into the arms of sleep. Something told her that Doug would be waiting there to catch her.

The streets were empty, and the early morning sunlight shone brightly over the tall steel and glass buildings, making them shimmer like towers of diamonds. Olivia smiled. She loved it when she had a dream with sunlight. It allowed her to be a daywalker, even if only in a dream.

After what felt like hours, she found Doug walking down the middle of Fifth Avenue, marveling at the peace and quiet that blanketed the usually loud city street. There was not a soul to be seen or heard, and it seemed as though everyone on earth had vanished, leaving just the two of them. The only sound she heard was the soothing beat of his heart as it called her to him.

She sat on top of the Saks Fifth Avenue building and enjoyed watching him as he wandered through the dreamscape. His muscular, broad-shouldered body was impressive amid the towering buildings. His blond hair seemed blonder here, and the white T-shirt clung to the expanse of his back with torturous perfection. The jeans fit him in a way that only a great pair of old blue jeans can fit a man, curving around that apple-like ass and skimming down strong legs.

That was another difference between who he was now and the boy he had been before. His body had filled out into that of a man, opposed to a young man still raw and not fully developed. Not anymore.

He had remarkable strength in the dream realm and seemed far more cognizant of where he was than most humans would be. Olivia cursed. She should have realized sooner that these dreams were more than dreams. No ghost or mere memory of her lover could create the frequency and intensity of the dreams that they shared over the past decade. There had to be a corporeal connection, and besides, since most vampires didn't dream, that in itself should have been a dead giveaway.

A relationship between a human and a vamp was next to impossible—not to mention against Presidium law. So what now? If he was her bloodmate, she would have to turn him, and she had zero plans to do that.

"I know you're here," he shouted. "I can feel you, and I swear I can still taste you."

Holy shit. Olivia gaped at him in utter surprise. He'd never spoken to her in the dreamscape or seemed so aware of what was happening. Then again, neither had she. She watched him stride confidently down the street and knew exactly when things had changed.

That kiss.

It had to be the kiss and that brief taste of his blood. That physical contact had somehow intensified their connection—cemented it somehow. What had Millicent said? Blood imprinting. When she tasted his blood, did she imprint on him? Perhaps when the floodgates had opened for her, they opened for him too, and allowed deeper access to each other's memories and feelings.

Feelings? All she could think about was feeling him. She wanted to feel him again. Touch him. Taste him.

She had a hard enough time getting him out of her head before that kiss, and now it was even worse. Olivia always absorbed blood memories from live feed, but this was far more intense, as if she'd absorbed him and the two of them were now connected. Sounded like blood imprinting. Son of a bitch. She wished like hell there was someone she could ask about all this crap.

The czar and the rest of the Presidium came to mind, and any joy she felt immediately got squashed. It was bad enough her progeny was playing with humans and making messes. What the hell would they say if they knew she was dallying with a human who was her likely bloodmate? Nothing good, that was for shit sure.

The old phrase what-they-don't-know-can't-hurt-them came to mind, and her smile returned. Dreams weren't real, right? So it wasn't as if she was breaking any Presidium laws by dreaming. At least that's what she told herself as she flew to street level and landed silently about a block behind him.

She walked toward him, and the distinct sound of her high heels clicking on pavement shattered the silence. Doug held his ground as she moved. Seconds later, she slipped her arms around his waist, rested her head on his shoulder as her hands spanned the tensed muscles of his abs, while she pressed her body against his.

"Miss me, lover?" she whispered into his ear. "I can't stop thinking about touching you."

Her hands slipped lower to unfasten the fly of his jeans, but Doug grabbed her wrists, pulled her around so that she was in front of him with her back against his chest. She had worn a long black nightgown made of silk and lace that covered hardly anything. Leaving something to the imagination was always more intriguing than letting it all hang out.

"I want to see you," he said between kisses on her cheek. "I need to know if you're real, or if I'm making it all up, like that kiss in the alley." His erection pressed against her lower back as his hands brushed down her

bare arms. "Was that you, Olivia? Was it another dream or a hallucination from hitting my head?"

He didn't know what was real and what was imaginary and probably felt like he was going insane. Olivia wanted to tell him, but where would she begin? How could she explain something she was still trying to understand?

Doug licked the hypersensitive skin along her neck as he murmured, "Even if it is all just dreams, I don't care. It feels pretty fucking real."

He gripped her shoulders and nuzzled her curly red hair off her neck. She arched back, lifted her hands over her head, and threaded her fingers through his short hair, bathing in the feel of his masculine hands as they massaged her breasts. A lusty moan escaped her lips as Doug trailed hot kisses along her neck, and he pinched her nipples as they peaked in response. She pressed herself further into his grasp, desperate to get closer, while he nibbled on the exposed skin.

"I feel like I've been looking for you forever—my whole life," he murmured. "Every time you get closer, but no matter how much I get, it isn't enough. I want more. I want it all."

His hands wandered to her waist and rested on the gentle curve of her hips. She pressed back and ground against him, which elicited a moan of pleasure as his lips pressed against the crook of her neck.

"Then what are you waiting for?" Olivia spun in his arms, grabbed his face with both hands, and whispered against his lips, "Take it."

He captured her mouth with his greedily, and she opened for him, letting him plunder. Devouring her as though she might vanish from his embrace at any moment, he scooped her up and carried her toward the abandoned taxi parked at the curb. Olivia kicked off her stilettos, wrapped her arms around his neck, and deepened the kiss—licking and nipping at his firm, warm lips—all the while wishing it were more than a dream.

He sat her down on the hood of the cab and stood between her legs, which she promptly wrapped around his waist, tugging him hard against her. Heat pressed enticingly against heat. Doug cradled her head in his hands and suckled on her lower lip before breaking the kiss. He rested his forehead on hers and brushed his thumb along the skin of her cheek as her hands rested on his ass.

He pulled back abruptly and lifted her chin, forcing her to look him in the face, and when their eyes met, all the breath rushed from his lungs. Familiar turquoise eyes stared at her beneath a furrowed brow, and she watched as the pieces came together.

"It's you," he said under his breath. "I'm not crazy, am I, Olivia? The second I laid eyes on you tonight outside the club, I knew you were mine. I've dreamt of you since I can remember, but I never thought you could be real." He moved closer, brushing his lips along the corner of her mouth. "And then, there you were on a New York City sidewalk in living color."

She studied his face, and her fingers trailed along the strong line of his jaw. The sun in the dreamscape bathed them in a golden glow and made her recall their stolen kiss in the alley. She had been weakened, but not burned, by the light of early dawn; his blood gave her life, making her heart beat for the first time in centuries, and even some of their memories were the same…all the evidence was right in front of her.

His blood. Just one small taste of his blood. Staring into those painfully beautiful blue eyes, the impossible became reality, and Olivia knew there was no mistaking it now. No pretending. She could have kept up the dream trysts and made love to him again in this plane, God knows she wanted to, but how could she do that knowing what she knew?

How could she allow this to continue? It would only be torturous for both of them. She had to end it, make him think it was nothing more than a dream, and never come to him again. She was vampire. He was human. She had no right to play with his new life and drag him into the darkness. She would not doom him to eternal darkness when he had a promising human life ahead.

She stared back, praying her eyes did not betray her sadness. Olivia pressed his hand against her cheek and closed her eyes. She was weak. She wanted to cuddle up against his chest, let him hold her until sundown, turn him into an immortal, and keep him with her forever. But that would be a selfish, shitty thing to do.

He deserved a real life. A human life. A wife. Children.

All she could bring him was death and blood.

"I'm not who or what you think I am," she said quietly.

Before he could protest, her eyes flicked open, and sadness was replaced with the cold detachment she learned to master as a sentry. Olivia put both hands on his chest and shoved him away with more force than she had ever shown him. She watched as he stumbled backward but managed to keep his balance. The look of confusion on his face broke her withered, beef jerky excuse of a heart.

Barefoot, she hopped onto the hood of the cab in one

fluid motion, her red hair flowing over her shoulders as the sun set with time-lapse speed. The long black negligee clung to her feminine curves, and she knew her nipples poked through the fabric, her body cruelly contradicting her words.

"It's just a dream, Detective Paxton," she said in a shaky voice. She never attempted to glamour a human in a dreamscape, but she had to give it a try. If it worked, he would forget and move on with his life without her. Olivia steeled her resolve and kept her eyes locked with Doug's, dropping her voice to the low, seductive tone of the glamour effect.

"Detective Paxton," she murmured. "Dreams end, just like this one will. Eventually, we all have to wake up and deal with the reality of the life we've been given. We're nothing to each other. Do you understand? I merely look like the woman you've dreamed of and nothing more. You'll have no memory of asking me to dinner, this dream, or the kiss in the alley." Tears stung her eyes as she fought to keep her voice steady. "The next time you see me, I will merely be a person to interview and nothing more. I mean nothing to you, Doug Paxton."

Seconds later, she shot into the air in one swift leap and streaked across the orange sky like a bullet. She prayed for silence and some kind of sign that her attempt to glamour him worked; however, as she fled the dreamscape, his gritty voice echoed.

"You're wrong about that, sweetheart," Doug shouted. "Dreams may end, but you and I are in it for eternity."

Chapter 5

THEY CAUGHT THE CASE NOT LONG AFTER COMING ON DUTY that night, and while he wasn't pleased another murder had taken place, he *was* thrilled to have something to get his mind off the crazy, fucking dream he had. It was the most realistic dream he ever experienced, and if he didn't know better, he would swear Olivia Hollingsworth had actually been there with him.

The dreams were no longer of an unknown redheaded beauty—now they were most definitely of Olivia. Between that weird hallucination in the alley and the dreams, he was starting to think he was going insane. Maybe he hit his head harder than he thought when he tripped outside the ME's building.

Doug stood over the corpse of the young woman and squelched the ugly head of rage that threatened to consume him. He had been on the job long enough that seeing dead bodies shouldn't affect him, but he would never get used to seeing brutalized women or children.

He squatted to get a closer look as Tom spoke to the college kids who found her. Washington Square Park had gotten cleaner and safer over the past few years, and most of the park had been renovated, but the bathroom facility was still under development. The city labeled it a *Comfort Station*, but with all the drug use and sex trade that went down in the crumbling brick building, Doug thought *comfort* was probably the least appropriate word.

Doug looked over his shoulder and through the open door to see Tom interviewing the shaken up kids. They looked like they were going to puke, but he didn't have pity for them, only for the dead girl on the cracked tile floor. The three of them could go home or go on Facebook and blather about how traumatized they were, but the only place the girl was going was to the medical examiner's office and then the funeral home.

He turned his attention back to the victim. Her bleached blond, blood-splattered hair covered her face, but the wounds on her throat and arms were similar to the ones sustained by Ronald. Her purse had been found in the corner of the busted-up bathroom and still had her money and credit cards, so it wasn't a robbery gone bad.

Based on the outfit, she had obviously been out clubbing. One of her heels was broken, and the other had fallen off during the attack. Her black dress was pushed to her waist, and her underwear was around her ankles. She had been raped on top of everything, but this was no run-of-the-mill sex crime.

Doug stood, needing to put distance between himself and the victim, but a mark on her hand caught his eye.

"Hey," he called to one of the techies from the examiner's office, "pass me a pair of gloves, would ya?"

He took the gloves from a guy who looked like he had been on the job for about a day and half.

"You got all the pictures of the body and the crime scene, right?"

The young man nodded wordlessly. Doug pulled on the gloves as Tom came in with the victim's purse in his hands.

"Victim's name is Brittany Diamond. She's twenty-five and has a Nebraska driver's license." Tom made a *tsking* sound. "Looks like another set of big city dreams have been snuffed out. Whatcha got, kid?"

"I'm not sure." Her left arm was draped over her abdomen, but it was the dark mark on her hand that captured his attention. Doug carefully lifted her pale hand and turned it, so that both he and Tom could see. Doug's jaw clenched as he looked at the familiar stamp. The lettering and the gothic design that encircled it was smudged but still readable, and right there, as plain as day, it said *The Coven*.

"Son of a bitch," Tom breathed.

"It's the same nightclub stamp that Ronald Davis had on his hand." He looked closer at it and then at Tom. "This one is black, but Ronald's was green."

"They use a different stamp each night, don't they?" Tom jotted down the information into his notebook.

"Yeah." Doug released her hand gently. "I guess we're heading back to The Coven."

"Looks like you've got an excuse to see that sexy redhead again." Tom's gravelly voice echoed through the space. "This makes two patrons that have turned up dead in just over twenty-four hours, and it looks like they were done by the same sicko. Both hacked up with very little blood at the scene."

"Doesn't make her a suspect, Tom," Doug said more defensively than he intended. "All we know is that both were at her club the night they died."

He stood and stripped the gloves from his hands, unable to look at his partner. He could feel Tom's gaze on him. Doug handed the gloves to the pasty-faced kid and headed out of the bathroom. If he didn't get some fresh air soon, he was going to blow.

"No," Tom said slowly, as he followed him into the darkness. "But it does mean that we need to pay another visit to the club and interview more of the patrons."

"Absolutely." Doug sucked in the warm evening air and ran a hand over his face. He glanced around and noted that the area around the construction site wasn't well lit and had been fenced off, but obviously hadn't stopped those kids from trying to hang out here. Hands on his hips, he turned to face his partner. "We've got two dead kids who hung out at the same club the night they were killed, which makes that nightclub our best lead."

He started toward the car with Tom by his side and silence lingering.

"The club is connected, and that's why we're going back." He snagged his keys from his pocket. "I'm not going there because of Olivia."

"Oh," Tom sang as he tugged the passenger side door open. "So, it's *Olivia* now, is it?"

"Just get in the fuckin' car," Doug said with the hint of a smile. "The club is probably getting going right about now but shouldn't be too crowded. Places like that don't usually fill up until well after ten."

"Whatever you say, kid."

Doug started the car and pulled the blue sedan into the street with only one thought on his mind—seeing Olivia again. He wove his way through the heavy city traffic with the ease of experience, and tension settled in his neck as the club came into view.

He double-parked their car right in front of The

Coven, and it took about three seconds for the bouncer to spot them. Doug was surprised to see there was already a line of people waiting behind a velvet rope. The line was two or three across and at least thirty deep. All of them were dressed in what one would expect to see at a club called The Coven. Lots of tattoos, chains, black leather, and eye makeup on both men and women.

"Ms. Hollingsworth has quite a popular spot," Doug said to the bouncer as he stepped onto the sidewalk. "It's barely nine o'clock, and you've already got a solid line."

"What can I do for you officers?" His deep baritone was barely audible above the noise on the street and the pulsing beat that thundered through the door. He shifted his stance so that his back was to the line of impatient customers, clearly wanting to minimize how much they heard.

"It's Damien, isn't it?" Doug asked as he surveyed the enormous man, who nodded silently. "My partner and I have a few more questions for Ms. Hollingsworth, and we'd like to interview the rest of the staff as well."

Damien tapped his clipboard as he looked from Doug to Tom, and just when Doug thought he would need to lean on him, he simply nodded and waved them in.

"I'll let her know that you'd like to speak with her." He snagged the phone from his pocket and texted something, probably to Olivia.

"Question for you," Doug asked with a nod. "Can we see the stamp you're using tonight?"

"Sure." Damien reached into his jacket and pulled out a small red stamp. He pressed it onto the paper on his clipboard. It was the same design as the one Ronald and Brittany had, just a different color. "Tonight's clubbing is brought to you by the color red." He grinned and looked at Doug. "Blood red."

"Right." Doug gave a sidelong look to Tom. "What color did you use last night? Black?"

"Yup." He stuck the stamp back in his pocket. "Why?"

Doug nodded toward the line and then looked back to Damien. "I'm assuming you'll be here for a while. There are a few questions we'd like to ask you, but I'll come by after I have a chance to speak to Olivia."

"I'll be here." Damien's eyes narrowed, and he nodded curtly. "No problem."

When Doug yanked open the heavy wooden door, his senses were immediately assaulted by the deafening music. He and Tom stuck out like sore thumbs; they may as well have worn their uniforms into the place. They were also probably the only guys without makeup on. The strobe light pulsed with the gritty beat of the music, and colors flashed over the dancing mob, making it look like one massive, pulsing creature.

The high arched ceilings reminded him of many old churches he'd been in, complete with gorgeous art deco stained glass. Doug surveyed the surprisingly small space and estimated there were two hundred people, and he bet the capacity was around that number, thus the line outside.

To the left was a long bar crammed with people angling to get their drinks and waving money at the bartenders. Maya, the blond they had interviewed the night before, and a pink-haired broad he had not yet met, were serving drinks. The back wall had massive white star, lit by a black light. The thing took up almost the entire wall, and sitting on top of what had probably been the church's altar, was the DJ's spinning station with a woman at the helm.

A little blond waitress who looked like she belonged on a farm was hustling from the bar to red leather VIP booths on the far right side of the place. There were a few tables scattered around the outskirts of the dance floor, but that was the limit of the seating.

They cut through the swarm of people, and when they got to the end of the bar, Maya was standing there, waiting with a big smile and her eyes fixed on Tom. Doug glanced at his partner. As he suspected, Tom was staring right back at the petite bartender.

"Well, hello, officers," she said. Maya threw her long blond hair over her shoulders and leaned on the bar with both elbows, which accentuated her cleavage. "What brings you back to our little corner of the world?"

Before Doug could answer, a familiar voice floated over him.

"I was going to ask the same question."

Olivia.

Doug turned to his left and looked into a pair of serious green eyes. Wearing a suit almost identical to the one from last night, she had a powerful, regal air. Her ivory skin glowed amid the flashing lights and gave her an ethereal look. Her gaze searched his and softened before Tom spoke up.

"Looks like you rendered him speechless again," Tom barked.

"We need to ask you about another patron," Doug said evenly, trying to ignore his partner. "A young woman was found murdered in Washington Square

Park earlier today, and she had your club's stamp on her hand. It was the black stamp that Damien said you used last night."

Olivia's face remained blank, but he sensed something under the surface—a storm behind her eyes. He stuffed his hands in his pockets because he didn't trust himself. He wanted to reach out and stroke her cheek just as he had in his dreams and kiss her full, rose-colored lips forever.

"We can talk in my office." She nodded toward to the back and brushed past him. "It's quieter there, and we'll have privacy. As you can imagine, I'd like to keep my customers out of this, if possible."

Doug spun on his heels with Tom close behind. She stood waiting for him a few feet ahead, but once she saw him following, she continued toward the back of the club. As she wove her way effortlessly through the sea of bodies and slipped in and out of his view, he imagined for a moment that he wasn't a cop, but simply a man following a beautiful woman through a club. Stalking her, and eventually claiming her, in the time-honored tradition of boy chasing girl.

She stood waiting at the other end of the bar, chatting with the pink-haired waitress. Doug watched the interaction and got the sense that their relationship was more than employer and employee. In fact, all of the people who worked here had a familial way in how they dealt with one another.

Doug sidled up next to Olivia as he and Tom stood by the end of the bar while she spoke with the punk-rock-looking bartender.

"These are the detectives I was telling you about,"

Olivia said with a nod in their direction. "I'm sure they'll have questions for you, Suzie, and Sadie. I want you to give them your full cooperation." Olivia flicked her attention to Doug. "Gentlemen, this is Trixie. She's not only my best bartender, but my friend, and she'll answer any questions you have. She works every night and may have seen something that could be of use to your investigation."

"What's up?" Trixie shouted and leaned on the bar. Her dark eyes, lined with heavy makeup, looked them up and down. "I'd be happy to talk to you guys, but the stink from the overflowing garbage can back here is making me wanna puke."

"Oh, for heaven's sake," Olivia said in a huff as she lifted the hinged section of the bar and stuck her hand out. "Give it to me. I'll take it out."

"I knew it." Trixie laughed, tied off the overstuffed bag, and yanked it out of the can. "No one hates a messy bar more than Olivia," she said as she handed it to her boss.

"Let me take that." Doug grabbed it, and his eyes met hers, but she didn't let go.

"You're going to take the garbage out for me, detective?" she asked incredulously.

"Call me old school, but taking out the garbage is a man's job."

Her challenging gaze didn't falter. "I assure you that I'm quite capable of handling this myself, and in case you haven't noticed… I'm a woman."

"I noticed," Doug murmured.

For a moment, neither moved. Her green eyes glittered, and just when he was going to relent and let her take the damn garbage out herself, she let go of the bag.

"Fine." She spun around. "Follow me."

"Be right back, Tom." Doug said without looking back.

Doug didn't hear Tom's response, or anything else for that matter. All he could hear was the thundering beat of his own heart. It was ridiculous to insist on taking out her garbage, at least by the standards of today's society, but Doug was old-fashioned. He couldn't stand there and watch the most beautiful, sophisticated, sexy woman he had ever laid eyes on carry a smelly bag of garbage into a crappy city alley.

He followed her down a narrow hallway to a black door with a red sign above it that said *Emergency Exit*. Olivia pushed it open and held it for Doug as he stepped through and tossed the bag into the banged-up green dumpster at the end of the alley. The sound of the door banging shut echoed through the dimly lit alley, and when Doug turned around, he found himself face to face with Olivia. Her distinctly spicy, feminine scent filled his head and heightened his desire.

"You're quite the gentleman, detective," she said quietly as her eyes locked with his. "Your mother raised you well. I should thank her."

"Not really." Doug's jaw clenched, and his hands curled at his side. "She died when I was little. Don't remember much about her."

"I see," Olivia said on a sigh. "Then I suppose I only have you to thank."

As if reading his dirty mind, she leaned closer so that they were only a breath apart, and just as he was about to throw caution to the wind, she pulled back. She raised a finger to her lips and looked past him to the dumpster.

"Did you hear that?" She cocked her head and listened intently.

"I don't—" She pressed one long finger to his mouth, silencing him, and making every inch of him harder than a rock.

"Quiet, or you'll scare it," she whispered.

Olivia dropped her hand from his lips and stepped around him. She made no sound as she moved across the pavement toward whatever it was that caught her attention. Doug watched her prowl toward the back wall, and as she squatted by the back of the giant steel structure, his fingers wound around the butt of his gun. He took two steps closer as she reached behind the dumpster, whispering soothing sounds the way one would to a baby.

A minute later, Olivia stood with a grin on her face and a dirty white and black kitten mewling in her arms. She whispered into the ear of the pathetic-looking creature, and she turned those large, soulful eyes to Doug. As she peered over the quivering ears of the orphan, his heart squeezed in his chest. He didn't think she could get more beautiful, but he was dead fucking wrong, and he wished like hell he could trade places with that cat.

"I don't think she's hurt," Olivia said.

She held it up and inspected it top to bottom as she walked past Doug to the door of the club. Olivia tugged the door open with one hand, cradled her charge against her chest with the other, and looked at Doug, who had not moved.

"I'm sorry." Her face fell, and she spoke quickly. "You're trying to run an investigation into a murder, and you're wasting time with me throwing out garbage and rescuing stray cats. Please, come in my office while I clean her up, and I'll answer any questions you have."

Doug didn't move but kept his eyes locked with hers as she continued to stroke the now quiet kitten's head. This woman was an enigma. A total mystery. One minute she was a tough-as-nails businesswoman fighting for the right to take out her own garbage, and the next she was a complete sucker for a stray kitten.

"No problem." He ran a hand over his hair and shook his head as he walked toward her. "I have no shortage of questions."

They reached the door marked: *Authorized Personnel Only*, and she went directly inside with her attention focused on the cat. Doug followed her and closed the door behind him, but to his surprise he turned to find an enormous German shepherd standing in front of Olivia, guarding her.

The dog snarled, while the black and brown fur on his hackles prickled in warning, but Doug stood calmly staring the dog down. He learned a long time ago that if you showed fear, you were a dead man, and that was true whether you were facing man or beast.

"Van!" Olivia snapped her fingers, and the dog whined before sitting reluctantly at her feet. "No."

The dog growled at Doug before he turned his attention to the tiny kitten in Olivia's arms. He sniffed it and whined, his curiosity clearly getting the better of him.

"You'll meet her in a minute. Go to bed." She pointed to what was obviously the dog's bed in the far corner, and he obediently trotted to it but shot Doug a look of contempt over his shoulder as he settled.

Van and Doug looked back to Olivia and the cat. She

had gotten an old towel from a drawer in her desk and promptly cleaned the kitten off, which was met with a series of mewling protests. Doug watched her intently and so did the dog. Then to Doug's great surprise, Olivia wrapped the kitten in the towel and placed it on the bed next to the enormous German shepherd.

"You were homeless once too," she said to the dog as she scratched him behind his ears. "Remember? Well, she was in a stinky old alley, which makes the pound you were in look like the Ritz Carlton. So be nice. Oreo is part of the family now."

Doug held his breath, certain that the dog was going to gobble the cat in one big bite. However, as Olivia stroked the kitten's head, the dog sniffed it and began to lick it and clean it as if it were a puppy.

"Oreo, huh?" Doug raised his eyebrows. "That's a ballsy move, naming it after a cookie and then putting it in front of that big brute."

"Van is probably more of a pussycat than the pussycat." Olivia sat in the leather chair behind her desk and folded her hands in her lap, as if she were the one interviewing him, keeping one eye on the unusual duo. "Looks can be deceiving."

"A concept I'm familiar with," Doug said evenly.

"Sorry." She straightened her jacket and brushed cat hair off it. When her eyes locked with his, he noticed her body visibly tense. "I guess I'm a sucker for strays and hard-luck cases. I seem to have a talent for rescuing the needy. Now, what did you want to ask me, detective?"

Doug cocked his head, moved closer to the desk, and didn't take his eyes off hers. He studied her carefully and could tell that he had her on edge, but what he *didn't* know was if it was because of the case, the stray cat, or *him*.

"We had another murder victim turn up." He watched for her reaction, but her face remained calm. "She had the stamp from your club on her hand, just like Ronald Davis."

Doug pulled the picture from his notebook and held it out to Olivia. Olivia tried to maintain that serene facade, but he didn't miss the tiniest widening of her eyes when skin met skin. She cleared her throat, tore her gaze from his, and turned her attention to the photo.

"She's dead?" Olivia asked tightly as she looked at the girl's graduation portrait. They pulled it from her high school website because Doug was not a fan of bringing morgue photos on civilian interviews. The smiling face full of hope was a far cry from what he had seen earlier today. She turned her stormy eyes back to his. "You think that whoever killed Ronald also killed this girl, don't you?"

"Yes, at least that's what we suspect. Both spent some portion of their last night alive *here*." He took the picture back and noted she was careful not to let their hands touch again. "You recognize her, don't you?"

Olivia nodded. "She was here with Michael Moriarty and his little gang of thugs. He said something to upset her, and she ran out in a huff."

"Did he follow her?"

"Hardly." Olivia let out a short laugh. "I doubt if he even knew her name. The guy has always got one girl or another hanging on his arm." She lifted one shoulder. "No accounting for taste, I suppose."

"Where did they find her?"

"Not far from here." He put the picture away

quickly and noticed the subtle change in her demeanor. "Washington Square Park."

He could tell she was unnerved by seeing the picture of Brittany, though he resisted the sudden and ridiculous urge to scoop her up in his arms and comfort her. Doug cleared his throat and straightened his back, wrestling to hang onto his waning professionalism.

"We need to speak with your staff, and I need to show her picture around the club. I realize you may not be happy about that, but—"

"Not a problem," Olivia said with a curt nod. "You'll have our full cooperation, of course." She cast a loving look at Van and the kitten, curled around each other and sleeping contentedly. "Too bad someone wasn't around to rescue Brittany," she said, her voice edged with sadness and a twinge of anger.

"We're going to find whoever did this."

"I can promise you one thing, detective," Olivia said as she turned her eyes to his. "If someone in my club was responsible, I will do *everything* within my power to assist you."

"I'm glad to hear that," he said as he put the notebook away and looked casually around the small office.

He noted the lack of personal photographs. The only pictures she had were of her dog and one large print of a sunrise over the mountains. Clearly not married and no boyfriend. Good. The very idea of it made him want to kick some serious ass. It wasn't dignified to feel jealous over a woman he just met, but that didn't make it any less true.

He turned to go, his hand lingering on the doorknob but not turning it. Mustering up his courage, he finally asked the question he had been dying to ask all night.

"So," he asked without turning around. "Is there any chance of you taking me up on my offer?"

He dropped his hand from the knob, silence stretching between them as if condemning him. Doug swore under his breath, turned around intending to offer an apology, and found Olivia standing inches from him. He hadn't heard the chair move or squeak, giving away her movements, yet here she was, just a breath away.

"What did you say?" Her brow furrowed, and she looked at him with wonder.

She was tall, and in those towering heels, only a few inches shorter than he was. Her skin was exquisite, void of a single line or freckle, which gave the impression of someone quite young, but based on her records, she was in her early thirties and had owned this place for the past ten years. Truthfully, she had the air of an older person, and that made her a walking contradiction.

"Dinner, remember?" he asked in a barely audible tone. His lips lifted as his eyes met hers. "Mexican. Chinese. Burgers. Hell, anything you want."

"I remember, detective… I wasn't sure if you would."

"There are some offers a man just can't forget, Olivia." His eyes drifted over the soft angles of her face, and he hardened with need. "You are inescapable, and I can't help myself when I'm around you. At the very least, I want to get to know you better, and I'd like to do it outside of these unpleasant events."

"I—I really didn't think you'd remember," she whispered.

Her sparkling green eyes stayed locked on his, and

her body wavered dangerously close, as if begging to be touched. He should have stepped back and allowed her to pass, or she should have asked him to move, but neither happened.

Instead they stood there, hovering over a dangerous place. Doug swallowed hard as blood rushed from his brain directly to his cock. His mouth watered as the scent of cinnamon filled his head and danced over his tongue.

"It would take me an eternity to forget you," he said in reverent tones.

Her eyes widened, and her lips parted, as if in invitation, which was all the encouragement Doug needed. In a split second his mouth was on hers, and his fingers tangled in those long, red curls as they had so many times in his dreams. His head fogged with desire as her sweet tongue tangled with his, and reason left him, but there was one thing he was sure of—that kiss in the alley had been real.

He would never forget the taste of her.

Her arms slid around his neck as he backed her against the wall and pinned her there. He delved deeply into the cavern of her mouth and groaned as she kissed him back with equal fervor. She wrapped one long leg around his, pressing herself harder against his growing erection. Her small breasts crushed against his chest, and he braced both hands on the wall on either side of her, not trusting himself, afraid he might rip her clothes off and bury himself deep.

Nothing made sense. None of it. But he didn't care. All that mattered was getting more and getting closer. She licked and nibbled at his lips as she grabbed his hair and kissed him back aggressively—which was a major turn-on. He loved a woman who knew what she wanted and wasn't afraid to go for it.

A moment later, she tugged his head away abruptly, breaking the kiss, but her body remained pinned between him and the wall. He rested his forehead against hers and squeezed his eyes shut.

Damn it all to hell. What was he doing?

Doug shoved himself away from the wall and the feel of her body.

"I'm sorry," he said as he grasped for some shred of reality. "I'm not sure what just happened."

Olivia was stone cold. She didn't move, but her green eyes, only moments ago filled with lust, were now hard and unemotional. She straightened her jacket and smoothed her soft red curls as she brushed past him to the door.

"I think we're about finished here, detective. I have to refuse your dinner invitation." Olivia tugged the door open. Pounding music filled the small space, which only moments ago had been thick with the unmistakable rumble of passion. "You are welcome to speak with any of the club patrons, as well as my staff. I have business to attend to, but you know where to find me if you need me."

She arched one amber eyebrow as she held the door open and motioned for him to leave. The music spilled into the office, instantly drowning out their intimate moment. Doug eyed her carefully and let out the breath he'd been holding. He barely noticed that the dog was once again standing guard at her feet.

"I'm sure you won't interview my customers the same way you interviewed me?" she asked in a low, seductive tone as he stepped through the open door. "I can't imagine behavior like that would be good for the image of the NYPD."

He turned to answer her just as the door slammed shut in his face.

"Not likely," Doug muttered under his breath.

He ran his hands over his face and swore silently at his lack of self-control and loss of professionalism. Never in his life did he have personal contact with a witness on a case, and here he was making out like a horny kid in the back office of a nightclub with a broad who could, quite possibly, be involved in the murders.

However, as he cut through the sweaty crowd and made his way to Tom, who was interviewing the waitress by the VIP booths, he knew it was only the beginning. Things were going to get weirder. Doug got to the bar and looked back at the closed door of the office. That kiss in the alley *was* real, and she *was* in his dreams.

The taste of her still lingered on his lips. If he was taking a trip on the crazy train, then riding it with Olivia had to be the best fuckin' way to go.

Chapter 6

Olivia leaned against the door as her fangs broke free, and she let out a sound that fell somewhere between a growl and a groan. How could she be so irresponsible? What in the hell was wrong with her? First, she lets him kiss her. Kiss her? Hell, he jumped her bones—and she loved every second.

She made out with him like the lust-starved woman she was, and kissing him almost made her orgasm.

"Shit."

Her eyes fluttered open, and she ran her tongue along her smooth fangs as the taste of him lingered, a vivid reminder of the brief tussle they'd shared. The office looked the same as it had ten minutes ago, but everything else had changed, and she was allowing it to happen like some silly youngling vampire.

She had to stop this nonsense. She would not pull Doug into the vampire world, no matter how much she wanted him. It simply would not be fair. Hell, she had gone three hundred years without sex and survived. Olivia could not allow this to continue. The only fair choice would be to glamour Doug and make him forget everything.

Tonight, after they hunted for the rogue, she would find Doug and glamour him face to face. Attempting to do it in the dreamscape was a chickenshit way out, and it obviously didn't work. Shortcuts never work, and if she had not been all fucked up on a high of knee-bending lust, she would have thought to erase his memory while he was here in her office.

What if glamouring him in person didn't work either?

Olivia's fangs retracted, and she smoothed the front of her jacket as she made the deal with herself. It would work. It had to work. She would make him forget all of it, and she would live the rest of her existence… alone.

"What a mess." She sighed and was met with a soft meow.

"Hey," she said with a faint smile as she scooped up her latest charge. "You sure did pick a hell of a time to join this crazy coven." She kissed the top of its black and white head as it continued to meow. "I know. I have more important problems than my own drama, don't I?"

Van Helsing barked and sat at her feet with an accusing look.

"I know, I know." She reached down and patted his head. "You try running this coven sometime, mister."

On top of her personal drama, she still had the rogue vampire nonsense to deal with, which had only gotten worse. Moriarty's date from the other night was dead, and she'd bet the same rogue was to blame.

"No more dicking around."

Olivia closed her eyes and reached out to Pete. *The rogue took out another victim. Doug and his partner were here again asking questions. The girl they found was here with Moriarty last night and had the club's stamp on her hand. See if you can get a look at the body, and get a DNA sample to Millicent ASAP. Glamour whomever you have to—but get those samples—I want confirmation that it's the same rogue that took out*

Ronald Davis. This psycho is messing with my business, and it's really pissing me off.

Consider it done, Pete replied.

Both were killed in the village so the rogue vamp that did this is likely hanging around here. I want to find this asshole before it slaughters anyone else.

Van Helsing yipped at her feet and wagged his tail happily as he tried to sniff at his new friend again.

"Yes." Olivia sighed and ruffled him behind his ears. "We're going downstairs. Come on, boy. We'll get Oreo settled in the apartment."

Olivia needed to eat and had to change her clothes. Donna Karan was great for her civilian life but not for the bloody shit she would likely participate in tonight. Olivia went to the back wall of her office and pressed the button behind the sunset painting. A moment later, half of the wall slid open, revealing the passage to the apartments beneath the club. She and Van stepped through the threshold, and as soon as the door slid shut, the motion-sensitive lights came on and lit the stone stairwell down to her home.

At the bottom of the staircase was the front hall of their underground apartment complex. The simple, soft white lights were spaced evenly around the circular entry hall, creating a surprisingly warm entryway. Olivia caught sight of her reflection in the gilded mirror that hung above the black lacquer table but didn't linger on it. Seeing her reflection was a blatant reminder that she was frozen in time while the rest of the world wasn't.

Olivia's apartment door was farthest to the left, and the other three led to Trixie, Maya, and Sadie's apartments. The black lacquered apartment doors were identical, but the spaces inside were as different as the girls themselves. Olivia hadn't been in Maya or Trixie's places lately, and it was probably better that way. Trixie was a slob and had clothing hanging from every piece of furniture, and Maya's place was bathed in bubble-gum pink. Both apartments made her dizzy.

Olivia turned the brass knob and swung her apartment door open, and Van ran past before she could get in. He raced across the dark wood floors and skidded around the black leather couch as he headed directly for his food dish in the kitchen.

"Hungry, buddy?" Olivia asked as she shut the door.

The enormous German shepherd picked up the blue bowl in his mouth and looked at her through big brown eyes.

"I guess so," she said with a laugh.

Olivia placed Oreo on the floor and watched as the kitten investigated the kitchen, while she took the bowl from Van and tugged open the tall white kitchen cabinet. She made quick work of getting dinner for Van, pouring a bowl of milk for Oreo, and whipping up a large mug of blood for herself. She leaned against the edge of the marble countertop and surveyed the space as she waited for the microwave to do its job.

It looked like any other apartment in Manhattan, except for the noticeable lack of windows. She didn't need a kitchen, but she liked having one because she enjoyed cooking for Marianna or Damien from time to time. Her fridge was bare except for pints of blood and some milk and leftover lasagna from having Damien over for dinner last Sunday.

The microwave dinged loudly, announcing the job

was complete. Olivia snagged her mug and took a sip. The warm liquid coated her throat and instantly warmed her body. She chugged back the rest and quickly washed the mug before heading back to her bedroom to get ready. She knew better than anyone that she would need all of her wits about her when hunting the rogue.

Olivia passed the guest bedroom and hall bathroom, noting she still hadn't picked that room up since Pete and Marianna stayed with her a few months ago.

Olivia swung open the double doors to the master bedroom and let out a contented sigh. She *loved* her bedroom. The walls were painted the lightest shade of blue that she could find and reminded her of a summer sky. The king-size bed with the black leather headboard took up much of the room, but it was the softest bed on the planet, and it sure beat the hell out of a coffin. The apple-green comforter looked ridiculously welcoming, especially since she hadn't gotten a full day's sleep. However, she resisted the urge to dive on the bed and headed for her closet.

The only thing Olivia adored more than her bedroom was her closet. She wasn't exactly a clotheshorse, but there was no denying a hot pair of high heels or a well-fitting suit made her feel powerful, in control, and sexy.

She promptly stripped down to her white bra and lace thong. She draped her suit over the hamper and put her Louboutins on the one empty space of the shoe rack, which was really more of a shoe wall. Okay, so maybe she wasn't a clotheshorse but could probably be accused of hoarding shoes.

Van Helsing trotted into the room with the kitten behind him desperately trying to capture his tail. Olivia smiled when she saw that the milk had perked the little girl up. Van barked and hopped onto the tufted bench at the foot of her bed. The minute he got up there, Oreo started mewling to join him.

"Conspiring against me already?" she said through a laugh.

Olivia hoisted the kitten and placed her next to Van. She promptly did three circles in a row before curling up next to her new protector. Van made a satisfied snuffling noise before placing his head on his front paws and watching Olivia's every move.

"I knew you were a sucker." She arched an eyebrow and wagged a well-manicured finger in his direction. "See. You're really a cat in dog's clothing, aren't you?"

The dog licked his lips and growled. Olivia shook her head. "If I didn't know better, I'd swear you just rolled your eyes at me."

Olivia strode to the stainless steel door at the center the far wall and hit the red button on the panel to the left. A gentle whirring sound filled the room as the door slid into the wall and revealed her *other* closet. She didn't want to go back to being a sentry, but that didn't mean she would leave herself or her coven unprotected. An armed vampire was a smart vampire... and one less likely to get dusted.

"I swore I wouldn't do it again," she said quietly.

Olivia breathed deeply as she stepped into the dark cavernous space, and her nostrils filled with the musky scent of leather and the pungent smell of silver as lights flickered on overhead. Memories of her days as a sentry flooded her with surprising clarity. Instead of allowing them to weaken her, she struggled to remember the strength, pride, and power she felt when she first worked for the Presidium.

The left wall was covered with ninja stars, knives, swords, chains, and small, easily concealed weapons. All the weapons were made with sterling silver and could cut through a vampire with laser precision. Simply getting scraped by silver burned like hell, but getting cut by it could kill, especially if it got into the bloodstream.

The right side was filled with guns of various sizes, but instead of a shoe rack, she had an ammo rack that ran floor to ceiling. She hated to admit it, but the ammo wall turned her on, even more than the shoe wall.

Along the back of the closet, opposite the entrance, hung various versions of her sentry uniform. Olivia pulled on the stretch leather catsuit and zipped it with ease. It molded to her body like a second skin, and she couldn't believe how comfortable it felt after all these years. Not only would it provide camouflage in the dark of night, it would also provide protection from the silver weapons she carried.

The tall boots and leather gloves covered her as easily as the rest, but when she pulled on the long leather duster coat, she felt as if she'd stepped back in time. She wasn't Olivia Hollingsworth, business owner and respected citizen. She was an executioner, and if you got in her way, her face was the last image you'd see before the world went silent.

But only for tonight.

Clipping the ammo belt around her waist, she immediately stocked up. She grabbed two black Berettas, along with several clips of ammunition, and slipped them into the harness, but of course, it wasn't regular ammo. These clips contained silver-coated wooden bullets that could not only incapacitate a vamp, but a direct shot to the heart or the head turned them to dust. She strategically placed several silver stars and knives in the lining of her jacket with a couple sheathed inside the top of her boots.

She required one last piece to complete the familiar ensemble and her traveling armory. Olivia went to the black box that rested on a high shelf directly above the row of uniforms. She carefully removed the box from its resting place, lifted the lid, and pulled the leather-handled, sterling dagger from its bed of purple satin.

She held it up and admired the sleek, deadly blade. It had the word *eternity* engraved down the center of the blade on one side and her name on the other. When a sentry was sworn in to their first tour of duty, they were given the Dagger of Eternity as a symbol of their rank among the Presidium.

Olivia secured the dagger in the sheath on her ammo belt and put the case back with the same care she used to remove it. She may not be a sentry anymore, but she still had respect for the position.

Suited and armed, Olivia gave Van a quick pat on the head and snagged a hair elastic off her dresser. All black was great for blending in with the night, but bright red hair didn't exactly *blend*. Olivia made quick work of tying her hair back in a long braid. Satisfied her curls were tamed, she headed out of her apartment.

"Take good care of Oreo while I'm gone, big guy," she called over her shoulder.

A familiar sound filled the air. Her gloved hand hovered over the doorknob of her apartment as Vincent's distinct presence rippled around her with the power of an elder—and her maker.

"Shit," she whispered.

"Now, now." His singsong teasing came clearly through the closed door. "Is that any way to speak about your maker?"

Olivia rolled her eyes, grabbed the doorknob, and opened the door for the man who had turned her into a vampire three hundred years ago.

"Well, what have we here?" He raised his salt-and-pepper eyebrows, as he looked her up and down in her full sentry regalia. He removed his hat and placed it under his arm as he gave her the once over. "Decided to play the game again, my dear?"

"Hello, Vincent," Olivia said wearily. Ignoring his comment, she stepped back and gestured for him to come in.

Vincent swept into the room with all the regality someone would expect from looking at him. Between the long steel-gray topcoat and the hat and cane, there was no mistaking how uptight and formal he was. He surveyed the apartment with the same look he gave her—disapproval. To top it off, Van Helsing came racing out of the bedroom, growling at Vincent as if he'd never met him. Luckily, the kitten didn't appear, which would only have given Vincent more fuel for his fire. He detested animals.

Vincent glared at Van Helsing. "I suggest you call off that mutt before I break his neck."

"Van." Olivia snapped her fingers, and the dog sat at her feet. He stopped growling but still looked at Vincent like he wanted to bite his balls off. She wasn't sure why Van didn't like Vincent. "To what do I owe this pleasure?" she said in the most pleasant tone she could muster. "I can't believe you came to New York. I didn't even realize that you were back in the States until you messaged me."

Vincent hated New York City. He detested America and rarely came across the pond in the last century, especially without more advance notice. The guy expected a fucking parade in his honor every time he came to visit.

Vincent sat in the overstuffed leather chair, crossed his long legs, and placed his hat in his lap. "It seems that you are having trouble managing your coven," he said quietly, while he rolled the handle of his cane between his fingers.

Olivia didn't sit, and if she wasn't in the mood to be cordial before that comment, now she really wasn't. She closed the door and stood in front of it with her arms crossed over her chest, trying to stop herself from telling Vincent to fuck off.

She was his progeny but had been on her own for the last two centuries, and the last thing she needed was Vincent butting into her business, her life, or her coven. Tension settled in her neck, but she managed to keep a civil tongue.

"I'm not sure what you mean," she said a bit too sweetly.

"Must we play these games, Olivia?" he said wearily. "I know about the mess your little blond vampire has made. She was turned five years ago, and as you know, she is still your responsibility. Therefore, her mess is yours, and since you are *my* progeny," he said, baring his fangs, "it is now mine as well. And you know how I loathe messes."

Anger and resentment flared hard and fast, but Olivia held her ground. She kept her sharp eyes on him and let him continue.

"Imagine my disappointment to have my holiday ruined." He smoothed back his dark hair that grayed in patches at his temples. He was distinguished, regal, and a snob. "I had planned on having a pleasant visit, yet it seems that is out of the question. My first stop was to the Presidium so I could pay my respects to the czar and his senators. Sadly, my visit turned into a reprimand from Augustus. He informed me that Maya killed a human and left a messy situation for the police to deal with." He made a *tsking* sound. "Quite unfortunate."

"What are you talking about?" Dread crawled up Olivia's back. She wasn't sure how Augustus found out, but that didn't really matter. All that mattered was protecting Maya and the rest of her coven. "Maya didn't kill that guy. Yes, I will admit that she fed on him and played with him all day, but she *didn't* kill him. They only found trace amounts of Maya's DNA, and according to Millicent, the prominent DNA in the wounds was from an unregistered vampire."

"Not according to Augustus," he said darkly.

"Augustus is a dick and a power hungry liar."

"Maybe," Vincent said evenly. "However, he is still the czar of this district, and as a former sentry, you know better than anyone that there is a chain of command that needs to be followed."

"Really?" Olivia's voice rose. "I guess he only bends the rules when it suits him or *his* progeny. His son, Brutus, let a youngling vampire out on the world with no training or guidance, and if you'll recall, he was only sent into hibernation. Brutus was *supposed* to be put down with that poor creature he created, but Augustus seemed perfectly fine with adjusting the punishment for his son."

"Be that as it may," Vincent said with an air of boredom, "he wants Maya put down. He's under the impression that while Maya may not have killed the boy, she's still responsible."

"That's ridiculous," Olivia scoffed. "How?"

"Augustus believes that Maya is the one who turned the rogue vampire, and therefore is indirectly to blame."

"What?" Olivia seethed, and her body shook with rage and frustration. "No fucking way. She didn't do that, Vincent."

"I was quite sure that's what you would say." Vincent held both hands up to silence her. "I volunteered to come and speak to you myself, and since *I* am your maker, Augustus is allowing *some* leeway."

"Why would you do that, or why would he even allow it?" She could not understand why he would dirty his hands with this business. Vincent hated messes, as he said, and he was volunteering to insert himself in the middle of this one. He made no mention of the dead girl, which led her to believe the czar didn't know about that yet. "What gives?"

"He's allowing it because he and I have been friends for longer than you've been alive," he bit out. He brushed his long, tapered fingers along the lapel of his topcoat in a calming gesture. "You are many things, Olivia. You are defiant, strong-willed, and unpredictable. However, you are not, nor have you ever been, *sloppy*."

Olivia's jaw set, and she bowed her head in deference.

She was all of the things he just said, but as far as she was concerned, they were strengths, not the weaknesses that he implied.

"I assured Augustus that we would clean up this mess and leave the city." He opened his gold pocket watch and glanced at it quickly. "You will gather your coven and come back to England with me tonight. You and your coven will be absorbed under my household."

Olivia's hands balled into fists as she gaped at Vincent, and every shred of restraint shattered in an instant. There it was. Vincent had been itching to get her back under his control, and he was under the misguided impression that now was his chance. Not likely.

After leaving her position as a sentry, she vowed that no one would run her life or control her again. Which was why she ran her coven more like a family than a military state, but all of that would change if she allowed her coven to be taken over by Vincent.

"Who the fuck do you think you are? I will do no such thing," she hissed. Olivia stalked slowly toward him, but he remained seated as calm as ever. "Maya didn't kill that guy, and there's no way she's creating unregistered vampires. She's a spoiled brat and cares more about getting her nails done than learning how to fight, but she wouldn't put her coven—*her family*—in danger. We will hunt down the rogue tonight and kill it."

"There is no need to go hunting, Olivia. You will simply leave the country with me tonight, and Augustus will forget this happened."

"You may be my maker, Vincent, but you're not my father, my husband, or my lover, and you have no say in my life. Your power over me ended after my first century as a vampire, and you know it. You have no right to come into my home and tell me what to do."

Vincent rose slowly from the chair but kept his dark, humorless eyes on hers.

"I don't like being defied, Olivia." His glanced at the ammo belt on her waist, and his eyes narrowed. He may have been older than she was, but she was the one sporting an armory under her coat. "However, what I like even less would be to see my progeny slaughtered by the Presidium. If you come back to England with me now, then Augustus would be willing to overlook this *indiscretion*." His voice dropped low. "But if you insist upon staying here, then there is nothing I can do to protect you. You will be entirely on your own."

"You did your due diligence, Vincent. However, I respectfully refuse. There's a simple way to solve this. I'll find the rogue and put it down. Then I'll bring Maya before the czar, and he can read her blood memories to see that she didn't do it. Plan made and problem solved." Olivia stepped aside and motioned to the door. "I wouldn't want to hold you up and ruin your holiday any further."

Vincent placed his hat on his head at precisely the right angle and moved slowly past her to the door. He paused and turned to face her with his hand resting on the brass knob. "I do wish you'd reconsider. Augustus expects someone to pay for this, and by all accounts, it's going to bc your little blond progeny. I'd be surprised if he would deign to read her blood memories."

"Someone will pay," Olivia said quietly. "You can bet on it."

"I hope it's not you and your entire coven." Vincent

bowed deeply before stepping out the door and whisking up the stairs in a flourish.

Van whined as Olivia went to the empty doorway, but he stayed by her heels, offering comfort.

"My sentiments exactly," she whispered.

She left soon after Vincent, much to Van's dismay. Olivia passed the entrance to her office, turned the corner where stone steps changed to wood, and flew up the old stairs to the exit in the roof. She popped the panel open and stepped onto the angled roof of the old church. Olivia pressed the slate panel closed and surveyed the New York City night warily. If the rogue was killing her customers, then odds were it was still lingering here in Greenwich Village.

She glanced at the digital watch on her wrist. Six more hours until sunrise. Six hours to find the rogue vampire and glamour Doug. Her lips tilted. Maybe.

Hey, boss lady. Pete's voice cut into her mind. *Meet me at Washington Square Park*.

Olivia leaped from the roof and flew toward the park, swiftly and silently. Not even the birds knew what it was that blew past them in the cool spring night. Minutes later she landed without a sound behind the construction site where Pete and Shane were waiting.

As his maker, she could detect his presence in the air almost the way a bat reads sonar waves. Too bad she couldn't detect just any vampire as easily. It would have made finding the rogue a hell of a lot easier. Leaning against the brick building hidden by shadows, he was almost invisible to the naked eye, but Olivia spotted him easily.

"You look good," Pete said with a nod of approval. "How long has it been since you put that on?"

"Not long enough," she said wearily. "Where's Quesada?" Hands on her hips, she scanned the area, sensing the other vampire in the vicinity. "I know you're here, Shane."

"I am here," said a baritone voice behind her.

Olivia didn't turn around but waved him forward, and a moment later, he was standing next to Pete with an emotionless expression. She looked him up and down as she nodded her approval.

"Good to have you on the hunt." Her eyes met his. "How much has Pete told you?"

"There is a rogue on the loose, and from what I have heard, you feel that your progeny is being unfairly blamed for creating it." He grinned, his white fangs flashing in the darkness. "I'm here to help you find it and kill it. Rogues are dangerous, messy, and savage. They have no honor or respect for the order of our society and do not deserve the gift of immortality. It will be my pleasure to assist you in destroying it."

"I see." Olivia held his stony gaze. "What about the czar? Aren't you breaking the rules by helping us before reporting to Augustus?" She wanted to see how much he knew and what he was willing to share. "From what I hear, you are all about the rules."

"As a former sentry you know that putting down rogues takes priority over all else." Shane's voice dropped low. "Augustus knows all about your progeny's role in this mess. I am here to not only help hunt and destroy the rogue, but also to ensure that you and your little troublemaker come before the Presidium tomorrow evening. You have one night to find this rogue. After that, your coven will pay the consequences."

"This is bullshit," Pete spat.

"Fine." Olivia held her hand up, silencing him, but didn't take her eyes off of Shane. "I had a feeling your help would come with strings attached. We'll take the help, and after we capture the rogue and prove Maya's innocence," she said with a sigh, "I'll also take an apology."

Shane smirked but said nothing. Olivia knew his kind. He was blindly devoted to the Presidium, and even more than that—to his duty as a sentry. She had no doubt he would be a fierce hunter. She also had no doubt that he would kill her and the rest of her coven if it meant following the czar's orders.

She turned her attention to Pete.

"We now have two dead humans thanks to this rogue asshole and—"

"Two?" Shane interrupted.

"Yes." Olivia winked. "Try to keep up." She looked back to Pete and did her best to ignore Shane. "Doug definitely thinks someone at The Coven is responsible."

"On a first name basis now?" Pete asked.

Olivia chose to ignore the comment and continued. "On top of that, Vincent—my maker—expected me and the rest of my coven to run off to England with him. Apparently, us leaving town is the only way Augustus would *overlook* Maya's involvement. He didn't even want us to hunt for the rogue."

Shane said nothing, but Olivia didn't miss the slight narrowing of his eyes at the mention of Augustus's willingness to bend the rules.

"What?" Pete's eyes glowed red, a side effect of his demon heritage. "Since you're here, I take it that you told him to fuck off."

"Basically." She looked at Pete through serious eyes. "When we get back to the Presidium, they're going to tell you to kill Maya. Isn't that right, Shane?"

"Yes," he said calmly.

"No damn way." Pete's jaw clenched. "We'll find the rogue and get it to confess to whoever turned it." He sucked in a deep breath, and his eyes flickered back to normal. He gestured to the crime scene tape that fluttered in the wind. "I got a look at the body in the coroner's van and took a DNA sample from the wound. The girl was killed just like Ronald Davis, so I had Millicent run the sample."

"It was a match?"

"Sort of," he said gravely. "It's a rogue, but according to the DNA sample, it's not the same rogue."

"Son of bitch," Olivia seethed. "There are two?"

Shane said nothing but listened intently as Pete continued.

"At least," he said grimly. "Their DNA sequences match them as siblings, which means we've got someone out there making their own little rogue coven and a bloody mess. The only good news is that Maya's DNA wasn't present on the girl at all."

"Well, it wouldn't be, would it?" She went into the decrepit bathroom, and the room was thick with the scent of stale blood. "She's been on lockdown since we found out about Ronald, but none of that really matters. Augustus has convinced himself, and the senators, that Maya made the rogue. If I know him, he's already sent word to Emperor Zhao, especially since I didn't agree to leave town."

She squatted and placed her hands on the floor,

hoping to capture some trace evidence of the rogue, but no luck. Olivia hoped there would be something to help her, but there was nothing here but stale blood and desperation—mostly her own.

"Damn it," Olivia said on a sigh. "We've got our work cut out for us."

"Since there are two, we'll cover a hell of a lot more ground if we split up, and I have something that should help us track down at least one."

Pete pulled a small glass vial out of the pocket of his long coat and held it up for her to see. Olivia leaned closer with a puzzled look as she stared at what looked like blood.

"What is that?" she asked hesitantly.

"A gift from Millicent and Xavier." Pete grinned and placed it in her hand.

"I guess Xavier still doesn't sleep much." Olivia cracked a smile. "What did he make for us?"

"He used the DNA sample from Ronald's wounds to create a synthetic version of that rogue's blood—we're calling him Rogue One. Xavier thought that it might help us track him down. Apparently, he's been working on something like this for a while and was psyched to have a chance to use it."

"Him?" Olivia arched one eyebrow at her progeny. "You tasted it already?"

"Yes, ma'am." He flashed his fangs and elbowed Shane, who clearly saw no humor in the situation. "Xavier should win the fuckin' Nobel Prize for the shit he comes up with. Anyway, I've got his blood scent now and so does Shane. So, in theory, if the rogue is in the area, then we should be able to track him." He narrowed his eyes, and they flickered red. "I can smell him in here, that's for shit sure, but Xavier said this may only last a few hours, so we should get moving."

"Synthetic blood as a tracking device? Cool." Olivia smiled and shook her head as she uncapped the vial and raised it in a toast to Pete and Shane. "Here's to Xavier, my brilliant friend," she said throwing it back like a shot.

The scent of rotting flesh filled her head, and the taste of dirt coated her tongue. Olivia fought the urge to vomit and grabbed the broken metal stall for extra support. The metal bent beneath her grip like clay, and for a second she thought she was going to pass out.

Her green eyes fluttered open and filled with tears. "Holy shit," she whispered. "That tasted like concentrated evil."

"Yeah. Evil dipped in dog shit." Pete grimaced and patted her on the shoulder. "I didn't know if you'd have the same experience, so I figured I'd let you try it for yourself. Why do you think it tastes so bad?"

"I have no idea." She wiped at her tearing eyes. "Jesus. Even the junkies I've fed on tasted better than this." She grimaced and shivered. "Well, that's not a scent or taste I will easily forget."

Olivia pushed past Pete and Shane to the fresh air outside and leaned against the brick wall.

"We split up, but keep communication open." She tugged her gloves on tighter and tried to focus on the scent of Rogue One that still lingered in the air.

"Since I have no ability to telepath with either of you, I will go hunting with one of you."

"Not me," Olivia said as she adjusted the gun in her

holster. "I've been to this dance before, but Pete has never hunted rogues, so you go with him."

Why do I feel like I just got stuck with the class dork? Pete's teasing voice drifted into her head.

He may be a stiff, but he's got centuries of experience, and I'll feel better if you hunt with him. You're going to be a father, remember?

"It's quite rude to telepath when I am standing right here," Shane said with mild irritation.

"Whatever." Olivia rolled her eyes. "If you find the rogue, don't kill it. Incapacitate it, and get it to the Presidium. We need it to confess or, at the very least, read its blood memories, so we can find out who turned it and get it to tell us where they're holing up during the day."

"Any ideas where to start?" Pete asked.

"Sewer and subway tunnels are most likely or any abandoned buildings in the area. I suggest we start with all of the above-ground options tonight while it's dark. I'm going to swing by Jerry's place and see if he's heard anything."

"Who is Jerry? And if he is an informant, why have I not heard of him before?" Shane asked coolly.

"He's my friend," Olivia said evenly. "Not an informant. He wouldn't talk to you or Pete because he doesn't know you."

Shane narrowed his eyes but didn't respond. It was only a half-truth. Jerry was her friend, but he was also her best informant. If anyone got wind of a rogue coven, it would be him.

"If we don't find either of them tonight, then we meet at the club tomorrow night and then go deal with

Augustus. You two take the East Village, and I'll cover the West Village. Agreed?"

"Agreed." Pete winked. "Boss lady."

Olivia watched Pete and Shane launch into the sky as she prayed they would find the rogue before sun up. The last thing she wanted to do was go before Augustus empty-handed. It could mean the end of Maya or even the end of her entire coven.

Chapter 7

Doug had a headache to beat all fucking headaches, and if he didn't get out of the damn nightclub in a few minutes, he was going to vomit all over these fishnet-and-eyeliner-wearing civilians. He'd been battling the loud music and flailing drunk dancers for the past hour and a half in order to question some of the people who had been there last night. The best lead came from the little waitress who looked even more out of place here than he did.

He went back to the end of the bar where Tom had been parked much of the time, interviewing Maya and Trixie. Tom was a good man and deep down, a good cop, but nothing fucked him up more than a pretty girl paying him some attention. Not that Doug was one to criticize weakness for a pretty lady, especially given his less than professional moment with Olivia in her office.

"Hey." He nudged Tom and gave a tight smile to Maya, who was lingering nearby. "I spoke to Suzie, the waitress, and she said that Brittany was here last night with Michael Moriarty and his crew."

"Michael Moriarty, as in the son of Tony Moriarty, owner of Moriarty Construction and our very own NYC crime family?" Tom took a sip of his water. "Guess we better pay a visit to little Michael."

"Anything, but let's get the hell out of here," Doug shouted. "This music is giving me a massive migraine."

"Thanks for your help, ladies." Tom tossed a tip on the bar and waved to Maya, who gave him a flirty wink and blew him a kiss. Doug shook his head. Tom either didn't see it or acted like he didn't.

Doug pushed open the heavy wooden door and sucked in a breath of city air. He snagged the pack of gum from his pocket and made quick work of unwrapping a piece and popping it in his mouth. He still had the taste of Olivia on his tongue, and it was messing with his concentration.

"Not a fan of nightclubs, eh detective?" Damien asked with a barely hidden smile.

"Not my thing, I guess." Doug waved Damien to the other side of the door, away from the people who were still waiting in line and hoping to get into the club. "Olivia and Suzie said that Michael Moriarty came here with a date but that she left before he did. Is that true?"

"Oh man." Damien ran a large hand over his head, and if Doug didn't know better, he thought the big guy was about to cry. Looked like Damien was a gentle giant. "Did something happen to her?"

"Yeah," Tom replied wryly. "Raped, murdered, and dumped in a public restroom. So help us out. What did you see?"

"She ran out of here last night right before closing." He fiddled with the clipboard, and his mouth set in a tight line. "She was crying and muttering something about how no one treats her that way."

"Would that someone be Moriarty?"

"Yes," Damien hissed as his eyes darkened.

"What about Moriarty and the rest of his group?" Tom asked. "When did they take off?"

"They left in his limo not long after that, but he didn't ask about the girl or where she went." Damien's brow furrowed, and a puzzled look came over him. "Come to think of it, I'm surprised he's not here tonight."

"Why is that?" Doug made a note and exchanged a knowing look with Tom. "He's a regular here?"

"Yeah. He can be found in one of the VIP booths every Friday and Saturday night for sure. Weeknights too, sometimes." A look of contempt came over his face. "He's been after Olivia for ages. I guess he figures that if he drops enough money here, she'll pay attention to him."

"Mm-hmm." Doug's jaw clenched, and he kept his eyes on his notes as he tightened his grip on the stubby pencil. "I can't imagine a classy lady like Olivia would be interested in the likes of Michael Moriarty." He tried not to sound like a possessive lover but failed miserably. "Anything else you can think of that might help us? Was she here the night before as well? Do you know if she knew Ronald Davis?"

"No, I don't think so, but if I remember anything, I'll be sure to contact you." Shouts and whining from the line behind them caught Damien's attention. "I better get back to the door. This mob can get ugly pretty quick."

"I don't doubt it." Doug handed the big bouncer his card. "If you remember anything else that might be useful, give me a call."

"No problem." He tucked the card in the pocket of his slacks and returned to his post at the door.

Doug pulled out without saying a word, and they drove for five minutes before Tom finally broke the silence.

"I take it you're headed for Moriarty's apartment?"

Tom rolled down the window and adjusted the rearview mirror on the passenger side. "It's close to midnight. Don't you think it's a little late to be calling on him?"

"No," Doug said tightly. "By all accounts it was out of the ordinary for him to be absent from the club tonight, and he happens to be a no-show the night after his date ends up dead? That's far too coincidental, and besides, he's the best lead we've got."

"Okay." Tom adjusted his position in the seat. "I can see him as a possible killer for the girl, but what about Ronald Davis?"

"Not sure yet." Doug shrugged. "Who knows, maybe Davis flirted with one of Moriarty's dates, and he didn't like it."

"You're grasping at straws, my friend." Tom tapped his fingers on the side of the car. "But you're right about it being our best lead."

They pulled up in front of Moriarty's swanky Upper West Side apartment overlooking the Hudson River, and the doorman looked at them with disdain. Moriarty's family owned three apartments in the building, and chances were that this guy was buried in their deep pockets, so a hell of a lot of good he was going to be.

"You can't park that here." The doorman waved at them with his white-gloved hand and shook his head vigorously. His gold buttons blinked as they caught the light of the passing cars. "Move along."

Tom and Doug flashed their badges simultaneously as they exited the car, which had the seasoned doorman rolling his eyes and muttering under his breath.

"What was that?" Tom asked with a big smile. "I didn't quite catch that. Did you, Paxton?"

"No." Doug glanced past the doorman to the empty, but brightly lit, lobby. "We're here to see Michael Moriarty."

"He's not here." The older man clasped his hands behind his back and avoided looking at them. "He went out last night and hasn't been back since."

Doug and Tom exchanged a curious look.

"How can you be sure?" Tom asked. "You're on the night shift, so what if he came back during the day?"

"When I went off my shift at 6:00 a.m., I told Bert, the day shift guy, that Moriarty hadn't come back and to keep his eye out for him." He dropped his voice and leaned closer, clearly not wanting anyone to overhear, even though they seemed to be the only ones around. "Sometimes the kid goes on a bender, and when he comes home, he causes a scene. His father hates it, so it's up to us to get him to his apartment with as little fuss as possible. Spoiled brat, if you ask me."

"So, I take it that Bert told you he never came back and that it would likely be your problem again?" Doug suppressed a grin. He could only imagine the crap this poor guy put up with from Moriarty. "That can't be much fun."

The doorman nodded curtly and glanced at the camera in the doorway, clearly nervous that he'd be caught talking to cops on camera.

"Would you please call us when Moriarty shows up?" Doug handed him his card. "He's not in any trouble. We just need to ask him a couple questions."

As Doug pulled away in the shadow of the towering steel building, he couldn't squelch the nagging feeling in his gut that Moriarty was involved in this mess. His date had stormed out on him, then she turned up dead, and now he seemed to have skipped town. Moriarty was looking more and more like their prime suspect, but Tom was right, there was still no explanation for why he would have killed Ronald Davis.

~

"Tell me again why we're coming back *here* when we could be going home?" Tom asked as he slammed the door shut on the sedan. "We've been working all night. The sun is gonna be up soon, and I need some sleep. I'm old and tired."

"By all accounts, Moriarty and four of his crew have vanished. They never came back to their apartments, and nobody has seen them since they pulled out of here in his limo. The driver and car are missing too, and the last place anybody saw them was here. We could get old and gray sitting around waiting to get a copy of his cell phone records."

"I'm already old and gray." Tom shook his head and let out a weary sigh. "You said that the Hollingsworth broad lives here in the building?" He glanced at the spire of the old church. "That's just weird. This place was creepy when it was full of people, and now it's really fuckin' creepy. The place is closed, man."

"Yeah, but I think she and her staff know more than they're letting on, and I want to know what it is."

"Kid," Tom said on a sigh. "You're gonna be the death of me."

Doug pulled his jacket out of the car and questioned his motives as much as Tom did. When he looked up, the gothic lettering of the nightclub's sign glared at him accusingly. They shouldn't be doing this.

He pulled his jacket on and stepped onto the cracked sidewalk in front of the club. Damien, the velvet rope, and the throngs of people were gone. Doug glanced at his watch and saw it was well past last call. He tugged on the doors of the club only to find them locked, and his heart sank. He didn't realize until that moment how much he wanted to see her—to taste her.

"See, kid," Tom said wearily as he leaned against the hood of their car. "They closed shop, and I don't see any door to her apartment. Let's go, huh? We can come at them again after we get some sleep."

The high-pitched pinging sound of a bottle clinking down the pavement caught their attention, and Doug's senses went into overdrive. They exchanged curious looks. Doug looked to his left toward the sound, but the sidewalks were empty, and the narrow street was void of moving cars. The only movement was farther down at the intersection of Sixth Avenue, but here on King Street it was quiet—too quiet.

The clinking sound echoed again, and this time they could tell it was coming from the narrow alley on the side of the club. Doug placed his finger on his lips and nodded toward the alley. He reached inside his jacket and wrapped his fingers around the steel butt of his gun as he and Tom inched closer.

Tom drew his gun and secured it in front of him as he sidled up quietly next to Doug. Maybe it was Damien or Olivia putting garbage out? It could be a cat or a drunk making his home next to a dumpster, but Doug couldn't squelch the sense that it was something more. Maybe it was the case, or *maybe* it was because an unnatural quiet had settled over the street.

As they moved slowly along the front wall of the club toward the alley, the lights of the nightclub sign flickered before going out and leaving them in the dark. No working streetlamps, and the sky was just beginning to lighten. Great.

"I don't like this, kid." Tom glanced around nervously.

Doug peered around the side of the building, but the alley was even darker than the damn street. He froze as the clinking sound of the bottle rattled again, and seconds later, an old Heineken bottle rolled past their feet.

A low, deep laugh floated toward them and chilled him to his core.

Doug and Tom raised their guns and swung around, but a split second later, something flew toward them. A dark shadow, seemingly death itself, grabbed Doug by the jacket, tossing him through the air, down the alley, and into the side of the dumpster. Lights bloomed behind his eyes, and his entire body went numb, as he slammed into the cold metal before landing in a groaning heap on the concrete.

Tom fired two shots, but someone or something tackled him to the ground, and through the head-spinning haze of pain, Doug could hear him screaming. He willed his body to move, to get up and help his partner, who was on the ground with someone on top of him. Doug rolled onto his side, gasping for air with his face pressed against the gravel, as he fought to stay conscious.

The numbness ebbed cruelly, as sharp pain radiated down his neck and back. He reached blindly around for his gun, but he could barely see anything. The world was spinning, and his head felt like it was going to crack open. He could hear his attacker move slowly toward him with the same low laugh he'd heard a moment ago. He inched closer as Doug vaguely recalled he had a gun in his ankle holster. Grunting from effort and biting back nausea, he snagged the gun from its hiding place.

"Police," Doug shouted.

The man kept coming. Doug blinked as either blood or sweat dripped into his eye, and he squeezed off two rounds, one of which he was certain hit the guy in the chest. Through blurred vision he saw the guy jerk as the bullet impacted, but all it seemed to do was piss him off.

Behind him Doug saw Tom's motionless body, and Doug knew he was dead. A dark shadow whisked in front of him, picked him up by the neck with one hand, and held him in the air like a rag doll. All he could see was a figure, a dark outline in the middle of a fuzzy sea of gray, while white spots danced before his eyes as the grip on his neck increased.

Gasping for air as the pressure in his head reached dangerous levels, he kicked at his attacker, but the guy was unfazed. In a flash he swung him around and pinned him against the building with the same ease that Doug would swing a baseball bat.

He let out an *oooff* as his back met the brick wall, and the wind was knocked out of him again. The second Doug's feet touched the ground, he pulled at the steely claw curled around his throat, and with his last ounce of strength, kneed the bastard right in the dick.

All the guy did was flinch… and growl. He looked vaguely familiar, and somewhere in the recesses of his brain, he remembered this was a low-level criminal—one of Moriarty's buddies. He was about five foot ten, far shorter than Doug, with dark hair and crazy eyes. That's what he kept thinking. This guy must be crazy, hopped up on PCP, or coked out of his gourd. That was the only explanation that made sense—at least until he saw the fangs.

Vampire.

The word seemed silly, almost comical, and yet that was all Doug could think as the guy got right in his face and bared his teeth. He had fucking fangs, and a second later he drove them into Doug's neck. It was like getting stabbed with a million tiny needles all over his body.

His skin burned, and his blood seemed to boil, but before long the pain was replaced by an odd sensation of floating and the vague awareness that he was being bitten over and over again. The guy was chewing on him like a damn steak. His back scraped against the bricks as he slid down the wall, while this crazy freak chewed on his neck. Just as his leaden eyelids fluttered closed, he heard *her*.

"Consider that your last meal, asshole."

The creature released him, spun around, and hissed.

It was Olivia.

Olivia was here? Doug coughed, and the coppery taste of blood covered his mouth. He wanted to scream, to warn her to get the fuck out of there, but not a single part of his body would cooperate as he sat slumped against the wall. A split second later, a gunshot blasted through the alley and his attacker let out an ungodly shriek and exploded into flames.

As ashes fell over him like snow, the last sight he saw was his redheaded goddess, looming over him with a look of concern, a set of bright white fangs, and a big-ass gun. As Doug slipped into unconsciousness, he heard her whisper, "Forgive me."

Doug's body stung, throbbed, and twitched in the throes of death, and then… he was flying. Flying with Olivia, his limbs tangled temptingly with hers as they whisked through cool, peaceful tunnels of stone. Darkness swamped him as the light faded from his sight, and the world he knew slipped away. White-hot pain cloaked his body in the shadows, but the soothing sound of Olivia's sweet voice eased his suffering and calmed the fire. He cradled her in his arms as the smell of copper and rich earth enveloped him and swept him away.

Chapter 8

Cool, clean sheets and the familiar scent of cinnamon surrounded him, and for a moment Doug thought he was dreaming, but when he opened his eyes, it all came roaring back in full color. He sat up as nausea swamped him, and the room started spinning before he flopped back into the soft mountain of pillows.

Two cool hands covered his bare shoulders, and Olivia's tantalizing, spicy aroma filled his head, instantly quelling the knots in his stomach. There was no way he was in a hospital. The place smelled clean and fresh, but not like a hospital. Maybe it was heaven?

He let out a moan of confusion and grabbed his head with both hands as he fought to get his bearings. He was in a bed. That much he'd figured out. He was naked as the day he was born and had gotten his ass kicked, probably by the same guy who killed those kids.

He remembered being bitten and feeling like he was dying. He could swear Olivia shot the crazy bastard and turned him to dust. *I must be dead. Dead or crazy. Shit.*

You're not dead. He could swear he heard Olivia's voice floating through his mind. *Or crazy.*

"Olivia?"

Doug cracked his eyes open and was greeted by her smiling face and brilliant green eyes. Her red curls fell over her shoulders and tickled his bare chest as she leaned closer inspecting what he figured was a gash on his head. Doug grabbed her wrists and tugged her closer, holding her against him. Panic and fear slammed into him as the memories flickered into his mind bit by bit.

Doug licked his dry lips and managed to croak out, "Where am I?"

"You're in my apartment." She extricated herself from his grip and picked up a mug from the nightstand. She held it to his lips. "Drink this. It will help."

It smelled like Christmas morning and a great steak rolled into one. He sucked it back greedily and groaned as the warm, thick liquid coated his throat. Within seconds, energizing warmth spread across his chest and radiated through his body. He tipped the cup all the way back, trying to get the last drop, and had to force himself to keep from licking the inside of the now empty mug.

"Whatever that is, it tastes great," he rasped.

He wiped his mouth with the back of his hand, and he wasn't exaggerating either. The throbbing in his head instantly went away, and the nausea had been replaced by a cool, tingling sensation that washed down his arm and through his head. It was like bathing in a peppermint patty.

"What was that? Some kind of organic remedy? I've never tasted anything like that."

"I guess you could say that," she said humorlessly.

Olivia let go, rose from the bed, and went to a white dresser on the opposite side of the room. He watched as she tossed a bloodstained washcloth in a basin and cleaned up her makeshift nurse's station. She was wearing a black catsuit that looked like it was painted on and hugged every womanly curve. Ass-kicked or not, he had the ridiculous urge to jump her bones, but given his current state, that wasn't likely.

"Not to sound like an ingrate, but why did you bring me here and not call an ambulance?" His brow furrowed as he looked around the bedroom. "How did you get me here by yourself anyway?"

She ignored his question. "What were you doing in the alley?" Olivia asked in a voice edged with frustration. She turned, folded her arms over her chest, and studied him but kept her distance. "Why on earth were you there?"

"Tom and I came to ask you—" He stopped midsentence as more memories came charging back and looked frantically around the room. "Where's Tom?"

Olivia didn't answer, but sadness flickered over her face. "I couldn't help him," she whispered. "It was too late. I'm sorry."

"What?" he seethed as he pushed himself to a sitting position. "You just left him there?" His throat tightened as he choked on anger and sorrow, glaring with accusing eyes. "You left him in that alley to die?"

"He was already dead by the time I got there." She squared her shoulders and leveled a cold gaze at him. "I'm sorry. I was, however, able to get there in time to help you."

Doug swore loudly, pressed the heels of his hands against his eyes, and slammed his head into the brass headboard. His partner. His friend and the closest thing he had to a family was gone—and it was entirely his fault. Tom hadn't wanted to go back there last night, but Doug insisted, and now Tom was dead.

"He's dead because of me," he ground out.

"You couldn't have known what was going to happen." Her gentle voice soothed him, but it couldn't stop the tidal wave of grief and guilt. "It's not your fault, Doug."

"Where is he?" Doug asked tightly.

"We have his remains. I thought you'd want to have a say in how he's taken care of." The bed dipped as Olivia sat next to him and rested her delicate hand on his forearm. "I know it's difficult, but can you tell me what else you remember?"

"Nothing that won't sound crazy," he said as he rubbed his hands vigorously over his face. He dropped them in his lap, and Olivia linked her graceful fingers with his in a surprisingly intimate gesture. He brushed his thumb across the ivory skin of her hand and marveled at the smoothness; she was fire and ice all rolled into one. "We came back to talk to you. I heard something in the alley. Tom and I went to see what it was, and that's when they jumped us. And then…" he trailed off, unable to finish his thought.

He looked away and around the room. What was he supposed to tell her when he didn't trust his own memories? He fleetingly noticed that there were no windows in the room, and he didn't know how he knew, but he could tell they were underground.

"What else?" she asked quietly as she rubbed her thumb over his palm. Smooth strokes seemed to ripple through his whole body, like a pebble in a pond; that simple touch affected his body from head to toe.

"I'm not really sure," he said absently. "Tom fired at least two shots, but something or someone tackled him."

He bit back the grief and focused on his anger. Anger he could manage, but not grief, not the stabbing pain of loss. When his mother died he promised himself that he wouldn't get close to anyone else again, so he wouldn't feel that heart-wrenching emptiness. Grief, loss, and a broken heart were harder to face than anger and vengeance. Those emotions could feed the fire in his belly—the one that wanted to kill whoever did this to Tom.

"I got tossed against a dumpster, and after that it's all jumbled." Doug instinctively touched the spot on his neck where the guy had bitten him but found nothing. "And really fucking weird."

"Something wrong?"

Olivia watched him intently, and his eyes met hers as his fingers brushed the unmarred flesh on his neck. It should have been a hacked-up mess, bandaged or stitched, but it was smooth and free of injury. It was as though he had never been attacked at all.

He tightened his grip on her hand.

"Doug?"

"He bit me, Olivia," he said just above a whisper. He looked her straight in the eye, worried that she would tell him he was crazy or hallucinating, but to his surprise she remained calm and resolute. "He had fangs, and the guy fucking bit me. I thought he was coked up or drugged out of his eyeballs, but I've seen a lot of addicts in my day, and none had that kind of strength. He picked me up like I weighed nothing. At first, I thought the fangs were fake and part of a costume."

"What else?" Her voice, edged with tenderness, dipped low as her eyes searched his. "What else did you see?"

"You." Doug adjusted his position in the bed and looked at her intently. "I saw you shoot him."

"Yes."

Her voice was barely audible and her expression unreadable. Was it regret? Fear? Apathy? He didn't know, but since she didn't roll her eyes or call him crazy, he held his breath and waited for her to continue.

"It's okay." A smile cracked her face, and she squeezed his hand. "You're not crazy."

"You said something about this being his last meal, and you shot him."

"Unfortunately, I didn't get the one that killed your partner. Which means we've still got a rogue out there, and it could cause quite a bit more damage if we don't put it down. I'm just glad it didn't turn your partner. When rogues create other rogues, the turn never goes well, and the situation gets exponentially worse."

"Rogues? What do you mean *create* rogues?" Doug cocked his head, and that sick feeling in the pit of his stomach came rumbling back. He squeezed her hand tighter, and his jaw clenched. "How about we cut the crap, and you cut to the chase."

"I thought you were a good detective?" She arched one amber eyebrow as the corner of her mouth lifted. "Detective."

She slipped her hand out of his as she rose from the bed and paced back and forth across the room. He watched her carefully and tried not to think about the facts. They all added up to a big pile of crazy, like a sack full of cats kind of crazy.

"Let's look at the evidence, shall we?" She ticked the evidence off one finger at a time. "A man with herculean strength, who was far smaller than you, tossed you around like a doll. He had a set of fangs, bit you, and drank your blood. When I shot him, he exploded and turned into a cloud of ash. I live in an apartment with no windows beneath my nightclub, which is, by the way, called The Coven." She slowly moved toward the side of the bed as she spoke, but didn't take her eyes off his. "You're not dreaming now, Detective Paxton. So why don't *you* tell *me* what's going on."

Vampires.

The word ran through his head again and again like a broken record at a million miles a minute, but he couldn't bring himself to say it. Doug smirked at the ridiculousness of the idea as he ran his hand over his chest, shaking his head in disbelief. But the smile ran from his face when he realized something quite important was notably absent.

"Something wrong?" Olivia asked evenly. "I guess you could say that I stole your heart, but that seems rather dramatic."

"This has got to be another freaky fucking dream," he said with sheer disbelief. He looked at her for reassurance that he still had a heartbeat, that this was just a dream, but no such luck.

"We'll talk about the dreams another time," she said casually. Doug's startled gaze flew to hers when she acknowledged the dreams, but she didn't miss a beat and kept talking. "I think the fact that I've turned you into a vampire is more than enough for today's convo."

"Vampire?" Doug asked incredulously. "A vampire killed Tom, and then *you* turned *me* into a vampire?" He let out a short laugh and crossed his arms over his broad chest. "Bullshit. Tom was attacked by a dog or something."

"Sadly, it was not a dog, and this isn't bullshit. We have at least one more rogue vampire out there, and we have to find it and put it down before it does more damage." Olivia tore her gaze from his and went back to the dresser. She picked up a large black pitcher and poured more of that stuff into his mug. "Drink more of this," she said, crossing to him and holding it out. "It will make you feel better."

"What the hell is that stuff?" His eyes flicked to the mug in her hand. He wiped his mouth again, and his stomach dropped when he saw faint red streaks on the back of his hand. "Holy shit," he said accusingly. "You fed me blood?"

"Please stay calm," Olivia said quietly. Her green eyes softened as she moved closer. "Your transition was remarkably fast—fastest that I've ever seen actually. It's something I'm going to ask Xavier about, but in the meantime, you can't run off half-cocked. You have a lot to learn and significant adjustments to your new life."

"Fuck you, lady." Doug shoved the covers aside, not caring that he was completely naked. "You're nuts, and I'm getting the hell out of here, so I can find the sicko that killed my partner."

Before he could go anywhere, Olivia was on top of him. One second she was standing next to the bed with a mug full of blood, and the next she straddled him on the bed. She was strong. Strong enough to hold him there, and she moved like a ghost. She pinned his wrists against the brass headboard in what was supposed to be intimidating, but all it managed to do was turn him on.

"It's the truth," she said, her face inches from his. "And it will make everyone's lives a lot easier if you just accept it. If I hadn't turned you then, you would've died too," she said in a low, husky voice. Her green eyes edged with tears remained locked with his. "I—I couldn't let that happen."

"Why not?" Doug asked gruffly. His gaze wandered over her face. She reminded him of a porcelain doll. "Why not just let me die?"

Olivia opened her mouth as if to respond, but she shook her head and said nothing. Whether she was unable or unwilling, he didn't know. She shifted her weight as she pressed his wrists harder against the headboard, and Doug's body reacted instantaneously. He was, after all, completely naked with the woman of his dreams straddling him in such a way that all he could do was think about being inside of her.

Her heavily lidded eyes met his, and her nostrils flared as his growing erection pressed against her feminine core insistently. Olivia's exotic scent intoxicated him. She loosened the grip on his wrists as she tangled her fingers in his, holding him prisoner with her body.

"I couldn't let you go," she whispered, rocking her hips against him wickedly as she held his gaze. "Not when I just found you."

Doug groaned as waves of pure pleasure rocked him, giving him more satisfaction with that tiny move than any other woman had with full-on sex. Olivia leaned in, achingly slow, and ran her sweet tongue along the seam of his lips, teasing him and tempting him. She told him more with her actions than she could put into words, and that was when his restraint and last shred of sanity snapped.

Desperate for more, for connection, to feel something

other than grief and pain, he devoured her mouth with his and dove deep. He sat up in the bed, tore his hands from hers, and buried them in her silky red curls, kissing her deeply as she remained wrapped around his naked body.

He groaned as Olivia ground herself against him and ran her fingernails across the broad expanse of his back, while she kissed him eagerly, wrapping him in her leather-clad embrace.

His tongue slid along hers as she tightened her legs around his waist, as if she was anchoring him to reality. He needed to get closer, to taste her and convince himself that this was all real, that he had not gone completely off the deep end.

He explored the dark cave of her mouth wanting to taste every bit of her, but it wasn't enough. He needed more—all of her. He cradled her face in one hand as his thumb brushed her jaw, tilting her head back, allowing him better access to her graceful neck. Doug trailed kisses along her alabaster skin, down to that sweet lovely spot below the ear, and she moaned as she laced her fingers through his short hair and held him to her.

He breathed her in, reveling in that sweet, spicy scent that was so distinctly hers. The one he had been chasing his whole life—the one flirting along the edges of his mind in fantasy and reality. Were they even separate anymore, or had the two collided into an alternate reality?

Doug growled her name as her skin brushed his lips, and her fingers fluttered along the nape of his neck. As Olivia's long limbs tangled around him, all he could think about was getting closer. Need clawed at him.

Greedy and desperate, he clamored for something elusive, something slipping out of his reach, hiding from him, or perhaps, he just couldn't see what it was.

Doug growled as he licked the gentle curve of her neck and curled his fingers around locks of hair. All he could think was that he had to taste every part of her. It went beyond the need to be inside of her, to bury himself deep in the most intimate place a man can touch a woman. It was the instinctive need to become *one*.

Lost in pleasure, Olivia arched back as he tugged the zipper of the catsuit down, panting to feel her flesh against his. He pushed the offending fabric aside to feast on her gorgeous breasts. Impatient and eager, he took one rosy nipple in his mouth, suckling as she rocked against his cock and held him.

"Yes," Olivia breathed. "Taste all of me."

Please. Electricity shot through him in orgasmic waves as her mind touched his.

Olivia's voice whispered through his head erotically, and she ground her hips against him, writhing in his lap, begging him to take her.

To taste her.

A growl bubbled up from his chest; an animalistic noise erupted as the orgasm flared in hot, bright flashes, and fangs exploded in his mouth ready to grant her wish.

"Do it," she rasped.

Olivia guided his head to her throat, offering herself, but through the blind fog of lust came the tiny voice of reason. She wanted him to bite her and drink her blood? Revulsion battled with desire as his teeth hovered above her snow-white skin.

"*No*," Doug shouted.

Horrified, he shoved her away with all his strength. Doug watched in shock as Olivia went flying twenty feet across the room and landed surely on her feet in a crouching position in front of the bedroom door. His body hummed with lust, and if he still had a working heart, it probably would have beat out of his chest.

"Like I told you," she said breathlessly. Her green eyes flashed, and a smile curved her lips as she rose to her feet. "You have a lot to learn."

He swiped at his mouth but winced as his fangs made a long, thin cut on his index finger. He looked at the wound, which was dripping blood onto the white sheets, and watched in fascination as it healed closed in a matter of seconds, as though it had never been there at all. While the bloodstains on the sheets proved that he wasn't crazy—apparently, he *was* a vampire.

"Just toying with me, aren't you?" he said tightly. Anger, resentment, and frustration fired in his gut, although it did nothing to quell his lust. "This is all a game to you."

Doug flicked his angry eyes back to Olivia and revealed his fangs. Something dark and dangerous stirred inside of him as it dawned on him that she probably didn't care about him or want him. He was merely a pawn for her to use and control. All of this had been a ploy to get him to be just like her—the dreams, the kiss in the alley, and her office, every minute was part of her seduction to lure him into this insanity.

"What? Did you figure that if enough blood rushed to my dick, I'd forget my humanity and drink your blood? Why? Does that seal the deal?" he asked, his voice dripping with sarcasm. His eyes darkened, and his voice lowered. "I should kill you for doing this to me."

"I understand how you feel." Olivia smoothed her long red hair back and kept a blank expression on her face. An emotionless expression, he thought. Cold and calculated. "I wanted to kill my maker as well, but it would be ill-advised."

She zipped the catsuit back up, covering the milky white curves of her gorgeous breasts that he had been feasting on a moment ago.

He had his head up his ass.

"You want to know the truth?" he asked as he appraised her beautiful form and wrestled with his battling emotions. "I'm not sure if I want to kill you or fuck you."

"You could try to kill me, but since I'm older and more experienced, it would not end well for you. Secondly, I'm your maker, and killing me is against Presidium law, so it would also earn you a death sentence. And it would hurt my feelings," she said with a dramatic gesture.

She turned to leave but thought better of it and turned to face him again.

"By the way, I haven't *fucked* anyone in almost three hundred years," she said haughtily. "What makes you think that I'd break that streak for you?"

Doug blinked. Three hundred years? He had no retort for that. Man, he thought it was rough going three months without sex. His eyes wandered over the gentle curve of her leather-clad hip and the swell of her breasts, which made his cock stir to life again in spite of the fact that he was furious with her for turning him into a sideshow freak.

"Now stop bitching, and get dressed. There are fresh clothes laid out over there." She waved toward the small blue and white love seat on the other side of the room. "You have to be brought up to speed and register with the Presidium."

"What the fuck is the Presidium?" He got out of bed and grabbed the black leather pants from the small sofa, hoping to shift his focus to something other than jumping her bones. "Leather?" He held them up and looked at her as though she'd lost her mind. "So, not only do I have to feel like a freak, but apparently, I have to look like one too. I guess I should be happy that there's no cape."

"You're not Superman," she said with a roll of her eyes. "You're a vampire."

"Oh, excuse me for getting my fictional stories mixed up."

"The Presidium is the vampire government, and the leather isn't a fashion statement," she said while ignoring his last statement. "That is to help protect you. If you're going to hunt with us, then you'll be using silver weaponry, among other weapons. The leather will protect you to a point."

"Silver? Garlic? Crosses?" Doug snorted and shook his head. "So the movies have it right?"

"Not all of it." Olivia said as she tied her hair into a tight ponytail. "Sterling silver will kill us if it gets in the bloodstream and just touching it burns like hell. Garlic doesn't do shit, except stink up the joint and give a human bad breath. There's more, but seeing that today is the first day of the rest of your undead life, you have plenty of time to learn."

Doug grumbled something under his breath as he

turned his back on her and dragged the pants on. He had a million questions, but at this point, wasn't even sure where to begin. He could feel her watching him and tried not to think about how much she turned him on. It contradicted every other emotion he was having right now.

"You turned me into a sideshow attraction." He shoved his arms into the tight shirt, a Lycra and leather thing that fit him like a second skin, and pulled it over his head. "Like the fucking monster that killed my partner."

When he turned to her, she was standing inches from him. Face to face, her body hovered dangerously close. Her exotic scent filled his head, and without warning, his fangs burst free of their own accord. His gaze flicked to the smooth, silky skin of her throat, and his body hummed with desire—the gut-wrenching need to pierce that flawless flesh and drink.

"When did you get that tattoo?" she asked in a shaky voice.

Olivia placed her hands on his shoulders and urged him to turn around. Doug was only too happy to comply because he was afraid he would lose his senses and kiss her again. Although his body was willing, his mind was all kinds of confused, and he was not in the habit of hooking up with women who didn't really want him.

She lifted his shirt, and as her fingertips rasped up his back, he shut his eyes trying to keep his raging hormones under control. He had gotten the tattoo because of the dreams, because of *her*, but the last thing he wanted to do right now was to admit that little tidbit.

"Just a stupid thing I did when I was in college." He

tugged the shirt down and spun around to face her. "It doesn't mean anything."

Hurt, or something like it, flickered briefly over her features. "I see," she said quietly as she tore her gaze from his and walked to the door. "I'll be in the living room when you're ready."

"Two things." Doug grabbed a pair of combat boots off the floor and put them on as he spoke. "Number one. I'm going to stick with you until we find that sack of shit that slaughtered my partner, and then I'm going to kill it."

"Agreed." Her jaw set determinedly. "And number two?"

"Sunlight kills vampires, right?" He watched her nod curtly. "After we kill it, I'm taking a walk in the sun because I'd rather be dead than be like this."

"Part of what you will learn, Detective Paxton," she said as her voice hardened, and her eyes glittered like emeralds, "is not all vampires slaughter humans like the rogue that killed your partner or the one that almost killed *you*. Now, finish getting dressed, and drink the rest of the blood in the pitcher before you come out. Van and Oreo are out there, and if you're hungry, they might smell like lunch."

"Van? Your dog?" He cocked his head. "Is your dog's name *Van Helsing*?"

"Yes." She fought the urge to smile and join in the humor. "Don't change the subject. Drink all the blood in the pitcher. You were just turned, and for some reason, you woke up a day and a half earlier than expected. I don't want to take any chances, especially since your transition is showing unusual side effects."

Doug said nothing but glanced at the pitcher as a stabbing pain tugged at his gut. As much as he hated to admit it, he was starving. He could smell the blood from here, but oddly enough, it didn't smell like blood. He had smelled plenty of blood over the past ten years as a homicide detective, and the pungent, mineral smell was something he had gotten used to. However, that stuff in the pitcher did not smell anything like blood—it smelled delicious.

He also wanted to know what other side effects she was referring to, but hunger took over, and all he could think about was eating. It clawed at him, like an animal trying to get out of a cage, and before he realized what he was doing, Doug found himself standing on the other side of the room with the pitcher in hand.

"What the fuck?" he said in awe as he looked back to where he'd been standing a second before. Somehow, he'd managed to move twenty feet without even feeling it—like he willed himself across the room in the blink of an eye.

"You have a lot to learn, like I said," Olivia murmured. "I can't have you running around the streets of New York City starving." She stood in the open door with her hand lingering on the doorknob. "Otherwise, you *will* turn into the very monster you fear."

Chapter 9

Olivia shut the door behind her, leaned against it, and closed her eyes as she willed her quaking body to settle down. She shook with a volatile combination of lust, fear, loss, and anger from the intense events that had taken place in the past twelve hours. She had feared that by turning Doug, she would run the risk of losing him altogether, and her suspicions were confirmed.

He hated her. Hated what she was and what she had made him.

In addition to everything else, that tattoo on his back was a perfect image of the Dagger of Eternity. Why would he have that tattoo? Was it from the dreams with her? Had she shown it to him at some point in the dreamscape? Damn it, she couldn't remember.

What the hell did that matter, anyway? His body wanted her, but that could be chalked up to the surge of power and intensified sensations that were common when a new vampire was turned. Unfortunately, in his heart where it mattered, he loathed her, and he wasn't the only one. Right about now, she had a serious case of self-loathing.

Olivia didn't blame him for being angry, and if he had been any other new vampire, it would not have hurt to have him look at her with disgust—but Doug wasn't just anyone.

He was her bloodmate.

The evidence pointed in that direction, and when she turned him, any miniscule lingering doubt about who he was, or more importantly who they were to each other, was eliminated.

That small bit she tasted during their kiss in the alley had been *nothing* compared to the tsunami of emotion, heat, and life force she experienced when she drained him before the blood exchange. His blood memories flooded her in living color.

She was swamped by the loneliness from his life of self-imposed isolation, by the grief he felt when his mother died, the pride he experienced when he graduated from college and then the police academy, and the blind rage that filled his mind every time he saw a murdered woman or child.

His whole life flashed into her, his memories becoming hers in minutes, and finally, her heart beat in time with his as it slowly died out. During Doug's final moments as a human, Olivia was truly alive and joined with him as though they were one. Her heart started to beat and her lungs filled with air—she lived as he died.

That was a first. She'd never merged with the others when she turned them.

When she slit her wrist and let her ancient blood flow into his mouth, Olivia expected him to swallow it blindly, as most half-dead people did—yet the opposite happened. As the first trickle of rich blood dripped over his tongue, Doug grabbed her arm. He clamped onto her wrist and held it greedily to his lips as he drank, while his other arm slipped around her waist and cradled her body flush against him.

She didn't tell him when to stop feeding. He simply

pulled away and licked her wound closed without any prompting. He pulled her tighter and kept her wrapped in his embrace as he hibernated during the change. Olivia allowed herself to linger there and slumber briefly in his arms before waking to clean him up.

She never slept with a man in her bed. Not even as a human. She and Douglas had made love in the woods that one fateful night, and they certainly never slept together. Even she and Vincent never shared a bed when they traveled together—not that he didn't try. Doug Paxton was the first man she truly slept with—human or vampire.

It was the most intimate moment of her life.

Not that Doug had any idea how monumental that was, and would it even matter? Would it make a difference if he knew who they were to each other or who he used to be? At the moment, he hated her and the idea of being a vampire so much that he would rather kill himself.

Olivia hadn't had any intention to turn him. She planned on glamouring him to make him forget, and all of those grand plans went out the window when she saw the rogue feeding on him in the alley.

Something inside of her snapped.

She couldn't let him die again. She loved him.

While she had a penchant for rescuing people and animals, she at least thought about what she was doing. Some of her coven members had been alert enough for Olivia to ask them if they wanted to be turned. Not Doug. It was probably the most selfish decision Olivia had ever made, so she couldn't blame him for hating her.

Wonderful. She finally found the love of her life after

three centuries, and he despised her. Would it even matter that she loved him? That she madly, truly, deeply loved him? Not likely.

Olivia swallowed the lump in her throat and fought the tears that stung her eyes. She loved him for who he was all those years ago and for the man he was today. She loved his protective nature and his need for the truth. She adored staring into those brilliant blue eyes and the rush of his skin as it brushed along hers.

She loved him.

Liar, she thought to herself. If she really loved him, would she have turned him in the first place? Would she have condemned him to an eternity of darkness? She could be dead wrong about the bloodmate legend, and they may not become daywalkers, but she took his human life anyway. He was right. She should have let him die, and if she hadn't been such a selfish bitch, she would have.

Olivia shoved herself away from the door and stalked into the kitchen with Van Helsing at her heels. She'd kept him out of the bedroom because she wasn't sure how the dog would react to the newest member of the coven, or how Doug would react to the dog, for that matter.

She'd never heard of any vampire transitioning so quickly. Her gut instinct told her it was because he was her bloodmate, but it was only a hunch. All she had to go on was rumor and innuendo, which was not her usual way of operating. Perhaps Xavier or Millicent would have insight into why Doug's transition was so fast.

Olivia grabbed some blood from the fridge, stuck it in the microwave, and furiously punched buttons. She watched the red mug spin slowly and wondered what other surprises lay in wait. She knew he would have questions, and she prayed she would have answers. The truth was she had plenty of questions herself.

A knock on the apartment door tore her from her thoughts. It was Pete. Olivia had called him earlier and asked for help after she found Doug in the alley. Even though he wasn't thrilled his friend had been turned, it didn't stop him.

"Come in," she shouted.

Pete swung the door open and stepped inside, but the moment he did, his eyes glowed red. "He's awake already?" He flicked his glowing eyes to the guest bedroom and lowered his voice. "It's only been twelve hours. I thought the change took at least two days."

"Yeah, me too." The microwave beeped loudly. Olivia snagged her mug and drank the blood as she gave Pete one sarcastic thumb up. "Awesome."

"What's that about?" he asked, looking from her to the closed bedroom door. "Why did it happen so fast?"

"I'm not entirely sure," she lied. "Nothing about Doug's transition has been like anything I've experienced. The others, even you with your demon blood, took at least two days to wake up and complete the transition. Doug's only took twelve hours. Shit. Maya's took almost five days, and when she finally did wake up, I was worried it would be a bad turn, but it had worked out fine."

"Yeah, she's no trouble at all," Pete said drily. "Maybe it's because he was so close to dying when you turned him?"

"No." Olivia shook her head and took another sip. "You all were on death's door. I wouldn't have turned you otherwise." She glanced at the bedroom and tapped the mug with her fingers. "I'll talk to Xavier and see if he's got any ideas. He's been around awhile and has seen more weird shit than anyone I know."

"Well, whatever it is, I'm sure you'll figure it out." Pete glanced at the clock on the wall. "We've still got two hours or so until sundown."

"Did you get the samples from Tom and Doug's wounds to Millicent?" She tightened the grip on her mug. "Were either of these rogues responsible for the attacks on Ronald or the girl? I definitely picked up the scent of Rogue One, but the son of a bitch was gone by the time I got here."

"Yes." Pete took off his gloves and stuck them in his pockets. "The DNA in Tom's wounds were from the rogue that killed Ronald—Rogue One—but the one you killed, that attacked Doug, was yet *another* rogue sibling. Meaning, the one that killed the girl is still out there too."

"Shit," Olivia downed the rest of the blood. "That means we still have two out there, and I'm betting on more than that."

"Yup." Pete nodded toward the bedroom. "How'd he take it?"

Before she could answer, the bedroom door opened, and Doug emerged looking more pissed off than he was before. And hotter, if that was possible. Dressed in full sentry garb, one of Pete's uniforms that she kept here in case of an emergency, the man looked dangerous and sexy as hell. He oozed power, rage, and vengeance.

"Pete?" Doug asked warily.

He stalked into the room slowly, body wound tight

and hands balled into fists at his side. Doug looked ready for a fight. The tension in the room was so thick, even Van Helsing didn't move, but he kept his big brown eyes on the men as he stood by Olivia's feet. Oreo sat next to Van Helsing, which seemed to be her favorite place to be.

"Hello, Doug." Pete stuck out his hand but dropped it when Doug didn't move to accept it. "Not the reunion I was hoping for."

"You're one of them too," he said almost inaudibly. "No wonder you've been MIA, and here I was blaming your new marriage. Guess I owe your wife an apology—or my condolences."

"If you mean that I'm a vampire—" Pete said evenly. "Yes. I am. Just like you, partner, and as far as my wife goes, I definitely got the best part of that deal. She's the sexiest shapeshifter you'll ever meet, and that's saying something."

"Shapeshifter? There are shapeshifters too?" he asked as he furrowed his brow briefly before holding up one hand to keep Pete from answering. "Never mind. Tell me later." Doug stood his ground and flicked his eyes to Olivia. "You turned him too?" he asked quietly. "Didn't you?"

"Yes." Olivia looked away and rinsed out her cup as Van whined by her feet, sensing her uneasiness. "He's part of my coven, like you are now."

"Do you make a habit of seducing men and then turning them into freaks?" His voice rose, and he walked slowly toward Pete. "Did you fuck her?"

"Whoa!" Pete's hands flew up in surrender. "I'm a married man, dude." He gave Olivia a slanted glance. "Did I act like this big of a dick when you turned me?"

Doug went to grab Pete by the jacket, but Olivia flew across the room and tackled Doug, pinning him against the wall next to the front door. Pete could have handled himself, but she wanted Doug to be sure who was in charge.

"First of all," she seethed, her lips just scant inches from his, "who I *fuck* is none of your business."

His jaw clenched as she spoke, and his hands, which were curled around her waist, tightened. She tried not to remember the last time his hands were on her, but it was no use. She didn't want to notice the way his thigh pressed against hers, or how his chest flexed beneath her weight, but it was an effort in futility.

Olivia was certain she would never escape him or his taste ever again. He was tattooed on her soul, the way that Dagger of Eternity was tattooed on his back.

"Second, I only turned Pete as a favor to his wife, Marianna. Like you, he would've died if I hadn't." She dropped her hands and stepped away, hoping she didn't look as turned on as she felt. "Pete helped us clean up your situation and made it palatable for the humans."

Doug crossed his arms over his chest and turned his stormy eyes to Pete. "What did you do?"

"I crashed your car and set it on fire before it went into the Hudson River."

"What? You could've hurt someone." His eyes narrowed. "Don't have any respect for human life now that you're a bloodsucker, huh?"

"Anyway." Pete let out a sigh and continued. "Right now, the cops are assuming it was an accident. I glamoured two local beat cops who were on duty by the pier around sunrise. I told them that they saw you and Tom on a high-speed chase. Your car crashed, caught fire, and went into the river. Right now, they're dragging the river for both of your bodies. Soon you'll both be presumed dead. If it's any consolation, the whole department is pretty broken up about it."

"You just dumped him in the river?" Doug asked through clenched teeth.

"No." Olivia's voice softened. "We have his remains at the Presidium morgue. I thought you might want to have him cremated. The point is that they won't find your body or Tom's." She picked up her coat, heavy with the weight of hidden weaponry, and pulled it on as she focused on keeping her voice neutral. It would do no good to have her weeping over Doug's loss, no matter how heavily his grief weighed on her. "Did he have any family?"

"Not really." Doug leaned against the wall and rubbed his hands over his face. "His two ex-wives hate him, and he didn't have any kids. No family to speak of, except for me." He looked her straight in the eyes for a moment before he said anything else. "Thank you for not tossing him in the river. I'd like to see him before he's cremated, if that's alright."

Olivia fought the ridiculous urge to cry. She turned on her heels, stalked into the guest room, and grabbed the long coat, almost identical to hers and Pete's. Without saying a word, she came back in the living room and tossed it at Doug, who caught it in midair without taking his gaze off her. His blue eyes glinted back and wrinkled at the corners, sending a clear message that he'd meet any challenge she could throw at him.

"Put it on." She nodded toward him and pulled on her gloves. "You don't have any weapons yet, but after you're registered, *then* I'll give you back your gun. Loaded with new ammo, of course."

Doug said nothing and simply pulled on the coat. It fit him perfectly. He looked like he was born to be a sentry—maybe he had. Something about him was unlike any human she'd encountered. What was it about Doug that made him so unique? Was it only the bloodmate legend, or was there something more?

"There are leather gloves in the pocket." She tore her gaze from his and went to the front door. "Put them on. Like I said earlier, sterling silver will burn you quick. You'll heal, but it hurts like hell, and if it gets in your bloodstream, then you're close to fucked and will beg for a sunrise."

"I guess a stake through the heart is the real end game though?" Doug asked humorlessly.

"Sure." Olivia smirked and arched an eyebrow. "But who wouldn't that kill?"

"Zombie?" Pete asked, looking from her to Doug. "Gotta get those guys in the head, right?"

"Oh, for fuck's sake," Doug said wearily. "There are zombies too?"

"Nah," Pete said through a laugh as he slapped Doug on the shoulder. "I'm just messing with you."

To Olivia's surprise, Doug cracked a smile and shook his head. "Still a ball-buster, eh, Pete?"

"Absolutely." Pete winked at Olivia. The smile on his face faltered, and his brow furrowed with confusion as he kept his focus on his maker. "Looks like we're partners again, Paxton."

"What?" Olivia asked as an imminent sense of dread crawled up her back. "What's wrong?"

His expression stern, Pete held her gaze but remained silent for what felt like forever.

"You didn't hear me?" he asked quietly. "Are you okay?"

Olivia's stomach dropped to her feet as she realized what he meant. He had tried to telepath her, but she didn't hear him. Panic swamped her as she instinctively reached out to touch his mind with hers. *Pete? Can you hear me?*

"I don't know if he can, but I can hear you, and it freaks me the fuck out," Doug snapped. "What in the hell is going on now?"

Olivia and Pete looked at Doug and then at each other.

"What the hell?" she whispered.

"Try the rest of the Coven," Pete said calmly. He ran a hand over his mouth and looked from her to Doug and back again. "Maybe it was a glitch in the universe or something."

"Right," Olivia said in a shaky voice. *Trixie, Maya, Sadie... can you hear me? I want you to meet our newest coven member.*

"Ha," Doug said sharply. Hands on his hips, he paced the room. "I should have known that the rest of the broads in your club are bloodsuckers too."

"Shit." Pete's eyes glowed as he watched Doug before turning back to Olivia. "I didn't hear whatever you telepathed, but it sounds like Doug did. What is going on, boss lady? I don't like this one damn bit. Doug's vamp turn takes hardly any time at all, and now *you* can only telepath with *him*. Not only is this fucking weird, it's going to make communicating when we hunt a pain in the ass."

Van Helsing whined and rubbed against Olivia's leg.

Given how dizzy she felt, it was probably the only thing keeping her from falling down. She murmured soothing sounds and rubbed the dog's head as he tried to calm her in return. Oreo, seemingly unfazed, had curled up and fallen asleep on the sofa.

"You mean you used to be able to do this telepathy bit with all other vampires?" Doug asked with confusion and genuine curiosity. He crossed his arms over his chest and studied Olivia, while maintaining his distance. "What gives, Olivia?"

Bloodmates. That was the only answer that came to mind, but she sure as hell wasn't throwing that little bit of crazy into the mix. Olivia squared her shoulders as the queasy feeling in her gut subsided, and she leveled a cold look in Doug's direction, struggling to keep control over herself and the situation.

"We can only telepath with our maker, progeny, or siblings."

"Yeah," Doug interrupted. "But Pete just said you couldn't hear him, and based on the look on your face, I'm betting that Trixie, Maya, and Sadie didn't hear your last shout either. So why am I the only one who can hear you?"

"I don't know," she said quietly. "It may be only temporary. Maybe it's something in your blood. At any rate, we have other problems to worry about, like getting you registered with the Presidium, and facing the music with Augustus."

"Shane and I didn't have any luck last night. We picked up some scents here and there, but so far, the only one that got dusted was the one that attacked Paxton."

A series of knocks on the door and muffled giggles

in the hallway captured her attention. "I called them down here," Pete said. "I figured you'd want them to meet Doug. We should get introductions out of the way before we head to the Presidium."

Olivia nodded. "Brace yourself, detective." Olivia rolled her eyes and went to the door. She tightened her grip on the knob as she leveled an apologetic look to Doug. "Get ready to meet the rest of the coven and your new family."

Pete rubbed his chin and nodded to Doug. "Welcome to the family, brother."

The nervous look on Doug's face almost made Olivia laugh out loud. She tugged the door open to find Sadie, Trixie, and Maya in the doorway waving frantically at Doug. They flew into the room and tackled Doug in a massive group hug. His arms at his side, he looked at Pete for help but got none.

"Give the poor man some space, ladies," Olivia said more sharply than she intended. The three women peeled themselves off Doug, but Maya lingered on his arm. Olivia's fangs emerged, and she lifted her lip as she spoke. "Back off, Maya."

Maya looked immediately contrite, stepped away from Doug, and sidled in between Sadie and Trixie. Doug just gave them a curt nod and an awkward wave before adjusting his coat.

"Great." Olivia ran both hands through her hair and forced herself to smile. "You already know Maya. After all, it was her little game that started this adventure. Trixie is our other bartender, and Sadie is our DJ. I think you met them, but now you know them, or at least what they are."

"Hey," Trixie interrupted. "Why did Pete call us down here and not you? Are you pissed or something? I tried to telepath you earlier, but it was weird, man. It's like you weren't there."

"When was that?" Olivia asked quickly.

"Not long after you got back here with officer hottie," Trixie said with a wink in Doug's direction. "I heard you come in, but when you didn't answer…"

After she turned Doug and did the blood exchange… that's when it all changed.

"I thought it was just me," Maya said quietly, avoiding Olivia's gaze. "I—I tried to talk to you a little while ago, and when you didn't respond, well, I figured you were still upset with me."

Olivia's heart broke when she saw the hurt flicker across Maya's face. "It's not because of either of you." She looked at Doug, who was intently watching all of them. "I'm not sure what's going on, to be honest. Listen, until we figure things out, if you need something and I'm not here, then you reach out to Pete. Got it?"

The girls nodded and sat on the couch, making themselves at home once again. Sadie scooped up Oreo, and Olivia could hear purring from across the room. Maya lay her head on Trixie's shoulder and sniffled as Van put his head in her lap.

They were her family. Dogs. Cats. Vampires. What a motley crew. She looked back to Doug and noticed the look of contempt was replaced with curiosity. A step in the right direction.

"What about the waitress and Damien, the bouncer?"

"No," Olivia said sharply. "Both are human, and as far as I'm concerned they'll stay that way. I gave Suzie the week off, and Damien will be here during daylight hours as well." She glanced briefly at Doug. "He knows about us."

"How nice for him," Doug said under his breath. "Listen, this little family reunion is warming the cockles of my no-longer-beating-heart, but can we get this freak show on the road? I want to find the creature that killed Tom and then get this shit over with."

Olivia's chest tightened. She tried to suppress the rejection she was feeling, but it was no use. He would rather fry in the sun than stay a vampire and be with her. Awesome.

"Agreed." She turned her attention to the girls. "Maya, you have to come with us and see the czar. We can't dance around this anymore, kiddo. You're going to let him, or one of the senators, taste your blood and read your memories in order to prove you didn't turn the rogue that killed Ronald Davis and started this mess."

Maya nodded sheepishly but said nothing as she stroked Van's head. Her uneasiness flickered through the room, and Olivia watched her nibble her lip nervously. Her large blue eyes were filled with fear and tugged at Olivia's heart. This girl, this youngling vampire, was terrified, and Olivia had been doing nothing to reassure her. Guilt swamped her, and before she knew it, she swept across the room, leaned down from behind the couch, and wrapped Maya's petite shoulders in a hug.

"It's going to be alright," she whispered against Maya's hair before kissing the top of her head as the girl sobbed quietly. Van whined and snuggled deeper into her lap. "I'm not going to let the czar kill you." She stood up and squeezed Maya's shoulder reassuringly as she fought the tears that threatened to come. "I love you, Maya. You are my family, and there's no way on earth that I'm going to let the czar or his senators hurt you. Understand?"

"Mmm-hmm." Maya bobbed her head up and down and wiped the tears from her face.

Olivia released Maya and turned her attention to the other girls as she paced from the couch to face them.

"Trixie and Sadie, I want you to stay here. I closed the club for the week, said we were doing renovations, but I want you two on watch. At sundown keep an eye on the perimeter of the building. If you get wind of the rogue, you telepath to Pete, but you *do not* take it on yourselves. Is that clear?"

The women nodded. Olivia noticed Doug watching the situation closely and evaluating the other women. Sadie was smart and almost as old as Olivia, but Trixie was still young and had a tendency to be unpredictable, which could cause more trouble. It made her feel better that Sadie would be here to keep an eye on Trixie.

"Okay. I killed the rogue that attacked Doug," Olivia continued as she tried to regain her bearings, "but I wasn't able to get the one that killed his partner. It was gone by the time I got there."

"There are more." Doug interrupted, and everyone looked at him in surprise as he stalked slowly across the room toward Olivia. "One of these rogues could make another, couldn't it? I'd bet we're looking at more than two. The guy that attacked me was definitely one of Moriarty's boys. He and his crew are missing, and no one has seen them since they left here the other night."

"Glad to see you thinking like a detective again."

Olivia gave him a nod of approval. "You're right. Rogue One is still out there, so is the one that killed Brittany. That's two… at least."

Silence fell over the room, and Olivia locked eyes with Pete. She didn't need telepathy to know what he was thinking.

"Shit." Pete tugged his gloves on. "Whoever is making these rogues is making his own little rogue coven, isn't he?"

"Most likely," Olivia said evenly. "If there is a rogue coven being built, then they're definitely holing up somewhere together. We've got to find their nest."

"So these rogues—" Doug asked slowly. "They are turned by other rogues, and that's why they're crazy?"

"Yes." Olivia nodded. She was relieved that he was asking the right questions and looking to solve the problem. At least it was a step in the right direction, and it gave her some shred of hope. "Well, that, or they're turned by someone who didn't do the blood exchange properly by not giving them enough blood. Essentially, they are starved and crazy with hunger… the turn doesn't go right, and they get stuck in a feeding frenzy state."

"So they're like a bunch of hopped-up crack addicts?" Doug asked in a matter-of-fact tone. He pursed his lips. "That's the first explanation I've heard that's made any fuckin' sense since I woke up."

Olivia nodded, and to her surprise, the hint of a smile played at his lips before he looked away. A modicum of progress.

"Good." Olivia tugged her gloves back on. "We have to get going."

"You girls better not engage them if they show

up here." Pete's eyes flickered red, a symptom of his demon lineage.

Olivia didn't miss the look of surprise on Doug's face, but to his credit, he said nothing.

"I mean it, Trixie," Pete said seriously. "You and Sadie stay inside and keep an eye on the monitors in Olivia's office, but if you see them, do not engage them. You call me, and I'll bring Shane."

"I don't know who this Shane guy is," Doug chimed in. "But if I were you, I'd bring a lot of guns too."

"Not a problem, partner."

"Shit." Trixie cracked her knuckles and let out a growl of frustration. "I wasn't turned yesterday. I may not be part demon, dude, but I'm not a dumb ass."

"Demon?" Doug asked, but then he held his hand up. "Tell me later."

"Don't worry about it." Sadie elbowed Trixie and made a face that told her to shut up. "We'll hold down the fort, Olivia. I did hang with you for that century you worked as a sentry, and I picked up a thing or two. We've got it covered."

"I'll leave Van upstairs too." Olivia squatted and scratched his favorite spot. "He'll be another set of ears and eyes for you."

"We should get going," Pete said.

"But it's not sundown yet," Maya said quietly. "I hate taking the tunnels." She ran her hands over the red bustier minidress. "I should probably change my clothes."

"Well, since my partner is dead," Doug snapped, "I think you can live with getting a little dirt on that *dress*." He stopped abruptly, and his features hardened. "It sounds like this mess all started with you anyway."

"Sorry," she added quickly. "That came out all wrong."

Doug lifted one shoulder and shifted his weight. Olivia could tell that he felt badly for barking at Maya, and it only endeared him to her further.

"It's okay," Doug said apologetically. "I just want to get going and get this shit over with."

Olivia crossed to the large chair in the living room and shoved it aside, revealing an opening to the tunnels. She sensed Doug watching her every move, but she couldn't bring herself to look at him and risk seeing that look of contempt. She dug deep down inside and grabbed onto the cold mind-set of the sentry she used to be. It was that icy attitude that got her through more hunting excursions and executions than she cared to remember.

Doug brushed past her and dropped soundlessly into the tunnels. Olivia hesitated before joining the others. For the first time in over three hundred years, she doubted her own resolve. She could kill the rogue, kill a hundred, but killing her feelings for Doug… that was one mission she didn't think she could complete.

Chapter 10

Doug had heard the expression, the underbelly of the city, and he thought he had seen it already as a homicide detective in New York City. He could not have been more wrong. As he and the others raced through the sewer tunnels beneath Manhattan, he realized how little he really knew about the city he lived in for the past ten years. He, like most humans, was oblivious to the world that existed above and beneath his feet.

He didn't know how fast they were running, but it felt more like flying. His body hummed with power as he pumped his arms and legs with little effort. Doug noted the way he could see and hear *everything*. Water trickling in the tunnels sounded like rapid gunfire. Rats scurrying away from their approach sounded like a herd of horses. The heartbeats of people on the street above sounded like flapping wings from a swarm of hummingbirds.

The entire world was amplified. Brighter. Louder. Sharper. It was as if he had been living in a two-dimensional, black-and-white world as a human, and now, as a vampire, everything was in Technicolor and high-definition. He might have been dead, but ironically, he never felt more alive, and he felt guilty as hell about it.

He shouldn't like what he had become. A bloodsucker. A monster. He should loathe it and detest it like he did when he first woke up, but somehow… he didn't.

Doug's jaw clenched as he battled with his emotions. Was he being brainwashed on top of everything else? Was he losing himself in this insanity?

He flicked his gaze to Olivia. She ran beside him, matching his speed, and in spite of how fast they were moving he saw her perfectly. She was as stunning as ever. Her red curls flew behind her, but she stared straight ahead, intensely focused on their destination.

We're almost there. Her thoughts touched his, tickled almost, along the boundaries of his sanity. *The main entrance is just around the bend here to the left*.

Doug said nothing. He simply kept pace beside her and looked straight ahead. He could sense Pete and Maya right behind them, but he didn't want to turn and look. It seemed like a bad idea to take his eyes off the proverbial road.

Seconds later, Olivia's hand rested on his, and they came to an immediate stop. He wavered briefly from the biggest head rush of his life. For a minute, while he stopped moving, it felt like the world around him hadn't.

"It will pass in a minute." Olivia squeezed his arm gently and held him. He looked into her worried green eyes as the dizziness subsided. "It's a common side effect after running at that speed for the first time."

"I'm fine." Doug pulled his arm from her grasp and stuffed his hands in the pockets of the long coat, even though what he really wanted was to hold her hands. "Thanks. Where are we?" he asked, quickly needing to change the subject.

"The Cloisters are directly above us." Olivia pointed up. "The Presidium is located underneath The Cloisters and Fort Tryon Park."

"I thought vampires lived in luxury." He looked at the wet, mossy tunnel they stood in and made a scoffing sound. "This is a shithole."

"We're not in the Presidium yet." Olivia smirked and arched one eyebrow as she reached above them and pushed in a rectangular stone in the wall.

A section of the wall swung inward, and bright light flooded the sewer tunnel, revealing a lush, decadent hallway to a whole other world. Crystal chandeliers hung from a curved ceiling, and portraits lined the brightly lit corridor.

The door swung shut, closing silently, and when Doug turned around there was no sign of the door. He tried to squelch the feeling of being buried alive and took in the rest of his surroundings as swiftly as possible. The floors were red marble and reminded him of a river of blood, and the walls were a sunny yellow. The paintings gave him the eerie sensation of being watched.

The four of them walked down the hallway in silence toward a massive arched doorway made of wood, which conjured images of medieval times, but the camera watching them with its blinking red eye brought him back to the present.

Before they reached the doorway, Pete stepped ahead with Maya clinging to his arm like a damsel in distress. The girl looked terrified, and by all accounts, she probably should be. Pete placed his thumb on a button to the left of the door, and a moment later, it swung open.

"Stay close," Olivia said as they followed Pete. "Lots of listening and no talking."

"No promises," he said evenly.

She shot him a look of warning but didn't respond.

After what felt like forever, they finally arrived at their first destination. Another ornate, wooden door fit for a castle swung open, but the room inside was decked from floor to ceiling with LCD screens and filled with cigarette smoke. An older woman sat behind a massive desk, puffing away on what was clearly not her first smoke of the day.

"It's about damn time," she rasped as she crushed the cigarette in an ashtray overflowing with butts. "You know, for someone who doesn't like to turn new vampires, you've done it twice this year already."

"Thanks for the reminder, Millicent," Olivia responded humorlessly. "We need to register him ASAP so he can help us hunt the rogues."

"Yeah, I heard." Millicent fiddled with her lighter. "Before you go hunting, be sure to see Xavier in the lab. He wants to know if that synthetic blood worked, and I think he's got a new weapon." She wagged a finger at Olivia. "No more younglings outta you this year. You've hit your annual limit."

"Limit?" Doug asked with a curious look to the others. "There's a limit on how many vampires you can create? That doesn't make any sense."

"Of course it does." Millicent walked up to him, her hands in the pockets of her suit jacket, and looked him up and down. "You're a big one. You sure can pick 'em, Olivia. Anyway, too many vamps can cause a food shortage."

"You mean, people," Doug said sharply.

"Yes, people. Come 'ere." Millicent grabbed his hand and brought him to the back wall that looked more like one enormous computer network. He went with her and surmised that even as a human, this older woman wouldn't have been someone to tangle with.

She punched buttons on the large touch screen, and a stainless steel platform slid out. She put his left hand on it and punched a few more buttons. A flash went off as his picture was taken, and a needle quickly pricked his finger, taking a blood sample.

Doug removed his hand and watched as the small puncture closed and vanished. He opened and closed his hand, rubbing at it absently as he moved back to stand with the others again.

She punched a couple more spots on the screen, and seconds later an electronic identification card came up with his picture. "Too many vampires, and we'd all eventually starve to death. We can survive on vampire blood if we have to, but too much of it, and we can get a little nuts."

The screen blinked, and a loud beeping sounded as Doug's ID flickered to life on the screen. Doug Paxton: Vampire 12-52-6459—Maker: Olivia Hollingsworth.

So that was it? He was a vampire, and the woman of his dreams had turned his life into a nightmare.

"There." She lit another cigarette and took a long drag. "Your newest coven member is registered. Now, don't go rescuing any more dying humans, or you'll answer to Czar Augustus. And from what I'm hearing, you're in enough trouble as it is."

"Thank you, Millicent."

The door swung shut soundlessly, and they continued down the stone hallway, turning several times and making Doug feel like a rat in a maze.

Doug stopped walking, and Olivia gave him a curious look. "What?"

"You said that once I registered, you'd give me a gun." He stuck his hand out and moved closer, daring her to deny him. "How about it?"

He invaded her space, but those emerald green eyes were glued to him, tracking his every move. Doug dropped his hand and stopped inches from her as her familiar scent wafted over him, testing his resolve.

"Gun," he whispered. "Now."

The corner of Olivia's mouth lifted. Eyes on his, she reached beneath her jacket with both hands and withdrew a sleek, black gun and two magazines. She held them up and ejected the magazine to show it to him.

"It's a semiautomatic loaded with mahogany and sterling rounds. Put one in the brain or heart, and these will turn a vamp to dust. But hit 'em anywhere else, and it'll just slow 'em down, so be sure you shoot to kill."

She placed them in his hands, and when her fingertips brushed his palm, fire flickered over his skin and his fangs broke free. Lust and need roared through his blood. Olivia's eyes glanced to his bared fangs, and her tongue flicked out, moistening that gorgeous mouth.

"Believe me." Doug leaned closer, his lips a breath away from hers, and whispered, "I won't miss."

"Good." Olivia blinked and stepped away as she squared her shoulders. "See that you don't."

Doug stuck the magazines in the pocket of his coat and reached behind him, tucking the gun in the waist of pants. He didn't miss the curious looks from Maya and Pete, but he couldn't blame them. He and Olivia stood there eye-fucking each other like a couple of horny kids, and until two seconds ago, he had forgotten the two of them were even there.

"Let's go," she commanded.

"Yes, ma'am," he said with an exaggerated salute.

Olivia gave him the finger as she walked on, and he chuckled. She was tough as nails, and despite everything that had transpired, she still turned him on. He admired the way she handled Maya and the rest of her coven. The woman was powerful and commanding, but she was also sensitive and empathetic.

He studied her carefully, and it dawned on him how alike they were. Olivia was a rescuer and a protector. She seemed consumed by the need to save people, cats, dogs… vampires. He wondered what drove her? Who was she really trying to rescue?

The hallway opened into a cavernous space that looked like something out of ancient Rome. White marble statues of gods and goddesses lined the circular room, and at the center were towering white columns, framing pristine double doors of black-and-white-swirled marble.

"Welcome to the Presidium's New York office," Pete said. He placed a hand on Doug's left shoulder and leaned in. "Looks like Caesar's Palace in Vegas, doesn't it?"

"You aren't kidding." Doug rubbed his chin as he they walked down the four steps and into the center of the room. He gestured to the statues. "Are these gods and goddesses?"

"Yes," Olivia said with a snort of derision. "These are a few of Czar Augustus's mementos from his human life in ancient Rome. For a guy who looks down on humans, I always thought it odd that he surrounds himself with so many keepsakes from his human life. This room leads to the Presidium's main chamber, which is where official proceedings take place."

"I would've expected decor more like your club." He continued to look around them, wanting to know any way in or out. "This seems odd."

"The czars rule for two centuries in each city, and then a new czar takes over." Olivia kept her voice down, and he noticed her hand resting on the gun at her hip. "It's like when a new president moves into the White House and redecorates. Augustus was a senator in ancient Rome, so he decorated like this."

They moved slowly through the massive room, and their movements echoed. As each sound bounced back, Doug realized that the sound waves were helping him *see* the room. He didn't know how or why, but he had a multidimensional view of the space in his mind. He'd heard of bats and dolphins using sonar to see and wondered if that was happening to him.

Doug said nothing as Olivia watched him but simply nodded his understanding. His senses were on high alert, and he couldn't escape the feeling that something bad was about to go down. They continued across the open space to the steps that led to the double doors, but before the four of them even hit the first step, the doors swung open to welcome them.

"Olivia, I'm scared." Maya clung to Olivia's arm like a child and refused to move forward. Doug couldn't get over how completely different she was from when he first met her. Her big blue eyes were filled with tears, making her mascara run down her face. "Please don't let them kill me."

"It's going to be alright." Olivia wrapped her arm

around Maya, and in a motherly gesture, kissed the top of her head. "Be strong and stick close to Pete."

"Yes, ma'am," Maya sniffled.

"You'll be okay, kid." Pete patted her on the back and then glanced at Doug. "You're not gonna cry too are you?"

"Fuck you, Castro." Doug tried to suppress a smile, but he couldn't stop it.

"That's enough," Olivia hissed. "It's game time."

They climbed the staircase and crossed the threshold into the meeting room, and Doug fought the urge to let out a whistle. There were five people on a platform, and the one in the center—Augustus.

Wearing elaborate white robes with gold and burgundy trim, he sat in what could be described as a throne. He wore a golden laurel wreath on his head and had the same arrogant look as the painting Doug had seen. The women and men on either side of him were clad in similar robes and seated on small gold chairs.

Olivia, Pete, and Maya dropped to one knee and bowed their heads, but Doug stood his ground and kept his attention on the czar.

"Clearly, you haven't trained this one in our ways, Olivia." Augustus narrowed his eyes at Doug. "Your little coven is quite a mess."

"I'm not getting on my knees for you or anyone else," Doug said tightly.

Shane appeared out of nowhere and flew to Doug's side, lowering his voice to above a whisper. "You should do as your leader commands."

Tension filled the room, but Doug didn't waver.

"Give it a rest," Olivia said, rising to her feet. "He's new, and we have other issues to worry about."

"Perhaps," Shane murmured, his face emotionless as he stepped back. "Rules must be followed to maintain order."

Augustus rose from his spot on the lounge as his dark eyes went to Maya, who was still on one knee with her head bowed. "You must be the little vampire who started this messy situation in my city. Come here, little one."

Maya sniffled and slowly rose to her feet as she looked to Olivia for reassurance.

Augustus walked calmly down the steps and took her hand in his. Maya, head bowed and eyes averted, sniffled and adjusted the skirt of her small dress as the czar stepped back and looked her over from head to toe.

"You're a lovely little thing, aren't you?" His gentle tone was in stark contradiction to the cruelty in his eyes. Augustus was the kind of man who got off on hurting people, women in particular, drunk on his own power. "Have you been making rogues, little girl?"

"No." Maya shook her head furiously as tears continued to fall. "I swear it to you."

"Yes." He sighed. "I doubt you're lying. I *could* drink from you and read those blood memories, but that seems… beneath me. Don't you agree?"

Maya nodded furiously but avoided his glare.

"I don't care who made the rogues," he said in a low tone. "However, this mess all started with you and your irresponsible feeding habits."

"Augustus—" Olivia interrupted.

"But since you are her maker, Olivia," he said without taking his eyes off Maya, "then really, this is your problem. She is your responsibility, and therefore this is your mess. As punishment for running such a sloppy, unruly coven, this little troublemaker will be put down, and if you don't find that rogue nest and eliminate it, then you and the rest of your coven are next."

"It's too bad you can't show Maya the same mercy you showed your son," Olivia said evenly. "But I suppose since he's your biological son and not your vampire progeny, that's why you were soft on him."

Augustus stilled, and Doug saw the monster lurking behind the mask of calm.

"My son," he seethed, "was sent into hibernation for fifty years *by you*. He more than paid his debt for his minor indiscretion."

"Seems like a different set of rules, and if memory serves, the emperor is not a fan of breaking the rules or vampires who do." Olivia's amber eyebrows flew up, and a smile lit her gorgeous face as her voice dropped low. "You don't think you're above the *emperor*, do you?"

"I enforce the laws in this region, and it is up to me to decide what is acceptable and what isn't. In addition, I'm certain that Emperor Zhao wouldn't want to be bothered with this mess your coven is making," he bit out. "Your maker offered you a chance to take your pathetic little troop and leave, but you refused. Since you've chosen to stay, you will accept my judgment."

"Fine," Olivia added quickly. "I'll contact Vincent and tell him that we'll leave with him tonight. All of us, including Maya."

"It's too late, Olivia." Augustus glared down at them. "Vincent is gone. You made your choice, and now you and the rest of your coven will live with it."

Doug watched as the two women on the platform

looked at one another briefly before nodding in agreement. The men to the right did the same. The senators seemed more like puppets than freethinkers, and they disgusted Doug. Apparently, humans hadn't cornered the market on being assholes.

The czar held all the power, and no one was willing to question him or stand up to him. Maya wept quietly, and sympathy tugged at his gut. She was just a kid. Not much different from Brittany or any number of victims he saw over the years. Vampire or not, Maya was a victim of the brutal world.

At least now Doug had a chance to stop a crime before it was committed.

"How about a trade?" Doug stepped forward and stood in the center of the room with his hands on his hips. He resisted the urge to draw his gun because he knew it wouldn't end well for anyone. Himself, he didn't care about. He was ready to die, but starting a bloody fight was too risky for Maya, Olivia, and Pete. "Me for her."

What the hell are you doing, Paxton? Olivia's panicked voice touched his mind. *This is not a game.*

"How dashing!" Augustus clapped his hands and looked curiously from Doug to Olivia. "You want to trade your life for Maya's? Now that is refreshing!"

The senators perked up and whispered giddily to each other, which only irritated Doug. They had been alive for so long, they only found pleasure in the torment of others. Nice.

"Yeah." Doug jutted his thumb toward Olivia. "Olivia and I will hunt down the rogues. When the job's done, then you can kill me instead of the girl" He shrugged casually. "No harm, no foul. A life for a life."

"Doug, no," Olivia pleaded. She placed her hand on his arm and pulled him to face her. Her brow furrowed, and her voice hovered just above a whisper. "Please."

Please don't do this. The pleading look in her eyes was matched by the tone in her voice, and it tore at his heart. Doug swallowed the lump that formed in his throat as he kept his resolute gaze locked with hers. "So, do we have a deal, Augustus?"

"Just when I think I'm bored to tears, someone comes along and spices things up. My goodness, I thought New York City was going to be exciting, but it wasn't until this rogue nonsense." Augustus laughed louder and ascended the stairs to his seat. "We have a deal, Detective Paxton. Put down the rogues, and I will release the girl, taking your life in exchange for hers." He frowned and played with the roping on his robe. "To ensure that you do as I command, the girl will remain here."

"Damn it." Olivia dropped her hand and stepped away from Doug, turning her full attention to the czar. "How do I know that you won't harm Maya before we return?"

"She will stay under my protection." Shane flew down the steps next to Maya. "I have been a sentry for four centuries and have pledged my life to the Presidium. You have my word that she will not be harmed."

"How chivalrous," Augustus said with sarcasm. "You beat me to the punch, Sentry Quesada. You see, neither of the sentries will be aiding you, Olivia. You and your newest progeny will hunt on your own." Augustus grinned wickedly. "Be back here in forty-eight hours, or I'll assume that you failed, and the girl will be put down… along with the rest of your coven."

Pete started to protest, but Olivia raised her hand to stop him. Doug's focus remained on Augustus, and though his fingers itched to grab his gun, he refrained from starting a bloodbath and let Olivia continue.

"You are absolutely right." She turned her attention to Shane and Pete. "I would trust any sentry with my life and the lives of my family." She smiled sweetly at Augustus. "Not that I think our esteemed czar would go back on his word, of course."

"Wouldn't dream of it." He sighed. "Now be gone."

Doug nodded to Augustus and followed Olivia, Pete, and Shane into the main hall.

"That is one cold bunch of assholes," Doug said tightly.

Olivia looked at him intently. "Not all of us are like that," she said quietly.

Doug stared into those pools of green, and the need to touch her, to cradle her beautiful face, clawed at him. He knew she wasn't a monster. He saw the look on her face when Augustus threatened her coven, and the fear was evident. Olivia was a good soul, and no matter what, she would never revel in the pain of another the way Augustus did.

Doug, however, was another story. Ever since he was turned, all he could think about was finding the bastard that killed Tom and drinking him dry. He tore his gaze from Olivia and headed toward the exit. Looked like he was a monster, after all.

Chapter 11

XAVIER STOOD ON A STOOL AT HIS LAB TABLE IN HIS STAINED, white lab coat, so engrossed in what he was doing that at first Olivia thought he didn't notice they were there.

A moment later, he raised his pudgy hand and waved them in without looking up.

"A friend of yours?" Doug had kept one hand on the gun tucked in the back of his pants since they had left Augustus and the senators. She couldn't blame him. He endured a whirlwind introduction to his new world, and he was handling it pretty well—aside from the desire to kill himself, or more to the point, let Augustus kill him. How on earth was she going to stop that from happening?

"Friends?" Xavier laughed loudly and flew down from his perch to meet them. "You bet your ass we're friends. I moved my lab to New York just so I could be close to her."

He leaped into Olivia's arms and gave her a vigorous hug. She laughed and hugged him back with equal fervor.

"Good to see you, old friend." She looked at Doug as she held the scientist. "Xavier is the best weapons man in the business, and his inventions have saved my ass more times than I can count."

"Right." Doug nodded, and Olivia could tell he was trying not to stare at Xavier.

He was a dwarf, and in his human life, he worked

with a circus, living on the rails until his maker found him and turned him. His shock of white hair made him look like a miniature version of Albert Einstein. Xavier gave Olivia a kiss on the cheek before jumping from her arms and flying back to his stool.

"What's the matter, big guy?" Xavier scooped up two vials of blood and looked intently at Doug. "Never seen a little person before?"

"Well, not one that's a vampire," Doug said bluntly.

"Fair enough." Xavier chuckled and held the two vials out for Olivia. "Pete told me that the synthetic blood from the rogue worked, so I whipped up more. I'm betting that the first dose you took wore off or will soon."

"It did." She nodded. "I dusted the one that attacked Paxton."

She took the vials from Xavier and watched Doug take stock of the lab. She noticed that one of the first things he did was survey the space around him, and it was one habit that would help when they were hunting.

"Here." She held one out to Doug. "Drink it. It's a synthetic version of Rogue One's blood and will help us track him. If he's in the area, we'll be able to pick up his scent pretty easily, and it will make it difficult for him to sneak up on us."

Doug uncorked it, took a whiff, and grimaced.

"Rogues created by rogues are usually a little crazy because they haven't been properly trained or guided by their makers." She shrugged and tossed the empty vial into a trash bin on the other side of the room. "The blood you drank earlier was from one of our human donors and had been cleaned."

"It may be more than that, Olivia." Xavier scratched

his head and smoothed his white hair as he gave her a curious look.

"Like what?" Olivia adjusted the gun at her hip and inched closer to the table.

"I'm not entirely sure." He pursed his lips. "It could be the essence of the vampire—Rogue One is pure evil. Or he was created by another rogue."

Doug swallowed again and chucked his empty tube in the trash as well.

"No helping the bad taste, I'm afraid. Maybe if I could figure out why it tasted like that, then I'd be able to fix it." Xavier hopped from the stool and waddled to the back wall. He pushed a button on the left, and the stainless steel wall slid open, revealing a deadly arsenal. Xavier grinned mischievously and ran a hand over his goatee.

"However, I can help with something else."

"Son of a bitch," Doug breathed.

Olivia watched him and smiled. The look on his face could only be described as a kid at Christmas. He ran his fingertips over one of the new guns with an expression of awe, wonder, and excitement.

"See?" Olivia sidled up next to him and elbowed him playfully. "There are some perks."

"I always did appreciate a nice weapon." Doug smirked and gave her a sidelong glance. "You're right," he said as his eyes wandered over her face. "There are some perks."

Olivia kept her eyes locked with his and wondered briefly if he felt a smidgen of the attraction that she did. Was it possible that he didn't hate her for making him like her? She opened her mouth but shut it again quickly.

What the hell was she doing? There was no time for childish nonsense or hormone-driven fantasy. She straightened her back and turned her attention to Xavier. She was afraid she might dissolve into a weeping mess, clinging to Doug and begging him not to leave her again.

"Did you finish the UV ammunition?"

"Yes," Xavier said enthusiastically. He pointed to two large stainless steel guns with laser sighting. "These are the prototypes." He lowered his voice and looked around, as if worried someone else might hear. "They are supposed to go to Shane and Pete, since they are our sentries, but it looks like the two of you get to try them first."

Olivia lifted both guns from their spots on the wall and handed one to Doug as Xavier passed each a full ammunition belt. They strapped on the belts and loaded up their new weapons with the ease of experience.

"Impressive," Xavier said as he watched Doug load his gun. His white eyebrows furrowed. "When exactly were you turned? You seem remarkably comfortable with your new *situation*."

"Today." Doug settled the gun in the belt's holster. "Why?"

"Hmmm." Xavier stroked his goatee and looked from Olivia to Doug. "It's unusual but not unheard of."

"Really?" Olivia said while inspecting her new toy, trying to seem nonchalant. "I was going to ask you about that. Doug's turn only took twelve hours, and he slipped into being a vampire the way I can slip into a pair of great heels. Any idea why he seems to be… well… a natural vampire?"

Xavier remained silent but continued to look back

and forth between the two of them. Olivia squirmed and couldn't help but think that Xavier suspected there was more to her relationship with Doug than being his maker.

"Anything unusual for you, Olivia?" He flew to his stool and looked Olivia up and down. "You have turned a few vampires in your day. Is there anything different about his change as far as you are concerned?"

"She can only telepath with me now," Doug added. "No one but me."

Olivia shot him a look that could kill. "It's nothing," she said through clenched teeth.

"Doesn't sound like nothing," Xavier said quietly. He looked back and forth between them before waving his hand dismissively. "Then again, it could be an aberration, you know, a one-time thing. If your telepathy with the rest of your progeny doesn't return in a few days, let me know."

Olivia felt Doug staring at her as his voice touched her mind intimately. *My gut tells me it's not nothing, and based on your tense body language, you know more than you're letting on.*

"Tell us more about these new weapons, Xavier," Olivia said, breaking the mental connection with Doug, which was similar to slamming a door in his face. "What do we need to know?"

Doug swore under his breath and paced behind her with his hands on his hips. He wanted answers, but now was not the time for that conversation, no matter how much she may wish it were.

"Now," Xavier continued, "if these bullets perform as I believe they will, then you don't need to hit a vamp in the head or heart. The UV light within the casing of the bullet should turn our rogue friends into dust upon contact. Questions?"

"Nope." Doug shook his head and rested his hand on the gun at his narrow hips. "Point and shoot. Got it."

"Thank you, Xavier," Olivia said before placing a kiss on his white-haired head. "You always come through. We'll be sure to return these prototypes when we're done."

"See that you do." Xavier squeezed her hand and whispered, "Be careful, Olivia. It's been a while since you hunted as a sentry." He flicked his gray eyes to Doug. "It worries me that Augustus is sending you out there without Shane or Pete."

"It's a game." Doug folded his arms over his chest and turned his serious eyes to Olivia. "He wants to see if we can do it. If we do, then he gets the rogues put down and gets to kill me in exchange for Maya. If we get killed in the process, he gets rid of both of us and kills the rest of Olivia's coven." Doug shrugged. "It's a win-win for him and will entertain him at the same time."

As Olivia and Doug made their way through the catacombs beneath the Cloisters, she tried not to think about what Doug said. It was a game to Augustus. Maya. The rogues. Getting her and Doug to hunt alone—all designed to entertain his bored two-thousand-year-old ass.

Olivia led the way up a dark, stone staircase, and they reached what looked like a dead end, but she pulled an iron handle to her left, and a massive door hidden in the wall swung open. They stepped through the opening and into the Unicorn Tapestry room of The Cloisters.

Olivia didn't miss the low whistle Doug let out when the fireplace closed behind them.

They stood silently in the dark, almost reverently, as Doug moved closer to inspect the famous tapestry.

"I've never been in here," he said quietly. "I've lived in the city for over ten years and never stepped foot in here before today. I was never much of a museum guy, I guess, but if I had known about all the cool shit in here, I would've made a point to come. Gotta admit though, I never thought I would come in through a secret entrance in a fireplace."

"There are several entrances, but this room is my favorite. The Hunt of the Unicorn is beautiful and tragic. Unicorns were hunted to extinction by humans so long ago that their existence has been turned into nothing more than fantasy."

"Did you ever see one?"

"No," Olivia said through a laugh. She put her hands on her hips and shot him a playful look. "Just how old do you think I am?"

"Not sure." Doug faced her with a look of amusement and inched closer. "But if memory serves, it's best not to answer this question from a woman. It's a no-win scenario."

"Well, wise guy," she said, meeting his challenge. "The unicorns went extinct over three thousand years ago, and for your information, I'm only about three hundred, thank you very much."

"Don't look a day over twenty-five," he murmured.

His bright blue eyes studied her intently as his towering form invaded her space. *May I kiss you, Olivia?* His mind whispered through hers as he brushed the line of her jaw with his thumb. Olivia nodded silently. There was something both innocent and erotic in the way he asked. The enticingly wicked sound of his voice rippled through her mind.

Olivia's feet seemed nailed to the floor as he wavered closer, and his legs brushed temptingly along hers. Bathed in moonlight, Olivia held his hand against her cheek as Doug leaned down, gently capturing her lips.

Tenderly at first, caressing her mouth with his, he cradled her face in his hands as though she might break. Olivia sighed as his tongue slid between her lips and tangled slowly, tenderly with hers. He suckled her bottom lip briefly before releasing it and placing a kiss at the corner of her mouth.

"I'm addicted to the taste of you," he murmured against her lips.

The sound of footsteps in the hallway captured their attention, breaking the spell.

"It's the night security guard," she whispered, stepping from his embrace abruptly. "We have to go."

Doug followed Olivia as she whipped around the corner and made swift work of opening one of the ornately carved doors. Moments later, they were standing in the outdoor garden overlooking the Hudson River.

"What if they see us?" Doug glanced over his shoulder, but the guard was nowhere to be seen. "How exactly do we explain our presence?"

"Mel is the guard on duty tonight, and if we had to, we could glamour him. Believe me, it wouldn't be the first time." Olivia watched as confusion washed over his handsome face. "Vampires can erase or create memories, like hypnosis. Anyway, I'd rather not. I don't enjoy glamouring humans unless necessary."

Olivia walked through the gardens and hopped onto a wooden bench beneath the wisteria-covered arbor. She sucked in a deep breath and reveled in the multitude of scents in the night that filled her head and made her smile. There was great beauty in the world and having amped-up senses could be a perk, highlighting the smallest of luxuries in nature.

"Why not?" Doug jumped on the bench next to her and looked out over the river with the glittering city lights reflected on the surface. He turned to face her, his eyes sparkling. His voice dropped low, to just above a whisper, as his eyes locked with hers. "Tell me. Why don't you like glamouring humans?"

"Because it's too personal and intimate." Olivia's voice wavered, but she cleared her throat, hoping to steel her resolve. "I don't like invading the mind of another being without permission. It feels like I'm violating them somehow, and it's bad manners."

"You speak with your mind," he said with a lopsided grin. "I have to admit, the first time I heard you, I thought I was going insane. *But it also turned me on*." Doug linked one strong arm around her waist and yanked her against him. "So why is it okay for you to touch my mind? I mean, I know you're not changing my memories, but you're still… slipping inside of me."

Olivia's stomach fluttered as he leaned closer and nuzzled her neck, trailing kisses down her neck. *Why is it just me?* She shut her eyes and arched back, allowing him better access, and his clean, fresh scent filled her head, making her dizzy with desire. *Why can our minds whisper to each other?* Olivia clung to him and moaned as he kissed his way up to her ear, nibbling her lobe seductively. *Why can't I think of anything but you?* Lust fogged her, threatening to consume her.

"I would love nothing more than to take this further," she said breathlessly. Olivia squeezed her eyes shut, refusing to touch his mind, fearing it would break her last ounce of self-control. "But we are running short on time."

Doug silenced her with a kiss. A knee-buckling, head-spinning kiss that would have stolen her breath, if she had any. He dipped her, so she was perched beneath the fragrant arbor. Olivia tangled her arms around his neck and sank into the kiss, allowing him to take control and take as much of her as he wanted.

It was liberating.

Doug broke the kiss and whipped her to a standing position as his hands settled on her hips. "After sunrise," he said firmly, "you are going to answer my questions… among other things."

He released her from his grasp and looked out over the city. "Where do we go first?"

Olivia smoothed back the stray hairs that came loose during their kiss and adjusted the gun at her hip. She tried desperately to seem unaffected by his sudden display of affection but failed miserably. Doug gave her a sidelong grin and folded his arms over his chest, which was puffed up like a rooster.

"We're going to the medical examiner's office first to see if any other bodies have turned up." She stepped onto the stone wall. "Then we go back to the area around the club and the park because that's where they've been hunting. Chances are that's where they're nesting. They'll stay in a pack out of instinct."

"I'm supposed to be dead, right?"

"Yes."

"What if someone sees me?"

"You'll be moving so fast that even if they do catch a glimpse, they'll think they saw a ghost." Her lips curved into a smile. "Time to fly."

"Fly?" he asked skeptically.

"Like a bird." Olivia arched one eyebrow and leaped like a bullet into the night sky. "Or a bat." She dropped down and hovered in midair, staying there for a moment, while Doug gaped. "What's the matter, detective? Chicken?"

"Not on your life." Doug's blue eyes crinkled at the corners as he looked at her mischievously. "How about a little coaching for a newbie?"

"Remember when you were in the tunnels tonight and you ran like the wind?"

"Yeah?" He peered over the edge at the steep drop but leaned back quickly.

"Did you think about it, or did you just do it?"

"Shit." A grin cracked his handsome face, and he rubbed his head, reminding her of a little boy. "You're right, but this is a little different, don't you think? I mean, running is one thing, I've been doing that my whole life, but flying is another."

"Use your mind as much as your body." She winked. "From what I've seen so far, you're good with both."

Doug gave her a cocky grin, meeting her challenge, and in one giant leap, he shot into the air. Olivia watched as he swooped through the sky like a stealth bomber, until he finally stopped and hovered next to her. His eyes were alight with excitement, and his body hummed with power. Now she was the one gaping like a stunned sheep.

"What's the matter, Olivia?" he murmured wickedly as he drifted closer and his foot tapped hers. "You act like you've never seen a guy fly."

"I guess I didn't expect you to do it like you've been doing it all your life." She shook her head in wonder. "You were *born* to be a vampire."

His features darkened. "I was born to be a *cop*." His jaw clenched, and he drifted back, increasing the distance between them. "Let's go."

He flew ahead through the inky night towards the Village. As they sped through the city night together, she prayed he would eventually forgive her.

They landed on the roof of the medical examiner's building, and Olivia once again marveled at how easily Doug stepped into his new life—into her life. He had been quiet since they took flight, but she sensed the tension in him as he absorbed the sounds and sights of the city in an entirely new way. His brilliant blue eyes scanned the roof as they walked to the door, but Olivia stopped him before they went in.

"Hang on." She placed her hand on his chest as her other hand rested on the doorknob. His muscles flexed beneath her fingers, and much to her relief, he didn't flinch or shrink away, but held her gaze, meeting her challenge. "Stay behind me, and follow my lead."

"I've been in the medical examiner's office more times than I care to count, and I know my way around. I may not have been supernatural, but I managed just fine."

"I know that." Olivia dropped her hand and cursed herself for not saying the right thing. She turned her back on him as she opened the door. "I just think it would be wise to avoid contact with the humans. Your ex-girlfriend might freak the fuck out if her presumed-dead ex walked into her autopsy room in the middle of the night." She tried to keep the hurt and jealousy out of her voice but failed miserably. "Let's make it quick, and then we're heading back down to the Village."

"How did you know about Miranda?" Doug's fingers curled around her bicep, and Olivia fought the rush of lust that followed as his hand pressed into her arm. He furrowed his brow as he loomed over her, his mouth temptingly close. "You seem to know a lot more about me than you've let on. Why is that?"

"We don't have time for this." She tugged her arm free and yanked the door open. "Stay close and follow me."

"Whatever you say," Doug bit out. "But this conversation isn't over by a long shot."

Olivia flew down the empty stairwell to the bottom floor with Doug hot on her heels. As soon as she opened the door, the distinct scent of Rogue One slammed into them violently, knocking every other thought out of her head.

Her fangs erupted, and Doug growled in her ear before he pushed past her and raced to the double doors of the autopsy room with his gun drawn. Olivia swore under her breath and flew down the hallway after him.

She blew through the double doors and found Doug on the floor cradling the lifeless, bloodied body of Dr. Miranda Kelly. Sadness tore at her for the loss that Doug was suffering, but the scent of the rogue lingered, not allowing any time for mourning. Gun drawn, she surveyed the surroundings.

"They fucking slaughtered her," he growled. "Why? Why did they come here and kill her? What possible motivation could they have had to hurt Miranda?"

Olivia watched through sympathetic eyes as Doug placed a kiss on her hair and gently laid her broken body on the floor—anger carved deep into his features as he rose to his feet slowly.

"I can still smell that piece of shit, and when I find him, he's going to pray for sunrise and a quick death. I'm going to dissect his ass like a frog in a high school biology class."

"The blood doesn't bother you?" Olivia watched him carefully and noted that he seemed immune to the overwhelming scent of blood, which was unheard of for newly turned vampires. By all accounts, it should have triggered his bloodlust and hunger, driving him mad with thirst, but the only emotion he experienced was rage.

"No," he rasped. Doug looked around the room with his usual inspecting, intent gaze. "The place is destroyed. Maybe they were looking for something. What could she possibly have had that they would've killed her for?"

The computer was smashed, her files were strewn around the room, and blood spattered much of the floor. She glanced to the camera in the corner. It was torn from the wall, so whoever was in here knew enough to take out the camera. Olivia glanced at the autopsy table.

"The blood in these drains is fresh." Olivia leaned closer to get a clean scent. "It's not Miranda's blood. Maybe Rogue One let one of the rogues get picked up by accident?"

"What do you mean?" Doug squatted next to Miranda.

"The healing doesn't usually start for almost twenty-four hours. If Rogue One has been busy making new vamps, or his rogues have, then maybe they got sloppy, and a vampire that was in the middle of the change got picked up and mistaken by the humans for dead."

"Maybe." He stood, his face stamped with anger. "Or maybe it woke up on the table and killed her?"

Doug went to Miranda's desk and picked up the open file.

"Son of a bitch," he whispered before turning to face her. "Moriarty. He was the guy she was working on."

Olivia nodded, but before she could say anything, the subtle sound of wind whistling down a tunnel captured her attention as she swung her gun in the direction of the refrigerator compartments. Doug drew his gun right along with her, and they moved toward the noise.

One of the square stainless steel doors was open a crack. Olivia knew it led to the network of tunnels beneath the city. She pressed one finger to her lips and motioned to the partially opened door before yanking on it. It was empty, and the trap door that led into the tunnels was wide open.

"Sloppy and frantic," she whispered. "They killed her and escaped through there. Come on. We'll track them."

Doug didn't move. He was looking at Miranda's lifeless body, and Olivia knew he hated the idea of leaving her. She couldn't blame him, but they didn't have the luxury of taking her with them.

"We have to go, Doug." Olivia laid a hand over his. "The only thing you can do to help her now is find the vamps that murdered her and put them down."

His intense blue eyes filled with fury and flicked to hers briefly before he dived into the open drawer and slipped into the tunnel below. Olivia slid in behind him and closed the trap door, shutting it securely. The last disruption they needed was a human to stumble upon their network.

He crouched low and moved silently down the tunnel in front of her. They followed the scent for what felt like forever, but Doug stopped when they came to an intersection with five passages. She scanned the area not only with the enhanced night vision of a vampire, but also with the sonar vision that allowed her to sense far beyond where she could actually see.

Doug closed his eyes and held his gun out as he absorbed the subtle sounds around them. Olivia squatted down on her heels and watched him with genuine awe because he figured it out himself.

She didn't have to tell him about reading sound waves, and she didn't want to overwhelm him with information. Doug Paxton was full of surprises, and the most natural vampire she had ever met.

They're down there. His voice touched hers on a whisper. His eyes flicked open, and he pointed to the corridor to the right. *I sense movement, and it feels like something big. Not rats. I think there are two or three.*

Once a cop, always a cop. Olivia looked at him with pride, and a smile played at her lips. *It makes sense. This tunnel will take us to the Village, and there's an entrance to the street by Washington Square Park. Stay sharp. Chances are their nest is somewhere around here.*

Doug nodded, and as they moved toward the inevitable battle, Olivia prayed he would be as deft at kicking ass as he had been at everything else.

Chapter 12

THE NEED TO KILL PULLED AT HIM AND HUNG AROUND HIS neck like a fucking albatross. The image of Miranda's mutilated body flashed through his mind as he and Olivia made their way through the network of tunnels. He used his rage to drive him forward as they followed the stink of the rogues—the monsters that killed two of the only people he cared about.

He didn't love Miranda, but she was a good woman and didn't deserve to die. But then again, neither did Tom, Brittany, or Ronald Davis. He vowed that if it was the last thing he did, he would eviscerate the motherfuckers who were responsible.

Lost in his thoughts and focused on the path in front of them, he didn't hear the sounds at first, but Olivia did. Her delicate hand grabbed his, and they came to a halt, crouching in the tunnel back-to-back with guns drawn, both of them struggling to discern which direction the footsteps were coming from.

"They're coming from both directions." He squeezed her hand and took solace in the weight of her body leaning against his.

"Damn it," she whispered. "They're herding us like fucking cattle."

"And it sounds like a lot more than two or three."

"Go," she shouted. "There's an abandoned subway

tunnel about twenty feet ahead on the right. Shoot anything that moves."

Doug kept her hand wrapped in his and started flying down the tunnel, but as he rounded the corner and went through the opening to the abandoned subway, something slammed into him, cutting him across the face or biting him. Doug squeezed off several rounds as he flipped through the air before landing on both feet. He watched two vampires explode with bloodcurdling shrieks.

She landed at his side, and they quickly realized they were outnumbered—badly. She shifted her position so they were back-to-back, and as they drew their other guns, Doug and Olivia took in the horrifying scene that surrounded them. Standing on the abandoned, broken tracks, they were surrounded by at least twenty vampires. Snarling, drooling, and wild with hunger, they began to close the circle.

"Sweet Jesus," he whispered.

"I doubt he'll hear you," she said as her body tensed against his.

They started firing, and all hell broke loose. Doug hit several with the UV rounds, and they burst into flames in shrieks of agony. As he reloaded, two rogues leaped on him and started biting his neck. One tried to bite his arm, but the two layers of leather he wore afforded him some protection.

Doug roared in fury as he grabbed a small wild-eyed woman and threw her into the wall just before putting a bullet in her head. He tugged the other one off his back and ripped his head off in one swoop. Strength and pure power flowed through him as he fired his weapons and killed one creature after another. Rapid gunfire, bursts of flames, shrill death cries, and clouds of dust filled the air, stinging his eyes and coating his mouth with dusted vampire.

Olivia moved faster than he thought possible and killed several more with the sure shot of a sniper. He ducked as she threw silver stars past his head that sliced through two vamps like butter. He reloaded and shot several more, turning them to ash, but when he swung around to check on Olivia she pointed her gun and screamed, "Get down."

Doug ducked as she discharged her weapon and turned a charging vampire into a cloud of ash. The cavernous space fell silent as the two of them, covered in blood and dust, looked around to be sure they got them all.

"What the fuck was that?" Doug asked in a low voice as he scanned the room. "So much for two or three. There had to be at least twenty of those things. Who the hell is making all of them?"

"I don't know," Olivia said. "Whoever did this started making these vamps awhile ago, and at the rate they're growing, the city will be overrun in a matter of weeks. Rogue One wasn't here, and I don't remember seeing Moriarty in the melee."

"Nope." Doug shook his head. "Me either."

"This isn't the nest either," she said as she inspected the area. "It's too exposed. Too many tunnels in and out. Damn it. We need another night to find the nest. It's almost sunrise."

Doug wiped the blood away wearily as two more vamps flew down from an arch in the ceiling and right at them. Olivia unexpectedly pushed him out of the way, but he recovered, jumping back onto his feet just as one of the rogues tackled her. She fired, and the one on top of her exploded just before Doug shot the other as it swooped around. As the last one exploded in a cloud of fire and its shrieks echoed around them, everything fell silent.

Muscles straining, his entire body vibrated, and his senses remained alert as he kept his gun pointed at the cloud of dust. He waited for more, but none followed. It took a moment for him to realize that Olivia was still on the ground and quiet.

"Olivia?" Panic swamped him when he saw her unmoving, bloody form on the ground.

Doug went to her side and gently lifted her into his arms. Holding her limp body, horror filled him when he saw the massive gash on her neck. If she had been human, she would have been dead. Her head lolled in the crook of his arm, and her eyes rolled back in her head.

"Oh my God." He picked her up and looked around the room, feeling helpless for the first time since this crazy mess started. "It's okay. I have to get you out of here before more show up."

He had some ammo left, but not enough to take on another swarm. She moaned, and he watched as the wound started to close, but it wasn't happening fast enough, and she was losing too much blood.

Blood.

That was it.

It's going to be okay, Olivia. He touched her mind with his with an odd familiarity, as though he had been doing it his entire life. Maybe he had. The instant he linked his mind with hers, everything felt like it was going to be okay.

As he flew through the tunnels carrying her limp body, he wondered if the dreams were more connected to her than he previously thought. He wanted more than answers... he wanted *her*. There was more to her—more to *them*. Hell. He glanced at her pale, blood-streaked face, and something inside of him broke as he realized the truth.

He loved her.

He loved the woman from his dreams, and no woman he ever met could stand up against that redheaded siren—until Olivia. She was a part of him. This unique, strong, feisty woman was everything he was searching for, but he had no idea what to do about it. Doug found himself in foreign territory in every way possible.

Unsure of where he was beneath the city, he followed the tracks because he didn't want to risk bringing her to street level. The sun would rise soon; it was a sense of weakness that lurked along the edge of his senses and grew with each passing minute. Olivia winced, and her fingers curled around the lapel of his leather coat as she nuzzled against his chest and said something under her breath.

As Doug skidded to a halt, dirt and rocks sprayed from under his boot heels, and he leaned closer so he could hear. She tugged on his jacket, pulling him to her. Her lips brushed against his cheek as she tried to get the words out.

Sentry safe house. Her voice, faint and weak, wrapped around him like a blanket, surrounding him, comforting him, and assuring him she was still with him. *By the abandoned City Hall subway station. Further south. Keep going down the tracks. Looks like an old utility closet.*

"Good girl." He placed a kiss on her forehead. "Hang on."

Doug shot down the tracks, whipping around curves like a train on the rails, praying they weren't too far from the station she was talking about. As he rounded a sharp curve to the left, the defunct subway stop came into view, and like a freaking light at the end of the proverbial tunnel, he saw a steel door on the right near the main platform.

He came to a full stop, short of the faint rays of early morning sunlight that came through the cracks in the ceiling. The art deco design of the arches with faded ceramic tiles looked haunting and beautiful amid the vermin-ridden tunnels. It seemed a shame that this architectural marvel was buried here, hidden from the world.

The steel door appeared locked and rusted shut, but it was a door to somewhere, and if he had any luck, it would be a place he and Olivia could hunker down for the day. *Push the Danger sign on the door.* Her voice, weak and thready, flickered in his head.

Doug threw a prayer to the universe, held onto Olivia with one arm, and did as she said. The door gave way with an ear-shattering screech and swung open, revealing an old utility room with defunct fuses and levers that no longer served any purpose. Doug stepped inside as the door shut tightly behind them.

He surveyed the small room and marveled at how clearly he could see everything, even though it was black as pitch. Still holding Olivia in one arm, he looked at the filthy floor and grimaced.

"This place is disgusting."

A weak smile played at her lips. *Orange lever on the back wall.*

Doug pulled the lever, trying not to jostle her too much, and seconds later the back wall dropped into the floor as lights flickered on, revealing a virtual oasis. Doug whistled as he carried her over the threshold, and the door slid closed behind them.

The room was approximately thirty feet square with thick beige carpeting and aqua-colored walls, bathed in soft lighting. To the left was an oversized sofa, black coffee table, and a top-of-the-line media center. The right side of the room had an enormous king-size bed and a nightstand. The place looked spic-and-span clean as though the maid service from the Ritz Carton had just been there. Even the bed was made.

"Now this is more like it." He kissed the top of her head and carried her to the couch. "This place is nicer than my apartment."

He brushed a stray red curl off her forehead, and her brilliant green eyes fluttered open, locking with his. Doug sat down, holding her in his lap. He told himself it was so he could get a closer look at the wound, but that was absolute bullshit. He wanted her close, her body snuggled against his, safe and sound.

"You need blood, don't you?" he asked quietly.

Olivia's brow furrowed. "Yes, I'm sorry."

"Now you're apologizing?" he asked playfully as he shoved the sleeve of his shirt up and exposed his forearm. "After all the shit we've been through in the last twenty-four hours, you apologize for needing a little blood? That's some weak-ass stuff, if you ask me."

"Sorry," she murmured through a faint smile.

Doug lifted her head with one hand and held his wrist to her mouth. "Go on," he said gruffly. "Do it."

Are you sure? Her glittering eyes flicked to his as her voice whispered along his mind.

"Bite me, already." He pressed his wrist against her soft lips and watched with genuine fascination as her fangs unsheathed and sank into his flesh.

He wasn't sure what to expect. Pain, maybe? A pinch, like getting your finger pricked at the doctor? Doug gasped as her fangs pierced his skin because the last sensation he expected was pleasure.

Warmth washed through his body as a rich wave of pleasure rippled over him and made his dick as hard as a rock. This was wrong. Majorly fucked up.

Wrong or not—he was harder and hotter than he'd ever been in his life. Doug groaned and prayed for restraint. His fingers curled into a fist, tangling in her silky, red curls as she drank from him. All he could think about doing was stripping her naked and plunging deep inside of her.

Erotic images flashed through his mind. Memories of the dreams he had over the years and her voice, whispering wickedly in his ear as she drove him to the brink of orgasm. He saw her naked and writhing beneath him in ecstasy as she ran her fingernails down his back. All of these memories came roaring back in living color, tormenting him.

Olivia's body shuddered against his as she held his arm with both hands, her lips pressed against his skin erotically, and her tongue flicking back and forth on the sensitive flesh.

She moaned as she broke her hold on him and licked the wound closed. Doug barely noticed. He felt every spot where her body touched his, and when she adjusted her position the curve of her ass pressed enticingly against his cock, sending another rush of carnal pleasure rippling over his skin. The images in his mind faded, but the physical response was still in full force.

Doug opened his eyes to find her staring up at him through heavily lidded eyes. The wound on her neck had completely healed. A smile curved her lips, and she pressed her hand against his cheek, brushing her thumb along his hypersensitive skin.

"Thank you," she breathed. "You didn't have to do that."

Doug couldn't speak. His body was wound tighter than a drum, and the woman draped over him held him captive in every possible way. His heated gaze wandered up her throat and lingered on her full, ruby-red lips. Her mouth parted, and he glimpsed the sharp points of her fangs. He held her tighter, afraid she might slip away.

"Do you have any idea what you do to me?" he asked gruffly as his hand rested on her thigh. Doug pulled her closer and brushed his fingers along the deliciously sexy curve of her ass. "You ruined me."

"I'm sorry." Her brow furrowed, and she dropped her hand to his chest, trying to extricate herself from his grasp. "I know you hate me for turning you. Your body's reaction is because of the feeding, nothing more."

"That's horseshit." He held her in his iron-clad grip, and her confused eyes latched onto his. "My *body*, and the rest of me, is reacting to *you*, Olivia, and has been from the first time I dreamt of you all those years ago.

When I saw you that night at the club, it was like—like coming home. Something that I'd been chasing my entire life was there in front of me, but like the typical, stubborn asshole I am, I refused to believe it. You are in my head, wrapped around my heart, and buried under my skin."

He grasped her biceps and pulled her into an upright position in his lap, tugging her close, so that her face was only inches from his. Her scent filled his head and intoxicated him, but now she was looking at him as though he had completely lost his mind.

"You ruined me for any other woman, did you know that?" He brushed his lips along her cheek and ran his hand along the curve of her ass as it pressed against his erection erotically. "None of them could even live up to the idea of you, to the redheaded siren who haunted my sleep with promises of perfection. All my life, I thought I couldn't commit to anyone because of my fucked up childhood or some bullshit notion about fear of commitment. It was all because of you, wasn't it?"

He pulled back and lifted her chin with the tip of his finger, forcing those pools of green to look at him.

"You had my heart before I was even born."

Doug brushed his thumb over her lower lip. He watched as she licked the tip of his thumb and took it into the moist cavern of her mouth and suckled. All he could do was picture that gorgeous mouth wrapped around other parts of his anatomy.

Her eyes snapped open and captured his as her tongue wound slow, erotic circles around the tip of his thumb. Pulling one leg across his lap, she straddled him, pressing herself harder against his erection as she linked her arms around his neck, and he covered her mouth with his.

Doug buried both hands in her hair, angling her head, and devoured her with equal intensity. He licked and suckled at her plump lips, bathed his tongue with hers, and moaned as she ran her fingers along the back of his neck.

In a tangle of limbs, he reached between them and pulled down the zipper of her catsuit, baring her gorgeous white breasts. Olivia shrugged off her coat, tossing it to the floor and arching back, as she offered herself. Doug took one mound in his hand and lapped at the hardened, pink nipple as she held him to her, urging him on.

"I want to lick every inch of you and taste every curve," he murmured against the swell of her breast. Doug flicked the rosy peak with his tongue as he peered at her wickedly. "But you're wearing far too many clothes."

In a flash, still holding her in his arms and with her legs wrapped around his waist, he leaped to his feet. Olivia clung to him as he walked her to the wall and pinned her there. A smile played at her lips as she dropped her legs from his waist and stood. She licked his lower lip as her hands pressed against his chest and pushed him away.

Before he could protest, she unhooked the ammo belt and let it drop to the floor as she peeled the skintight catsuit from her torso and bared herself to the waist. He grinned and moved forward to take her in his arms, but she leaned back against the wall and kicked up her booted foot, placing it on his chest, keeping him at bay.

The spiked heel dug into his chest and probably should have hurt. It only made him want her more.

"How about a little help?" Olivia whispered wickedly with a nod toward her tall boot.

Doug's lips lifted as he held her gaze. He complied with her request and slowly unzipped the knee-high leather boot. He tossed it aside and ran his hands along her calf and down to her perfectly manicured toes. Olivia put both her hands above her head as she switched feet and pressed the heel of her other boot into his chest. Doug made quick work of removing it and tossing it onto the couch with the other.

"You're not quite finished," she rasped as she clasped her hands above her head.

Olivia arched her back, making her pert breasts jut temptingly toward him. Doug's gaze wandered over her. He had never seen anyone more beautiful or seductive, and although he dreamed of her forever, he hadn't really seen her until now. While she seemed like a seductive temptress, she was actually baring herself and putting herself in a position of vulnerability.

Eyes on hers, Doug shucked his coat and tossed it absently to the side as he inched closer bit by bit, until his leather-clad thighs brushed hers. He hooked his thumbs into the catsuit around her waist and pulled.

As he dragged it over the curve of her hips, he trailed kisses between her breasts and lapped at one nipple and then the other. Olivia's body quivered as his tongue ran down the center of her belly, and his fingers rasped over the lush skin on her ass as he bared her to him. He breathed in her musky scent and kissed the silky smooth skin along the inside of her thigh as he stripped her bare.

Doug dropped the garment to the floor as he rose to his feet and brushed his fingers along the sides of her legs, over her hip, and finally wrapped both hands around her narrow waist. Olivia's eyes, glazed with lust, stared at him with desire as his hand found its way to the nest of curls, and his fingers slid inside. She gasped and clutched his shoulders as he massaged her clit with his thumb and explored. Her eyes widened as the orgasm built inside, and his dick throbbed with every sweet sigh and sound of pleasure she made.

Fangs burst in his mouth, and a growl rumbled in his chest. Instead of being horrified, it urged him on. He massaged her bare breast in one hand as he worked the tiny bundle of nerves with the other.

"Yes." She whispered his name, and her hands dropped to the fly of his pants, impatiently releasing him. "I want to touch you."

When her long fingers wrapped around the length of him, he slammed one fist against the wall, struggling to stop from coming. She ran her hand up and down the length of him, matching his tempo as she ran her thumb over the head and back down again.

Just when Doug thought he was reaching the brink, Olivia released him from her grasp and smiled. Hands on his shoulders, she pushed him toward the sofa and urged him to sit. Fangs bared, she ran the tip of her tongue along her lips and straddled him.

Clinging to him, she held herself above the tip of his cock, lingering there for one exquisite minute before finally impaling herself on his shaft. Pleasure slammed into him as she sheathed him with her tight body. Doug cried out, gripped her hips, and suckled her breast as she rode him, fucking him fast and hard.

She tensed around him, milking him, as the orgasm crested, and her fangs emerged just before she sank them into his shoulder. Doug touched her thoughts with his. *Olivia.* Carnal pleasure scorched his body in a flash of lightning as he joined her in mind and body—tumbling, free-falling over the edge and into oblivion.

As he drove into her with one last thrust and the exquisite orgasm rocked him to the core, he could think of nothing but tasting her. Through the brilliant, blinding haze of pleasure, only one thought raced through his mind.

Blood.

On a curse, with her nude body curled around him, Doug bared his fangs and drove them into the tender flesh of her breast. Her warm, rich blood coated his throat, and lights burst behind his eyes. It felt as though his heart came roaring to life and beat in his chest once again. He didn't know how or why—he once again had a beating heart. As her sweet, cinnamon flavor bathed his tongue, all reason dissolved, and the world he knew exploded.

Chapter 13

Breathless and frightened, Olivia ran through the woods with her hand securely linked in Douglas's. They snuck away from the village and made love for the first time under cover of the moonlit forest, but someone had found them. In a panic, the two straightened their clothes and began to make their way back to the village quietly, but the distinct sound of footsteps behind them hurried them along.

"Someone is following us," Douglas whispered. He pulled her closer in the shelter of his tall, strong body, which only moments ago had been pressed deliciously on top of hers. He leaned against a large oak tree and looked around frantically. "I can feel their eyes on us."

Suddenly, an unfamiliar male voice wafted through the air. "You can run, but you can't hide."

Olivia snuggled closer to her lover and gripped his overcoat in her shaking hands. "We must go." Fear crawled up her back as the forest seemed to come alive. "I'm frightened."

"Come." He gave her a reassuring smile as he pulled her along. "I can see light from the lanterns outside the meeting house. We're almost there."

The bitter wind blew harder, stinging her face and eyes as she ran blindly. It was punishment. She knew it. Punishment for being a sinner and fornicating with Douglas before their marriage, and if her parents found out, they would be horribly ashamed. She knew the risk, they both did, and yet the fear of being caught didn't stop them. All that mattered was being together.

One big gust of wind came, blowing her bonnet off, allowing her unruly red hair to fly around her as the crisp fall wind blew harder. Olivia held her heavy skirts in one hand while she struggled to traverse the rocky, stick-strewn path back to town. Her boots, the ones with the tiny heel, the ones she begged her mother for, were not helping her cause.

She wiped the tears from her eyes just as something swooped down from the trees and blocked their path. The Shadow Man loomed over them like the angel of death, and though most of his face was hidden, she saw his fanged grin. Olivia opened her mouth to scream, but no sound came out as Douglas protectively pulled her behind him.

Somewhere in the recesses of her mind, she wondered if this was the devil coming to claim them and make them pay for their sins. The Shadow Man was dressed impeccably and reminded Olivia of English royalty she had heard about from her father. Though it was clear his intent was anything but regal.

"And what were you two doing out here, all alone?" The man's voice was deep and so quiet that Olivia wasn't quite sure if he'd said it out loud, or if she'd imagined it. His dark eyes flicked to Olivia. "A beauty like you should not be out in the woods at night." His voice dropped lower still. "You never know what might happen."

"Leave us, sir." Douglas's voice, strong and sure, cut between them. The stranger's head turned immediately

to Douglas, and she felt his body tense as she pressed herself closer to him. "We are expected back in town, and I must be getting Olivia home before her parents set to worry."

The man moved toward them slowly, his attentions directed to Douglas, and though Olivia strained to make out his face, she could not. "You will do no such thing." He was now a few inches away. "You will walk away and leave her here with me, is that clear?"

Olivia shook with pure terror and clutched Douglas tighter. His body hummed with tension beneath her fingers, and just when Olivia thought she would scream, Douglas defiantly stepped forward.

"I said, move aside, sir," Douglas ground out.

"Fascinating." Confusion and awe laced the Shadow Man's voice. "I've never before encountered a human who was not influenced easily by my people, let alone immune to our powers of suggestion."

"Human?" Douglas's voice wavered, and he stepped back, keeping Olivia behind him. "We will be on our way, sir."

As they attempted to leave, a claw-like hand grabbed Douglas by the throat and hoisted him into midair. Olivia stumbled backwards and fell as he held Douglas against the tree.

"Run," Douglas gurgled as he clutched at the hands around his throat.

Olivia wanted to scream, but still, no sound came. The man leered over his shoulder and hissed, revealing a set of demon-like fangs. Horrified and paralyzed with fear, she watched as he growled and bit her lover's neck.

She covered her ears and squeezed her eyes shut, praying it was a horrid nightmare, but she could not shut out the noises the creature made as he drank Douglas's blood.

The woods filled with a cry of triumph and then fell silent.

A gust of wind whipped around her as Douglas called to her weakly. Olivia opened her eyes, even though she was terrified by what she might see. The demon was gone, and Douglas lay on the ground at the base of the massive tree.

Crying, she scrambled across the rocky ground and cradled his head in her lap. His eyelids fluttered open, and his beautiful blue eyes stared up at her. She sniffled and wiped the blood from his cheek as he struggled to breathe.

"It will be alright," she whimpered. "I'll—I'll find someone to help you."

"Please don't leave me."

"Never," she whispered. "I am yours for eternity."

The life faded from his eyes as his last shuddering breath left his body. Sobbing, she held him in her lap and prayed for death herself. "I don't want to live here without you."

Tears fell onto his long blond hair while she quietly wept. A shadow flew overhead, blocking the light of the moon, and the Shadow Man landed silently next to Olivia, answering her prayers.

Olivia woke with a start. Still naked on the couch, covered by Doug's long coat, she sat up in the safe house room and tried to regain her bearings. They had sex.

Sex? That didn't fucking cover it. Granted, she had only had sex once as a human, with Douglas all those years ago, but it was nothing compared to the combustible experience they shared last night.

Doug was fully dressed and sitting on the foot of the bed with his arms resting on his knees. Olivia pushed the mass of red curls off her face and held the coat over her nakedness as his brilliant blue eyes watched her with his trademark intensity. Hurt washed over her when she saw the way he was looking at her, and the dream from last night came roaring back in living color. She wondered, fleetingly, if that dream had been shared with him, like so many others.

"What's going on?" His voice reverberated through the closed space. His brow furrowed as he stared her down and unknowingly answered her question. "Tell me, Olivia. Just cut the shit, and tell me. That dream I had last night was more like a memory, and if I didn't know better, I'd say that's exactly what it was."

She rubbed her hands over her face and pulled her hair back, wishing like hell she had a hair elastic. She flicked her gaze to his before looking around the room for her clothing. She stood, tossed the coat aside, and strode in all her naked glory to claim her belongings. She could feel his eyes on her, and to his credit he said nothing, but watched silently as she quickly dressed.

"There's something you aren't telling me." Doug swung his feet off the bed and stalked toward her as he watched her pull on her coat. He invaded her space, backing her against the wall, and placed both hands on either side of her head, caging her in. "What is it?"

Her body quivered with fear and anticipation as she

studied his ruggedly handsome face. What would he do when he found out the truth? Would he be relieved? Angry? Her hands balled into fists at her side as she reached deep down for the courage to tell him and prepared herself for his inevitable rejection.

"You—" she whispered in far shakier voice than she'd hoped. "You are Doug Paxton, but three hundred years ago you were Douglas Threadgood, my lover and fiancé. I take it that you shared the dreamscape with me last night after we..."

She trailed off, on the edge of losing all dignity and jumping his bones, or crumbling into a weeping heap and begging him to forgive her. Her throat tightened with unexpected emotion as she watched the stone cold expression in his eyes soften. Confusion washed over his face, and Olivia cleared her throat. She had to explain before she burst into tears like the sniveling, stupid girl she had been all those years ago.

"The dreamscape we were in last night wasn't exactly a dream. It was a memory." Her voice dropped low. "More specifically, it was *our* memory."

"Our memory." It came out as a statement, but he still looked at her beneath a furrowed brow. "Are you talking about reincarnation?"

"Yes." Olivia nodded as he leaned closer, and she pressed her body harder against the wall. "You look almost exactly like you did all those years ago. If we had a chance to look at your family tree, I bet we'd discover that you're a descendant of the Threadgood family." Her voice dropped to a whisper. "Physical similarities aside," she whispered, "your soul is unmistakable."

"I saw a whole bunch of stuff when I drank your

blood, but I didn't know what to make of it, and it felt like a funky LSD trip. When we made love and I drank from you, there were more images and memories." His mouth set in a tight line. "And if I didn't know better, I'd tell you that for about a minute and a half… I had a heartbeat again."

"I wasn't sure if you felt that too," Olivia breathed.

"Okay." Doug nodded slowly, dropping his hands from the wall. Olivia relaxed as he waved for her to continue. "If I can accept that I'm a vampire, then wrapping my brain around reincarnation shouldn't seem so outrageous. Keep going."

"Vincent, or as I called him that night, the Shadow Man, happened upon us in the woods. We snuck off and made love while most of the village was at the social." Her lips lifted at that part of the memory. "We were to be married that summer, but neither of us wanted to wait that long, and the only place we could get any semblance of privacy was out in the woods at night. Although, you didn't want to go to the woods because of the social, but I *convinced* you."

Doug folded his arms over his chest, and his face remained a mask of stone as he stared at her fiercely. She wasn't sure if he was angry, frustrated, or thinking she was nuts, but at least he was letting her continue.

"Vincent tried to glamour you, and it didn't work." She let out a short laugh. "That still aggravates him to this day. He couldn't figure out why you were immune. Although, now I know how he feels. I tried to glamour you in the dreamscape, but it didn't work."

"I remember," he said in a barely audible tone. "Go on."

"He told me later that when he drank from you, he

went into some kind of frenzy. He hadn't meant to kill you, but there was something about the taste of your blood that sent him over the edge." Tears filled her eyes, and her throat tightened. "I don't know how long I sat there weeping with your lifeless body in my lap, but it felt like forever. The next thing I remember, I woke up two days later at his Virginia estate as a vampire."

"He turned you after he killed me? And you stayed with him?" He clapped his hands and gave her a sarcastic two thumbs up. "That's great. Nothing says true love like running off with your boyfriend's killer."

"You have no idea what I felt or what I went through." Anger flared up her back as she closed the distance between them in a split second and got right in his face, but he didn't retreat. "He came back that night and turned me, but he didn't exactly *ask*. I had no choice but to stay with him. Not only was I alone and clueless about being an immortal, all vampires are tied to their makers for the first century of our new lives. So I was pretty much fucked."

She shoved at his chest when he said nothing and continued staring her down, but he didn't move. The look on his face sent a tidal wave of guilt through her. Did he think she wanted to be what she was? That she watched him die so that she could be immortal and live an eternity without him?

"Where was I going to go?" She screamed and pounded his chest with both hands before he grabbed her wrists and pulled her against his rock-hard body. "I died when you did, don't you understand?" The tears fell freely now, but she barely noticed because it felt so good to let it all out, to finally tell him everything. "I thought you were gone forever, and it was *my fault*. You were attacked right in front of me, and I did nothing but sit there like some silly, helpless girl, and my punishment was to live an eternity without you—as a monster."

He stared at her intently, but if he didn't say something soon, she was going to scream. Tension hummed in the air, but much to her relief, Doug pulled her into his arms and cradled her head against his chest. *I couldn't save you.*

"That's why," Doug whispered as he stroked her hair and rocked her gently. "The reason that you're rescuing damsels in distress, cats, dogs, and the rest of the world." He pulled back and brushed her tears away with his thumb as he cradled her face. "You've been trying to save me."

Olivia nodded as the tears fell. She clung to him desperately, worried that this too was a dream, and he would slip from her grasp like mist in the woods.

"You blamed yourself? All this time, you blamed yourself for what happened?" Doug placed a tender kiss on her temple and whispered in her ear. "Then I guess I was right…you had my heart before I was even born."

"Yes, and you've had mine." She linked her arms around his neck and buried her face against his broad chest. "I swear I wouldn't have turned you if you hadn't been dying. You do believe me, don't you?" She sniffled and pulled back, looking him in the face again. "When the dreams started, I actually thought that it was your ghost visiting me, but when I met you that night at the club…"

"When did the dreams start for you?"

"About twenty years ago." Olivia smiled, hugged him

again, and pressed her cheek against his shoulder as she wrapped her arms around his narrow waist. "Actually, vampires aren't supposed to dream. I hadn't dreamed in over two centuries, so when I had the first one, I thought I'd gotten some bad blood. When they happened more frequently and *only* with you, well, I assumed it was your ghost. At the start of the dreams, you were quite young, and as you got older, the dreams got more… intense."

"You're telling me," he said on a sigh. "Do you have any idea how often I had to change my sheets?"

The two of them burst out laughing, and he took her head in his hands and kissed her passionately. Desire stirred swiftly as his mouth explored hers, and he held her against his hardening body.

"The dreams were nice," he murmured against her lips as he pulled the zipper of her catsuit down. "But it doesn't hold a candle to the real deal." He kissed the corner of her mouth before pulling back abruptly and giving her a funny look. "Were you really celibate until last night?"

Olivia arched one eyebrow as she made quick work of pulling his shirt over his head and undoing the fly of his pants.

"You bet your fangs, I was." His manhood sprang free, and the weight in her hand made her wet. "And I plan on making up for lost time in a *big* way," she said as she ran her hand up and down the hard length of him.

Olivia dropped to her knees. She looked at him as she cupped his balls and licked the head of his penis in slow, deliberate strokes. Doug groaned and threw his head back as she worked him in her hand and ran her tongue up and down this cock. He tangled his fingers in her hair, guiding her as his hips pumped faster, and she took him deeper.

"Stand up," he growled.

Doug pulled her to her feet, spun her around, and yanked her catsuit down over her shoulders. Olivia, eager to feel his skin against hers, rid herself of the offending garment, pushing it past her hips. Knowing what they both wanted, she bent forward, leaned both hands on the wall, and offered herself to him. She glanced over her shoulder and bared her fangs.

"Fuck me," she rasped.

He curled one arm around her and drove his shaft deep inside. Doug placed one hand over hers, tangling their fingers together as he rocked his hips, spearing into her time and again.

"More," she whispered. "Harder. God, please don't stop."

He gave in to her commands and pumped into her willing body rapidly, but still it wasn't enough. Fingers linked. Bodies locked. She arched her back as he buried himself deep, and when the sweet, torture of the orgasm crested, she brought his arm to her mouth, sinking her fangs into his wrist. Doug swore as she pierced his flesh, and when the orgasm exploded, he leaned down and drove his fangs into the soft skin along the back of her neck.

The simultaneous orgasm and blood exchange was the most erotic, carnal experience of Olivia's life, and on a flash of light, Doug's voice touched her mind on a whisper. *Eternity*.

Both their hearts began to *beat*.

Bodies linked, limbs intertwined, blood flowing, their

hearts actually beat, and in that blinding, brief moment Olivia and Doug were *alive*.

She thought this part of last night's experience was a fluke, a one-time phenomenon because of her lengthy stretch of celibacy. However, as the tiny aftershocks rippled through them and their shaking bodies, Olivia knew it was more than a fluke. Whatever was happening between them was related to being bloodmates. As their hearts finally slowed to a stop and lay silent once again, Olivia wondered what other surprises lay ahead.

Doug slipped from her body, and she spun in his embrace, linking her arms around his neck and nuzzling him contentedly. She knew she had to tell him the rest. She had to confess that they were bloodmates, but not now. Now she wanted to enjoy the little peace they had found.

"We should get dressed." She tucked her hair behind her ear and pulled her catsuit on for the second time. "It's almost sundown, and we still have to find the rogues' nest."

"Okay," he said as he put his shirt on. Doug nodded toward the bed. "At least we don't have to change the sheets," he said with a wink. "So. Let me make sure I've got all this shit straight. As I now know better than anyone, there are vampires, and Pete said something about being married to a shapeshifter, right?"

"Yes." Olivia nodded. "His wife, Marianna, is an Amoveo. They're shapeshifters."

"Got it." He secured his ammo belt and weapon before pulling on his gloves. "And, apparently, there is such a thing as reincarnation. Any other mind-fucks that you want to drop? For example, why did my turn take only twelve hours instead of two days? Why do you and I dream when vampires aren't supposed to dream, and why have I slipped into this life seamlessly, when I should've had a fucking mental breakdown? And why the hell do our hearts start to beat when we drink from each other while we're… y'know?"

"Not sure, it's probably nothing," she said in a tone that didn't convince her any more than it convinced him.

Doug nodded and pursed his lips as he watched her take stock of the ammo she had left. She squirmed under his inspection but stood straight and steeled her resolve. She met his challenging gaze and gestured to the door. He knew she was holding back. Damn it.

"You know, I may not be an expert at relationships, but I know when a woman says *nothing*, it's a whole lotta something."

She met his challenging gaze and blurted it out. "We're bloodmates."

"Okay." Doug shrugged and looked puzzled. "What's that?"

Olivia burst out laughing. She belly-laughed until her stomach ached and tears streamed down her face. All this time she was terrified to utter the term *bloodmates*, scared that he would be furious with all it could imply, and the guy didn't even know what it meant. Olivia swiped at her eyes but stopped laughing when she saw his irritated look.

"I'm sorry," she said through fading laughter. "I'm not laughing at you. I'm laughing at my own foolishness. I was so scared to tell you that we're bloodmates—at least I think we are—that it never dawned on me that you wouldn't know what it meant."

"Why would I be angry?" He put his hands on his hips and inched closer. "Olivia?"

"It's a legend really. At least I thought it was until I found you. According to the legend, some vampires have bloodmates. If these mates find each other and bond with a blood exchange, then they become daywalkers." She watched his reaction carefully, but his expression didn't waver. He was pure concentration. "Vampires that can walk in the sun."

"Okay." Doug nodded slowly and ran a hand over the top of his head as he looked at her sideways. "That actually sounds pretty good. Why did you think I'd be upset? It's not like you pick bloodmates, right? I mean, it sounds like destiny or fate."

"The only bloodmate couple I ever heard of were targeted for termination by a sentry on orders from the Presidium. It makes sense, I guess. Vampires that can daywalk would threaten the Presidium's power. But…"

Olivia lowered her gaze and tugged her gloves on tighter. Doug took her face in his hands and forced her to look him in the eye. Her lower lip quivered, but she clenched her jaw, refusing to cry like some silly girl.

"I was afraid you would think I turned you so that I could bond with you and be a daywalker, not to mention that if anyone finds out, we would likely have a death sentence on our heads."

Now Doug was the one who started laughing as he pulled her into a loving embrace. He squeezed her tightly before pulling back to look her in the eye.

"Haven't you heard anything that I've said? I love you, Olivia, and from the looks of things, I always have. Human. Vampire. Daywalker or not. I love *you*, and as far as this whole bloodmate legend goes, it sounds pretty good." A lopsided grin cracked his handsome face. "I guess this means you're stuck with me and my over protective, chauvinistic ass."

He kissed her passionately and smacked her derriere as he released her.

"I'm still not sure about this, you know. I mean the daywalking part," Olivia said plainly. "Like I said, I thought it was a fairy tale for vampires. I never thought it was real. So don't plan any tropical vacations any time soon, okay?"

"Daywalking would be a bonus." He tugged on a springy curl and released it. "Getting you is the best part, and I'll take you any way I can get you."

"Good," she said firmly. "Let's get going. We only have until the next sunrise before Augustus kills my coven off." Olivia's voice dropped to just above a whisper. "Then again, if we finish our job, this won't end well for you, will it?"

They hadn't spoken about his self-imposed death sentence since they left the Presidium's offices, and she wondered if he had forgotten his offer. The resolute look in his eye told her he knew exactly what he had done.

"I'm not going to watch you die again," she said tightly. Olivia brushed past Doug and pushed the button, opening the heavy steel door. Before she could leave, he curled his hand around her arm and turned her toward him.

"It's going to be okay." His lips brushed her temple, and his voice surrounded her like a blanket as he hugged her. "Maya will be fine, and so will I. We'll figure it out together, but you have to trust me."

Olivia pulled back and gave him a sidelong glance as she stepped through the door. “It’s time to hunt.”

Chapter 14

When the sun went down, Doug's blood hummed and vibrated with the power of the night. He felt an ungodly strength when he was first turned, but something had changed after he and Olivia made love. The power surging through him now was nothing short of extraordinary. It was as though they were bolstering each other's strength.

When they finally reached the street, the sights and sounds of the city almost overwhelmed his senses, and it took a moment to acclimate to the onslaught. They walked side by side up Bleecker Street, and he marveled at Olivia's focus. She may have been looking straight ahead, but he could tell she was taking in several blocks with the sonar senses of a vampire. She was a far cry from the frightened young girl he saw in the dreamscape the previous night, and it was no wonder. She'd spent a good portion of the past three hundred years fighting, and from what he saw yesterday, she was damn good at it.

Lethal and beautiful were the two words that came to mind every time he looked at her. She could put a vamp down in a matter of seconds with her sharpshooting skills and her aim with the ninja stars, but she didn't need that to slay him. All she had to do was look at him, and he was a goner. Gone, baby, gone.

He hated to interrupt her concentration, but hunger

gnawed at him, and when they passed a traditional NYC hot dog cart, his stomach growled loudly.

"Holy shit, that smells great." He lingered for a minute by the hot dog cart before Olivia took his arm and pulled him away. She was giggling and shaking her head. "What are you laughing at, Liv?"

"It's not the hot dogs that you smell," she said evenly.

"Yes, it was, I—" Doug glanced back at the man working the cart and then back to Olivia's smiling green eyes. "It was the guy, wasn't it?"

"Mmm-hmm." She smothered another laugh. "I'm sorry, but the look on your face is priceless."

"Well, whatever. I'm hungry. So whether it's hot dogs or the hot dog man, I gotta eat, Liv."

"I like that." Olivia smiled and elbowed him playfully as they continued along the busy sidewalk. "Liv," she said when she saw his look of confusion. "I like it when you call me, Liv."

"Good, because it suits you." Doug wrapped his arm around her shoulders and pulled her against him as they continued on their way through the Village. "So what's for dinner, Liv?"

She turned down a quiet side street with several apartment buildings and only a few storefronts. "There's a massage parlor up here that's run by a friend of mine, and he'll have something. I don't advise live feeds, and Jerry has a fridge with emergency supplies for friends like me. We have to feed again before we hunt."

"Not that I'm looking to feed on people," he said quietly. "I'm not, but why don't you want me doing live feeds?"

"Blood memories," Olivia said as they stepped up to the small storefront with the blue neon lettering that read: Jerry's Massage Shack. "Anyway, Jerry will not only have food for us but, hopefully some information as well. He's my version of an informant. He's hooked into everything in this city and hears about all the shady shit that goes on in the vamp world. If anyone has gotten wind of who's turning these rogues, it's him. I tried to touch base with him the other night, but he wasn't around. Hopefully he's here tonight. Anyway—" She sighed wearily. "No live feeds, no blood memories."

They stood for a moment on the sidewalk, and he took stock of the lighter pedestrian traffic on this side street. If he and Olivia were walking the streets like regular folk, then he presumed the rogues would do the same.

"What, dare I ask, are blood memories?"

Her features hardened, making her look older than she ever had. Her brilliant green eyes, rimmed with sadness, looked at him intently.

"When we feed on a living person, it's a direct line into their memories. Their blood and their memories become a part of us—forever." She frowned, and her voice quivered. "We can't pick and choose what we get, and believe me, there are some memories you simply do not want."

"Is that how you knew about my relationship with Miranda?" he asked.

"Yes." She stuffed her hands in her coat pockets. "That and more. Your memories only confirmed my suspicions about you and what a good man you are." She paused, and he could tell she was carefully choosing her words. "I saw how much you loved Tom. I felt your love for him, and I know he was like the father you never had. I'm so sorry that I couldn't save him."

Doug's throat thickened with emotion.

"You're right," he said gruffly. "I did blame you at first, and I was furious you saved me but not Tom, and turned me into a monster."

Olivia said nothing as she listened to him intently.

"Over the past twenty-four hours I've been reminded that being a monster is a choice, Liv. During my ten years working homicide, I saw humans make the choice to hurt, destroy, and kill every single day. They *chose* to be monsters and vampires are no different. Some of them, like you, Pete, and the girls at the club, rise above your basest instincts to embrace kindness, family, and friendship. Then there are guys like Augustus and whoever is making these rogues. Human or vampire, there will always be those who revel in destruction, choosing to be monsters."

"Thank you." Olivia's mouth lifted, and her eyes crinkled at the corners briefly, but sadness still lingered. "We do have monsters inside of us, Doug. Make no mistake about that, but the best way to keep it at bay is to avoid live feeds. They're like a drug—a high. The more you do it, the more you'll want it, and the harder it is to stop. Believe me."

She tugged open the door to the massage parlor, and he followed her inside. Her words haunted him. *We do have monsters inside of us*. He shuddered and lifted the collar of his coat, a human gesture he might have done if a cold wind blew against his neck. It wasn't the wind he was trying to shield himself from, but the truth. What if he couldn't keep the monster inside under control?

They sat in the rickety wood and wicker chairs of the gaudy waiting room, and Doug did his usual scan of his surroundings, trying to keep his mind off the nagging hunger. The walls were red velvet, and the rug was royal blue shag, reminiscent of the mid-seventies, but somehow it looked brand-new. Olivia spoke to the pretty girl at the desk, and Doug could tell by her scent that she was a vampire.

"So." He leaned closer and whispered in her ear. "How do you know this guy?"

"He ran a brothel in Vegas when I was a sentry there." She shrugged. "He relocated here about thirty years ago, and he's running the same game."

A shriek interrupted the awkward quiet of the waiting room, and Doug looked up to see an older, diminutive Japanese gentleman wearing a black and gold kimono and a wide grin scurry out through the curtain of beads, which undoubtedly led to the massage rooms. This had to be Jerry.

"Olivia, my friend." He swept over to them, his bald head glistening under the fluorescent lights, and when he opened his arms to hug Olivia, Doug noticed that his pinky nails were long and pointed.

"Hello, Jerry," she said as he released her. "This is my friend, Doug. He's training to be a sentry."

Doug shot a confused look to Olivia, and although he tried to recover quickly, old Jerry didn't miss a trick. She should have warned Doug what cover she was going to use. Jerry looked Doug up and down with an appraising eye, and his grin widened as he stuck his hand out.

"Nice to meet you." Doug shook his hand briefly and shifted his position protectively near Olivia.

"Right this way." He crooked a finger to them and held open the curtain of beads. "I have just what the two of you need."

Doug followed them through the small dark hallway lined with white doors on either side. When they reached the end of the hall, Jerry opened the last door on the right, and though Doug didn't quite know what to expect, this wasn't it. He thought it would be a small massage room, like many in the city, but this was more like a studio apartment.

The walls were painted with silver sparkly paint and a mirror above the leopard-print-covered bed. There was a zebra-skin rug in front of the white leather sofa, and the kitchenette along the back wall had white cabinets with door handles that looked like puckering lips.

"You like Jerry's apartment?" he asked in a singsong voice as he shut the door securely behind them. He floated, literally floated, to the kitchenette, and the fridge opened without him even touching it.

"It's—very *you*," Doug said as politely as possible.

"It sure is, handsome." Jerry pulled two containers from the fridge and put them in the microwave. "So, how long you been a sentry? I only hear about Pete and Shane." He pursed his lips, and Doug could hear him tapping his long fingernail on the counter. "I never hear about you."

"He's new and beginning his training. He's not a sentry yet, but I see potential." Olivia crossed her arms over her breasts and leveled a serious gaze at Jerry. "Now… what can you tell me about the rogue coven?"

"What you talking about, silly girl?" Jerry giggled nervously and began to wring his hands. "What rogue coven?"

The ding of the microwave went off, and the phrase *saved by the bell* went through Doug's mind. Jerry may have a direct line into the vampire world, but he was a shitty liar. It was blatantly obvious that this guy knew a lot more about the rogue coven than he would have them believe.

Doug shot Olivia a look when Jerry had his back turned and shook his head. She held up her hand. *I know*. Her mind touched his delicately and sent a seductive wave of warmth though him. Doug simply nodded because he was rendered speechless—telepathic or otherwise.

Olivia went over to Jerry, who was puttering nervously and getting them large glasses. She watched as he poured the steaming red liquid, and Doug's mouth watered. His fangs unsheathed, but he closed his eyes for second, willing them away, and by some fucking miracle, they retreated.

"Jerry," she said gently, with her hand on his narrow shoulder. "You don't have to be scared. I won't tell anyone that you gave us information. As far as the czar and senators are concerned, you gave us some blood and sent us on our way." She turned him, making him face her. "Now. What do you know about the rogues?"

His weary brown eyes looked at her with pure terror, and he shook his head. "You don't understand," he whispered. "The Maker can do what he pleases. I hear yesterday you kill many of his coven, but he will make more."

"I know," she said firmly. "The Maker? Is that what they're calling him?"

"That's what he call himself." Jerry handed a cup to Olivia and then to Doug before waving his hands at them and shaking his head. He went over and sat at his vanity and began to admire himself in the mirror.

"That all I know. Now take this big gorilla, and get out my apartment."

Doug chugged the blood and noted that unlike Olivia's blood, it provided sustenance for his body, but didn't do a thing for his soul. He placed the empty glass on the counter and glanced at Olivia. Everything paled in comparison to her. He studied her as she drank and sensed the frustration she was feeling. This guy was stonewalling her.

"I think you should start talking." Doug's voice, low and insistent, filled the room. "From what Olivia's told me, you've been helpful before, but she needs your help now more than ever."

Jerry avoided his gaze as he grabbed a tissue from the box and wiped his hands. "I not telling you anything."

Doug let out a loud sigh. "I don't have the patience or the inclination to dick around with you, *Jerry*."

"Is that so, big man?" Jerry slammed his hand onto the table and glared at Doug in the mirror. "I'm hundred and fifty years old, youngling. Not only that, but Emperor Zhao is part of my family. If I want to, I could crush you like bug. I could—"

Quicker than a snake, Doug grabbed Jerry with one hand, yanked him out of the chair by his neck, and held him in midair. Jerry's eyes bugged out of his head in shock as he clutched at Doug's hand and flailed his small feet helplessly.

He hissed and bared his fangs, but it did little good to loosen Doug's grip or weaken his resolve. Out of the corner of his eye, he could see Olivia gaping, but he kept all of his focus on Jerry.

"I don't give a crap who you're related to, and

based on your current position, I'd say the bug in our little situation is you." He increased the pressure on Jerry's neck ever so slightly. "Now, I may be a new vampire, but I'm an old cop. I know bullshit when I smell it."

Doug tossed Jerry across the room onto the bed.

"I don't know what you're afraid of, but I can promise you one thing," he said, drawing his gun and pointing it at Jerry's head. "You should be more afraid of me and of what I'm going to do if you don't share what you know."

Jerry scrambled back on the bed into the pile of pillows and looked to Olivia for help.

"Eyes on me, little man." He flipped the safety on the gun, and Jerry looked back to him. "That's better. Now. What do you know about the rogues and this guy, The Maker?"

"Washington Square Hotel." Jerry ran a hand over his bald head. "I hear they go there yesterday." He flashed a furious look to Doug. "That all I tell you. Now get out before I tell Emperor Zhao how bad you treat his favorite cousin."

"Washington Square Hotel?" Doug put the safety back on and holstered his weapon. "It's right by where both of the victims were found." He turned to Olivia, who now stood beside him. "It's a central location. Not only that, Moriarty stays there with his crew from time to time."

Olivia nodded. "Holing up at a ritzy hotel during the day would be a lot better than an abandoned subway station." She smirked and lifted one shoulder playfully. "Not that I minded."

Doug winked and then shifted his attention back to Jerry. "If you hear anything else, you go to the Presidium and fill them in. Right now, our only advantage is that we've got the element of surprise. They don't know we've figured out where they're holing up, but let me promise you something, Jerry." He leaned both hands on the footboard of the bed and leveled a deadly glare at the diminutive man. "If they get wind of the fact that we're onto them, and if one single hair on Olivia's head is harmed, I'm taking it out on your ass."

He and Olivia let themselves out and hit the city streets once again, heading toward the park. As they walked in silence, Doug took a mental count of the ammunition he had left, and it wasn't a good number.

"We're low on ammo."

"Got it covered, detective." Olivia gestured to the dark alley on the left. "Let's duck in here for a second."

Memories of their kiss in the alley came roaring back, and his cock stirred to life as he walked beside her. There wasn't time for fooling around—but later, all bets were off.

Olivia stopped in the cover of darkness and grinned, her white fangs flashing brightly.

"Let's fly, lover."

She shot into the sky like a bullet, and he could hear the beautiful sound of her laughter as she zipped through the night. Wasting no time, he flew up into the night to join his lover as she sped through the city sky. Doug didn't know who this Maker guy was, and he had no idea what kind of shit-show they were getting into, but there were a few things he was sure of.

He'd been reincarnated. He was a vampire. He was

in love with Olivia. And even though there was a solid chance he was going to die, he was having the time of his life… of any life.

Chapter 15

Olivia and Doug landed silently in a dark corner of Washington Square Park. It was close to midnight, and this part of the park was deserted, so there was little danger of humans seeing them. They made their way swiftly down the steps of the West Fourth Street subway station, and not surprisingly, found it empty.

They hopped the turnstile and walked to the end of the platform. Olivia took a quick look around, and satisfied there were no humans in the vicinity, she pushed the black tiles in the wall that read W Fourth Street. Moments later, a large section of the wall swung inward.

"Unbelievable," Doug murmured as he followed Olivia into the emergency armory storage facility.

The lights flickered on as the door sealed shut behind them, and Doug swore under his breath as he looked at the arsenal that surrounded them. Olivia smiled and took a brief moment to enjoy his wonder and awe at this latest discovery.

"I love seeing our world through your eyes. I've been doing this for so long, I forget what a shock certain things will be for you."

"Are there armories like this in other places?"

"Yes." Olivia snagged a new gun and a few rounds of ammunition and handed them to Doug. "We have several for the sentries, and they are the only ones who know where they are. I have my own weapons closet at my apartment, but I didn't want to risk taking the fight there. I figure the rogues are looking for us too."

"You heard from the girls?" he asked tentatively. "Or is your telepathy still limited to me?"

She adjusted the gun at her hip and checked the safety. "When we flew over here I tried to contact Trixie. She's my rebel, you know, so I thought maybe… but nothing."

"When did you turn her?"

Olivia stilled for a moment before looking up at him. She was worried she might see contempt or scorn, yet all she saw was curiosity.

"In 1980. I found her dying of a heroin overdose in the subway tunnels. She was heavily involved in the punk-music and drug scene here in the city, but her dreams of making it in the Big Apple didn't quite pan out."

"What about Sadie? You two seem closer than the others." His inspecting gaze wandered over her. "She seems like more of an equal to you than the other girls."

"Sadie's been with me since the night I split with Vincent and just before I became a sentry. Her family lived in a remote cabin in what was then considered the frontier, and they fell victim to an Indian attack. Vincent and I smelled the blood and went to check it out. Sadie was barely alive, but her parents and five siblings were dead." Olivia's mind filled with the memories of that night, and she grimaced. "She looked so innocent and alone. I couldn't leave her there."

"It was a long time ago." She shrugged and inspected her ammo. "I turned her, and Vincent was fucking furious. I guess he didn't like the idea of the student becoming the teacher. He left us there, and I didn't see him again for another fifty years."

Doug said nothing but watched her through serious eyes.

"Maya was assaulted and dumped in the alley behind my club." Her voice hardened as the memories of Maya's rapist came roaring back in full color. "When I turned her, I got her blood memories." Olivia's body shook with rage, and her hands clenched and unclenched at her side. "Like I said, there are some memories you don't want."

Olivia's eyes filled with tears, and her voice dropped to a whisper.

"I killed the man who hurt her. I let the monster out and took a human life, and you know what? I loved every minute."

Doug reached out to comfort her, but she held up her hand and stepped back.

"There are no free rides, Doug. I got *his* blood memories. I felt the fear, pain, and degradation of the twenty other women he had brutalized. Monsters don't go unpunished."

Olivia swiped at her eyes and turned her back on Doug, unable to look at him, fearing what he might think of her now that he knew the truth. She grabbed some ammo and a silencer off the shelf and held it out to him without looking.

"Here." She sniffled and bit back the tears, refusing to allow them to spill. "We'll want to use the silencer because we may have to do this above ground. I'd like to keep the human involvement to a minimum. These aren't UV rounds. They're silver and wood, so make sure you hit them in the head or the heart."

"Got it." Doug took them from her and restocked his supply in a casual manner. Silence hung heavily between them for what felt like forever before he finally broke the silence. "The only monster in that story you told me was the sack of shit you killed, and if you ask me, you did society a favor," Doug said.

Olivia turned slowly to face him but found him perusing the shelves, looking for more weapons to take. Relief washed over her. Doug wasn't the least bit bothered by her dirty secret. Maybe everything would work out after all? So far, her fears of what might happen or what Doug might say were worse than reality.

"So we stick to the plan." Doug snagged some silver stars and stuck them in the inner pockets of his coat. "We stake out the tunnel entrances under the hotel and get 'em as they're coming in before sunrise. Right?"

"Actually, I think we should split up." Olivia put the last clip of ammo in her belt and turned to face Doug. "If they come in early enough, then they won't need to use the underground entrances, and they could waltz through the front door."

"No fucking way, Liv." His eyes flashed. "I'm not letting you out of my sight."

"Doug." Olivia tried not to be annoyed at his macho chauvinism, but it was no use. "I was a sentry for a hundred years. In case you've forgotten, I can handle myself." Her voice rose as she spoke, and her body tensed. "I am not that scared, sniveling girl I was all those years ago."

Doug swore loudly, put his hands on his hips, and stared at the fluorescent lights in the ceiling. Just when Olivia was about to start screaming her fangs off, he ran one hand over his short blond hair, and a smile cracked his handsome face.

"I sounded like a dick, didn't I?" He glanced at her sideways.

"Yes." She folded her arms over her chest. "A big, macho dick."

"I'm sorry." His expression softened as he placed both hands on her shoulders and looked her straight in the eye. "I know you're capable and could probably kick my ass if you wanted to, but there's one thing you need to understand."

"What?" She braced herself for more male posturing and formulated her blistering response in her head.

"I love you, Liv." His fingers gripped her shoulders tighter, and his throat worked as he swallowed. "I have been chasing you my entire life, and I kept every other woman at a distance because they couldn't live up to you, or the idea of you. I never thought I was worthy of love or marriage or any of that shit. I thought I didn't have what it takes to be a husband or a father." He stopped, and his brow knit together. "Wait—can vampires even have children?"

"No," she said through a laugh. Hell, the man wanted to have children with her?

"Really? Well, that's too bad. I'd love to have a spirited little girl with your curly red hair and green eyes, not to mention your bad-ass fighting skills." He kissed the tip of her nose. "Since she'd be as gorgeous as you, she'd have to be able to fight off all those rotten boys."

"Doug," she whispered in a shaky voice.

"No." He shook his head. "Let me finish. There's still a part of me that thinks I'm not lucky enough to feel this way, and I am fucking terrified of losing you. So," he sucked in a breath and continued, "you'll have to forgive me for being an overprotective dickhead. That's not going to change. I feel more alive with you as a vampire than I did as a human, so you're stuck with me. We stick together. No one hunts alone—that's non-negotiable."

He loved her. He said it and put his heart and everything else on the line. As her eyes searched his, she knew that no matter what happened, he would be there for her. Her eyes stung with tears, and a smile played at her lips. For the first time in centuries, she didn't feel alone.

"Okay." She nodded and looked at him warmly. "We stick together. We'll check the West Village again and then go to the hotel before sunrise. We can glamour the clerk and find out if Moriarty checked in and what room he's staying in, then ambush them when they come back to sleep for the day."

"That's my girl."

He leaned down and captured her lips with his as he cradled her head in his hands, kissing her desperately, as though he might never get another chance. Olivia wrapped her arms around his neck and kissed him back as if it was indeed their last kiss.

They walked the Village much of the night but didn't catch the scent or any sign of the rogues. After hours of coming up empty-handed, and with sunrise only an hour away, they agreed that it was time to hit the hotel.

They stepped onto the sidewalk in front of the luxury hotel, and the doorman smiled tightly as he looked them up and down. Doug buttoned his coat and gave the man a friendly smile as they approached. Olivia scanned the human and sensed his nervousness but wasn't sure what they did to make him uneasy.

As he opened the door for them, Doug leaned down and whispered in her ear. "The two of us look like we stepped out of the Matrix. Most of the clientele at this place are decked out in high-end designer duds, not black leather."

"Right." Olivia rolled her eyes.

She was about to make another remark, but when she stepped into the plush lobby with red walls and art deco paintings, she was rendered speechless by the stink of rotting flesh and dirt. The scent of Rogue One filled the lobby and wafted over her in unpleasant waves.

Doug stood still inside the entrance next to Olivia, but based on the tension in his body and the look on his face, he'd picked up the scent as well. She reached out with her sonar senses but didn't pick up on any vampires in the immediate vicinity. However, the perfectly manicured man behind the counter was looking at them like they'd landed from Mars.

"May I help you?" He looked them up and down with blatant disgust.

"Actually," Doug said almost inaudibly, "you can."

Olivia stepped up to the desk with him and placed both gloved hands on the gleaming black countertop. She leaned close and held the tall, slim man's gaze as she glamoured him.

"We need information about a guest," she said evenly. The clerk nodded, slack-jawed and eyes vacant, but he remained silent. "Do you know who Michael Moriarty is?" He nodded again as drool dripped down his chin and his hands rested limply on the counter. "Good. Has he been staying here?"

"Yes," he said on a sigh.

"Excellent." Her voice remained soothing and clam. "What room is he in?"

"Mr. Moriarty has all of the rooms on the ninth floor."

"Wonderful." Olivia put her hand out. "I'd like a copy of the master keycard please."

She maintained her focus as the clerk handed her the keycard from a drawer.

"When I walk away, you will remember none of this. Do you understand? It's been quiet, and you saw no one come or go. Is that clear?"

He nodded like a bobblehead doll. Olivia released her hold on the weak-minded man, and they whisked to the first floor hallway, leaving the clerk alone and bewildered. They ducked around the corner, and Doug snagged her around the waist with one strong arm and placed a kiss on her head.

"You are something else, do you know that?"

"I have my moments," she murmured. Olivia held up the keycard and flashed him her fangs. "Time to clean house."

They flew up the stairwell, and the stench of the rogues grew more pungent. It was strongest at the ninth floor landing and stuck in Olivia's throat.

"We do one room at a time," she said, peering through the small window at the top of the door. "And we do it as quietly as possible."

"Shit." Doug ran a hand over his mouth. "I can't imagine this is gonna be fuckin' quiet. Vamps make a lot of damn noise when they get dusted."

"Not much of a choice." Olivia gripped the door handle and drew her gun. "Ready?"

Doug nodded and drew both guns, but he captured her gaze before she ducked through the door. "Be careful, Liv."

"You too, detective."

Olivia ran the key through the reader on the first door, swung the door open, and they whipped into the room with guns raised. Olivia had seen plenty of death and destruction in her day, but this place looked like something out of a horror film.

The next three rooms they checked were the same, and all told, there were over thirty dead humans, but no vampires. Doug said nothing, though she sensed his rage building, knowing it was only a matter of time before he completely lost it. His anger ticked up twice as much with the dead women.

With only one room left, no sign of the rogues, and sunrise thirty minutes away, Olivia was beginning to think they found a new place to nest and had abandoned this one. She and Doug stood outside the last room, and just before she opened it, a familiar scent filled her nostrils. She flicked her wide eyes to Doug and saw that he'd picked up on it as well.

Jerry.

"That little weasel," Doug seethed.

He kicked the door open, and side by side, they stepped into the room with guns raised. "Wait," Olivia shouted. "Don't shoot."

Jerry was chained to the bed and blindfolded. Thick ropes of silver were wrapped around his neck and gagged his mouth, while all four of his limbs were lashed to the bedposts.

Michael Moriarty stood calmly next to him with a gun pointed at his head.

"Took you long enough," Moriarty snapped. He inched the gun closer to Jerry, who was passed out cold. While Olivia was pretty damn mad that her snitch had snitched on her, she didn't want him to die. Moriarty flicked his beady eyes to Olivia. "Your friend here decided to warn The Maker and tell him about your little visit."

"Who turned you, Michael?" Olivia tightened her grip on the gun. The faint scent of Rogue One filled the room like a phantom. "Tell us, or you're going to end up like the rest of the rogues."

"I gotta admit—I freaked the fuck out when I woke up at the medical examiner's office, but once I got a taste of her and drank her sweet blood… everything felt better."

"You killed Miranda?" Doug said through clenched teeth. "Too bad you and your maker missed our little party in the tunnels."

"Yeah, he was pretty steamed that you two wiped out his brand-new coven." He jutted his chin out. "I mean, there was a hell of a party around here, and you had to go and ruin it."

"Moriarty," Doug said tightly. "You and me go way back, and you know I'm not going to play these games. You're gonna go down one way or the other. Human. Vampire. Cloud of dust. I don't give a shit."

"Paxton," he spat. "Even as a vampire, you're a pain in my ass. I know this will be a blow to your overblown ego, but this whole situation has nothing to do with you." Moriarty smirked and shook his head as he leered at Olivia. "What the hell did you do to piss him off so bad, huh? You know, you're the whole reason he came back to New York and started getting this coven together. Then, after you wiped 'em all out in the tunnels last night, I wanted to help him build it again. He was so steamed all he could think about was killing you and hitting you where it hurts, so he's moved on to phase two. He left me here with Jerry so I could give you a message."

"Me? Phase two?" Olivia's brow furrowed as she struggled to understand what this could possibly have to do with her. "What are you talking about, Moriarty?"

A smile slithered across his face as he leered at her. "Been back to your club tonight, Olivia?"

Panic slammed into her as she realized what he meant. "Oh my God."

Moriarty laughed. Olivia saw the microscopic movement of his finger tightening on the trigger, but before he could shoot, she flew across the room, tackling him against the wall. His gun fired and clattered to the floor.

Somewhere through the frenzy of rage, she could hear Doug's voice calling her name as she sank her fangs into Moriarty's neck and ripped his throat out. Blood sprayed over her as she tore his head from his body, turning him into a cloud of smoking ash.

Shaking with fury and drowning in panic, two strong hands gripped her arms and shook her, pulling her from the abyss. As her vision cleared, she found herself looking into a pair of painfully beautiful blue eyes—eyes that were laced with worry and a touch of fear.

"Liv?" He said her name gently as his fingers curled around her upper arms. "Liv, are you alright? Hey, can you hear me?"

She blinked as the fog lifted. Olivia allowed herself

to lean against Doug's body for support as she regained her bearings. It had been a long time since she lost it like that, and it was more unsettling than she remembered.

She glanced to the bed and saw the bullet had missed Jerry, and although Doug had released him from the silver, he was pretty banged up. The burns were healing; however, the little guy was pretty out of it.

"Wake up and get out of here, Jerry," she said in an unsteady voice.

"I'm sorry, Olivia." His dark eyes filled with tears, and his slim body shook uncontrollably as he struggled to remain conscious. "I was going to call you, but didn't want you to be mad at me for being big jerk."

The cold hand of panic grabbed her by the throat as everything that Moriarty said came rushing back. Olivia clutched the front of Doug's coat. "The girls and Damien."

A sob choked her as it all came together.

"Oh my God." Her wide eyes latched onto Doug. "The Maker—it's Vincent, and he's going to kill my family."

Chapter 16

As they approached The Coven, Doug's concern for Olivia grew with each passing moment. She kept trying to communicate with the girls since they left the apartment but was met with a deafening silence. Apprehension and worry rolled off her in thick waves, and when he suggested they get Pete, she balked at the idea. There was no time.

Doug could feel the pull of the sun as it began to rise. He hoped like hell that it wouldn't weaken him, but he figured it would affect this asshole Vincent the same way. The only positive thing he could find in their current situation was that they still had a full set of ammo and a boatload of sterling silver.

When they reached the club, they went to the back entrance in the alley. Doug grabbed Olivia's arm and turned her to face him. In the dim light he could still see her green eyes clearly, and they were hard, cold, and full of vengeance, but he also sensed fear. She was terrified that the girls and Damien were already dead.

"Wait a second." He took her face in both hands and paused, wanting to choose his words carefully. She resisted. "Hey. I know we have to get in there, but listen to me for a second."

Doug's gut clenched as he stared into the pools of green. She always tried to act so tough, and when he saw her lose it back at the hotel, she revealed her vulnerability.

"I know you're frightened and worried about the girls, but we can't go running in there half-cocked. We need a game plan." He dropped his hands and folded them over his chest, wanting to give her the freedom to take the lead, even though it went against his nature. "You lead, and I'll follow, but I want to make sure we're on the same page."

"It's quite simple really." Her jaw set defiantly. "We get in there and see what's going on inside the club. Then we blow Vincent's arrogant fucking head off."

"What about the girls?" Her stern expression faltered at his mention of the girls. "I know you don't want to accept it, but it's possible that they could be dead already."

"No." Olivia shook her head furiously. "They might be incapacitated, but they're not dead. I'd know it, Doug. They're a part of me, and I believe that I'd feel it if they were destroyed." Her mouth set in a grim line, and her voice dropped. "I *will not* lose them."

Before he could say another word, she spun on her heel, and instead of going to the door, she shoved the dumpster aside as if it weighed nothing, revealing yet another entrance to the network of tunnels. "You didn't think I would walk right into the club, did you?"

Doug smiled and shook his head as they dropped silently into the tunnels beneath the club. They flew down the corridor and then up a flight of stairs, stopping outside her office, but Doug grabbed her arm before she opened the door.

I can feel movement in the building, and if I can sense them, Liv… His mind touched hers. *Then they can obviously sense us, so I'd say any element of surprise is out of the question.* He released the safety on both of his guns. "Ready?"

Olivia nodded once and drew both of her weapons. She hit the red panel to the left of the door with her shoulder while Doug stood ready with both barrels pointed at the door. She squatted below Doug's guns and trained her weapons on the small office as well, but it was empty.

They slipped inside as the door shut soundlessly. Pounding music from the club filled the space, and he could feel the deep bass beat through his entire body. The club may have been closed, but it sounded like good old Vincent was having a private party.

Doug went to the door and listened intently, taking full advantage of his enhanced hearing. Even above the music he could make out the sound of a man talking. He didn't recognize the voice, and he heard a woman weeping softly.

Anger fired through him as he fought his instinct to open the door and start shooting. He had no idea what condition the girls were in, and he didn't want to jeopardize them further.

Olivia was at her computer and typing away on the keyboard, trying to pull up her security cameras. *Motherfucker*. Her voice shot into his mind with all the force she'd intended. *He disabled my security cameras.*

No more dicking around. Doug tilted his head to the door. *I'll go in first, and you follow. Vincent obviously wants you, and he is using your coven to get you. The more I think about it, the more I'm convinced he hasn't killed the girls. In my experience, guys like this want an audience, and if he were going to kill them then he'd want you to see it.*

Olivia's eyes widened briefly before her expression

settled back into a mask of calm. *Open the door*. She rose from her chair and raised her weapons. *Now*.

Doug threw a prayer to the universe. He turned the knob slowly, then swung it open and pressed his body against the wall before peering around the corner. The hall leading to the main floor of the club was empty.

The music tumbled around them, and the lights flashed as though it was Friday night and the club had a packed house—but they knew better. Guns extended, Doug stepped through the door and moved slowly down the short hallway with Olivia at his side. When they reached the opening to the main floor, she stopped dead in her tracks, and he felt her begin to shake.

Trixie was lashed to the top of the bar with several ropes of sterling and looked passed out, if not worse. She wasn't moving, and through the flashing, colorful lights, Doug could see smoke rising from her flesh as it burned beneath the silver.

At the center of the dance floor, her bouncer Damien was tied to a chair and gagged. His head lolled back, and blood soaked the white T-shirt he wore. Even with the music, Doug could hear the faint, dwindling sound of his heartbeat.

There was one other faint heartbeat coming from the German shepherd. Van Helsing lay bleeding on the floor by Damien's feet, and his tail lifted briefly, acknowledging Olivia's presence.

They inched farther into the club side by side, and as they reached open space, they shifted so that they were again back-to-back and ready to battle. Doug, facing the DJ platform, swore loudly when he saw Sadie. She had thick chains of silver wrapped several times around her body and tied to the platform.

"Rogue One is in here somewhere, Olivia." His fangs erupted, and his body hummed with tension. "I can smell him."

He could feel her strong, lithe body against his, tense and ready to spring into action. He admired her restraint. It had to tear her up to see the people she loved in agony, but to her credit, she kept it together.

"I smell someone else too," she seethed. She stopped abruptly, and the muscles in her body tensed further. She turned her head to the left and shouted, "Where the fuck are you, Vincent? You're a sick old fuck. You started this whole mess to manipulate me into coming back to England, didn't you?"

Only the music responded as it continued to blare around them.

"Answer me, damn it!"

"You should know me better than that, Olivia."

The male voice, edged with sadness, drifted over from the far side of the club. They swung around toward the voice and aimed their guns in the direction of the VIP booths on the other side of the dance floor. The rapidly changing colorful lights were messing with Doug's vision, and for the first time since he was turned, his night vision was failing him.

He and Olivia moved toward the center of the dance floor.

"Vincent?" Olivia said sharply as she looked around the club. "You fucking coward. Show yourself."

Seconds later, to the left of the VIP booths, a tall, regal man stepped out from behind a small wall divider.

Doug fleetingly remembered that the hallway behind it led to the restrooms.

Vincent had his hands behind his back and moved toward them cautiously.

"Hello, Olivia." His voice was etched with sorrow. "This is not what you think, my child." His eyes widened when they landed on Doug. "My, my, my. I never forget a face, especially yours. The only human I couldn't glamour." His brow knit in confusion. "And here you are, and now you're one of us? Fascinating."

"Vincent?" Olivia's voice was shakier as soon as she set eyes on her maker. "Why are you doing this?"

Doug tightened his grip on both guns as a glint of silver caught his eye. Partially hidden behind Vincent's disheveled shirt and tie was a rope of sterling silver. It was wrapped around his neck, and Doug glanced down to see that the chain dragged behind him.

"Olivia," Doug said evenly. "It's not him. Vincent's not The Maker. Look at his neck."

As he uttered the words, Vincent's face twisted in pain as he was yanked backward and fell to his knees. A man Doug had never seen before stood behind him, holding the rope of silver in one gloved hand and a gun in the other. Next to him was the little blond waitress, Suzie. She wept quietly as he pointed the gun at her head. Doug immediately sensed that she had been turned.

"Hello, Olivia," the man growled. "Long time, no see."

"Oh my God," she said in a rush. "Brutus."

Olivia had never been more shocked in her three hundred years. Brutus, Augustus's son and the vicious piece of shit she made sure was sent to hibernation, was standing before her, larger than life. Olivia kept her guns trained on him, and the only reason she didn't fire was because of Suzie.

"Nice to see you haven't forgotten me."

"I should've put you down when I had the chance, you sick piece of shit."

"Do you really think that my father, a czar for the Presidium, would allow that? I don't think so." He tugged on the chain, causing Vincent to howl in pain and hiss at his captor. "Stop your whining." He sighed. "Actually, I'll stop it for you. You've served your purpose, old man."

A split second later, Brutus yanked viciously on the chain tied around Vincent's neck, and Olivia watched in horror as his head popped off like a macabre party favor. As he exploded into a cloud of ash, white-hot pain shot through Olivia and bloomed in her chest as Vincent died. She arched back and screamed in excruciating agony as Doug swept in and caught her with one arm, cradling her against his broad chest.

"Hurts like a bitch, doesn't it? I remember when our maker bit the dust. It hurt like hell. My father and I cried like a couple of younglings." Brutus laughed and pulled Suzie in front of him, still holding the gun to her head. "But you know what hurts worse? Starving in a hibernation chamber for fifty years and going mad with hunger." His hate-filled eyes glared at them. "The blood thirst? Damn, girl. That shit will make you crazy."

Olivia scrambled weakly to her feet with Doug's help and pointed her gun at him again, even though her head felt like it was going to split open like an egg.

"You did this?" Her voice wavered, and her vision

blurred as Doug's voice touched her mind. *Let me take him out with a clean shot to the head.*

Olivia glanced at Suzie's tearstained face. *No. It's too dangerous for Suzie.*

She cleared her head and sharpened her focus, looking for other vampires in the club, but her senses were wonky from the impact of Vincent's death. As her dizziness faded and her senses cleared, the distinct foul stench of Rogue One filled her head. Brutus was the rogue? How could that be? Olivia shook her head as if she could shake off the confusion.

"Do you know what I had time to do when I was in hibernation?" His voice dropped low as he walked slowly toward the center of the dance floor, taking Suzie with him as he stopped behind Damien's dying body. "I had time to think about how I'd kill *you* for putting me there."

Olivia and Doug countered Brutus's movements, keeping a safe distance but keeping him in their sights.

"Your father isn't going to be happy with you, Brutus," Olivia said as calmly as possible. "I'll bet he'll give me a flipping medal for dusting your sorry ass."

"Are you kidding?" Brutus laughed, and his long brown hair fell across his forehead. "He's been bored as hell, and I finally livened things up." He smacked Suzie on the ass, and she winced. "She interrupted me, lover. What was I saying? Oh, yes. Making you suffer, Olivia. Oh, I came up with many wonderful ways, but I ultimately decided that killing you would be too easy. So, why not bide my time and hit you where it really hurts? Wipe out this little family you've made for yourself." He kicked Damien's chair with his foot. "Even this *human*. Kill them one by one in front of you."

"*Stop it*," Olivia screamed. "Don't touch him!"

"Well, he's almost dead anyway." He lifted one shoulder. "I was going to kill this one too after I followed her home the other night," he said, squeezing Suzie closer to him. "But I decided to turn her instead and have some fun with her. I always liked blonds, and this one is a virgin. Bonus."

Suzie whimpered and tried to pull away as he kissed her head, but he was too strong.

"When I saw your little bartender leaving the club with that human buffoon, I realized that I found the perfect opportunity to get the ball rolling. I would've had a slaughter fest, and we did get off to a nice start, but you had to make a big fat mess with my rogues in the tunnels."

"No." Olivia shook her foggy head. "An unregistered vampire killed Ronald Davis. It was Rogue One, not you."

"Please." He sighed. "The Presidium's computers aren't hacker-proof. I glamoured a Google geek, and he changed my ID in the system so when they ran the blood sample it came up as an unregistered rogue. Then I ate him. Dinner *and* a show. Really, Olivia," he said wearily. "It is the twenty-first century. Get with the program."

"I don't think we've had the pleasure," Doug interrupted.

"No." Brutus winked. "But I met your partner, and he tasted great. Did you know that the sweetest bit of blood is that last pump of the heart as the life fades from the body?"

Before Olivia could stop him, Doug screamed and squeezed off two rounds, but Brutus, who was two thousand years old, shot up to the arched ceiling in a blink.

Frantic, they pointed their guns in the air, but Brutus was nowhere to be seen, and neither was Suzie.

A gust of wind whooshed behind them, and Olivia felt something slash her across the throat. She tried to get out of the way, but she wasn't fast enough. She covered her neck with one hand and could feel the blood seeping through her fingers as she stumbled, struggling to regain her footing and still hold her weapon out in front of her. Doug linked his arm around her waist and held her against him while keeping an eye on their surroundings.

Doug glanced to the front door and started backing up toward the entrance with Olivia tucked in his arm. *We have to get him by the entrance to the club*. His grip tightened on her.

What are you going to do? Her weakened voice whispered into his mind, and she fought the panic that welled up inside. She felt like she was dying and deep down she knew that she was. Telepathy was all she could manage.

Trust me and hope that Suzie gets away from the door.

"Now you're hiding?" Doug taunted him and shouted into the pulsing lights. All of his experience as a cop taught him that guys like Brutus were impotent losers, and if you egged them on a bit, they'd come running. "All this time, you wait for revenge, and now you're hiding like a little bitch in the shadows. What a pussy."

Snarling, Brutus appeared ten feet in front of them. When his boot-clad feet thundered onto the floor, with Suzie still in his grip and bleeding from the neck, he grinned, his fangs dripping with blood as he stalked toward them.

"Hiding behind a girl?" Doug glanced at Suzie

and then to Brutus. "What a pantywaist. Some two-thousand-year-old vampire you are. I was hoping for a fight, but it looks like you're too much of a chickenshit to take me on."

"Please," he sneered. "I could dust you in under a minute."

"Oh yeah, Brucilla? Looks to me like you only take on little girls. Hey Liv, wasn't that one you told me about only twelve? Nice. You're a coward and a pervert."

Doug let Olivia go, and as she slipped from his grasp to the floor, she prayed his gamble would pay off. Brutus was far older and stronger, and by all accounts, Doug shouldn't stand a chance, but then again, nothing about Doug was standard issue.

"Where's your dress?" Doug mocked him as he backed up to the large wooden doors. "Your daddy's dress is real nice. Maybe you could borrow his."

Brutus screamed in rage and tossed Suzie, who went flying across the room. Her petite frame slammed into the bar, and she landed in a motionless heap. Olivia watched through fading vision as Brutus flew at Doug with remarkable speed and force. He grabbed him by the throat, but just before Brutus leaped, Doug propelled himself backward with all of his strength, and the two men burst through the wooden doors like a couple of torpedoes.

Olivia instinctively rolled away from the rays of sunlight as an ear-shattering explosion rocked the air. As they landed on the sidewalk in the dawn of early morning, a high-pitched shriek of agony and defeat pierced the air as Brutus burned and exploded in a noxious cloud of black smoke and ash.

At least, Olivia prayed it was Brutus... and only Brutus.

The pulsing lights of the club mixed with smoke and the golden rays of sunshine, which fleetingly reminded Olivia of a dreamscape she once shared with Doug.

Tears rolled down her cheeks as she waited and prayed for Doug to emerge from the light, and like an answered prayer, the hulking shadow of Doug Paxton stepped into the club amid the smoky glow.

He picked her up and cradled her to his chest as he strode with her into the warm beams of sun that streamed into the club.

"You looked like you could use a little sun," he whispered as he placed a gentle kiss on her forehead.

For the first time in three centuries, the prolonged exposure to the rays of the sun didn't burn. She smiled as it bathed them, and tears fell as she reveled in the miracle of their love. In the miracle of *him*.

"Secure the building."

A familiar, deep baritone that Olivia hadn't heard in over a century filled the room as the music shut off and the lights ceased flashing. Doug's muscles bunched as he prepared to fly into the daylight. *Doug, wait.*

A minute later, the house lights came on, and twenty special-ops sentries charged into the club with guns drawn. Olivia watched with relief as some of them tended to her coven, Damien, and even Van Helsing.

Covered from head to toe in protective sun gear, a soldier zipped behind them like a ghost. In a matter of seconds, he hung a blackout curtain across the broken doorway and stood guard to handle curious humans who may want to investigate.

"Well, since you probably could've killed us by now,

and it looks like your boys here are helping our friends instead of staking them into oblivion, I think it's a safe bet you're an ally." Doug's fingers pressed into her as he held her tightly. She knew he was scared for her, but to his credit, he didn't let it show. "However, the woman I love is dying, and I don't have time for pleasantries or vampire bureaucratic bullshit," Doug stated bluntly. "So let's have it. Who the hell are you? And why couldn't you and your recon squad have shown up five minutes ago?"

"I am Emperor Zhao," he said with a regal bow. He walked over to them calmly, bared his fangs, and made an incision in his pinky finger. He held his hand in front of Doug and tipped his head. "If you would allow me? It will heal her swiftly."

Doug glanced at her, looking for reassurance, but all she could manage was a weak smile. Olivia had heard tales of the emperor's charity and kindness, but some thought it as much of a legend as the bloodmate stories. He gave the emperor a curt nod and watched as he held his finger over Olivia's mouth.

The rich, decadent scent of his ancient blood filled her nostrils, and she opened her mouth like a baby bird. As soon as the first, fertile drop landed on her tongue, his age-old power surged through her body like an electrical current. Icy-hot sensations flickered through her system as he healed her. Within seconds, the deep wounds on her throat closed, and she was rejuvenated.

"Thank God," Doug whispered as he rained kisses over her face and hugged her.

"Actually, it's Zhao," the emperor quipped.

"Thank you, Emperor Zhao." Olivia placed her hand

on Doug's shoulder as he put her down, and she once again stood on her own two feet. She bowed her head in gratitude but remained in Doug's comforting embrace. "And thank you for helping my coven. Forgive me for asking—how did you even know about this or where we were?"

"My cousin, Jerry, informed me of what was happening." He smoothed his red tie and glanced over his shoulder at the flurry of activity behind him. "He said you spared him in spite of the fact that he betrayed your trust."

"Jerry, huh?" Doug gave Olivia a sidelong glance. "He's quite a *character*."

"Yes," Zhao mused. "Every family has at least *one*, even us vampires. Speaking of family, we will see your coven is brought to full recovery, Olivia. It's the least I can do for the two sentries who put down this rogue coven and stopped what could have become a slaughter of this great city."

"If there's anything I can do to repay you—" Doug said as he pulled Olivia against him and kissed the top of her head. "I can't thank you enough for helping Liv."

"Yes." He flicked his dark eyes back to Olivia. "Actually, there is something. Detective Paxton, you and Olivia are going to be my new Czars of New York."

Chapter 17

Doug looked the massive vampire up and down, trying to figure out if he heard that correctly. The emperor exuded power and radiated authority, which was partially due to his physical size; the man had to be six foot four, and beneath his expensive navy suit, he looked like he was in incredible shape. His air of sovereignty and control went beyond the physical, and if Doug had to guess, Zhao was even older than Augustus and Brutus.

He had a head of thick, jet-black hair and sharp, dark eyes that didn't waver from Doug and Olivia. Doug held her tighter as he surveyed the heavily armed military escort Zhao had with him and noted that both of the girls and Damien were loaded onto stretchers and had blood drips hooked up. Looking at Olivia, there was no denying that this Zhao guy had an ancient vampire whammy cure in his blood.

"I'm sorry." Doug shook his head, not sure if he just heard what he heard. "Did you say you want to make us the new Czars of New York? I can't imagine Augustus will take kindly to that."

"Augustus is dead," Zhao said flatly. "As are his senators. I will not tolerate weakness or inconsistencies in the Presidium. Our race has survived for several millennia as a result of clear and thoughtful leadership. Allowing men like Augustus and Brutus to run free would be our undoing."

He raised one hand and two soldiers came directly to his side.

"Take the wounded to the Presidium offices, and see they are tended to. The human must be turned." He flicked a sorrowful gaze to Olivia. "You have already turned two new vampires this year, so I would have your progeny, Pete Castro, be his maker. I realize this human is important to you, and we will assure his transition is smooth. Also, the one that Brutus turned will need healing blood to assure her turn is successful. As you can see, they are receiving healing nourishment. However, the turn will be done at the Presidium."

Doug watched as the soldiers took her family out of the club through Olivia's office. He turned his attention back to Zhao, who stood ramrod straight with his hands folded in front of him. He looked like a politician but without the bullshit. He strode to the center of the dance floor and looked around, appraising the space. Doug and Olivia followed him as he continued to speak.

"New vampires should be made only with great thought and consideration. Becoming immortal is a privilege and should be given as a gift, not used as a virus to annihilate the world. Augustus was aware of what his son, Brutus, was up to, and that kind of enabling is dangerous and unacceptable."

"Not to sound like an ingrate," Doug began, "but why would you come here and deal with this yourself? Why not just send the hit squad?"

Zhao clasped his hands behind his back and nodded. "I must take blame for this mess. I permitted Augustus to forgo the execution of Brutus when he created the rogue nightmare in Las Vegas. Olivia disagreed, but to her credit, she followed the orders she was given." He took her hands in his and kissed them regally. "I should have listened to you, Olivia."

Olivia looked as surprised at the gesture as Doug did. "Thank you, Emperor Zhao."

"The two of you will take over New York City and the rest of the northeastern territory as of tomorrow." He held up one hand to silence them before they could ask anything else. "I am making you co-czars for three reasons. First, Olivia has the required experience as a sentry and the wisdom that comes with it. Second, Detective Paxton, in addition to your experience in law enforcement, you have proven yourself to be loyal to our people and have adapted to becoming vampire in a remarkably short amount of time, which is likely a result of your angel bloodline."

A smile cracked Zhao's face, but Doug and Olivia looked at the emperor as though he'd stripped naked and done a jig.

"What did you say?" Doug looked at Zhao as though he'd lost his mind. "Angel bloodline?"

"Yes," Zhao said with a faint smile. "You have angel blood in your lineage, and it is that unique heritage that has allowed you to transition seamlessly into our world. It is what kept you from being glamoured during your first human life with Olivia all those years ago."

"Angels?" Olivia said with genuine wonder as she linked her arm around Doug's waist. "I don't mean to be disrespectful, emperor, but are you sure? I mean, how do you know that?"

Emperor Zhao threw his head back and laughed heartily.

"Have you not studied our origins, Olivia?" His eyes crinkled at the corners. "The first vampire was a fallen angel, cast from heaven when he swore that man would love *him* more than God himself." Zhao turned his dark eyes to Doug. "He gave some humans eternal life and allowed them to drink from the immortal blood of an angel, but as with many privileges, the gift has changed over time."

Sadness washed over him, but he straightened his broad shoulders and continued.

"The blood of our forefathers, the blood of our very origins, runs in your veins, Detective Paxton. Who better to watch over one of the greatest cities in the world?"

Doug and Olivia clung to one another.

"I'm no angel," Doug said on a laugh.

"Perhaps not, but your ancestor was," Emperor Zhao said with a knowing grin.

"This is nuts. How the hell can you even know that?"

"You have an aura around you, a pale blue light, which is a dead giveaway to your heritage." He turned to Olivia. "Your progeny, Pete—his demon blood gives his light an amber hue."

"A light?" Olivia looked at Doug and shrugged. "I don't see it."

"You're far too young, my dear." His smile faded. "Augustus saw it, which was why he was so quick to agree to take your life in exchange for Maya's. As bloodmates and daywalkers, you will have more freedom to manage the territory and maintain control over this part of the realm."

"But." Olivia's eyes widened. "We—I mean—*I* thought that you hated the idea of daywalkers and that the elders viewed us as a threat. I heard that the last time a bloodmate pair revealed themselves, they were targeted for termination."

"Not by me," Zhao said in a voice tinged with sadness. "Regrettably, some vampires do fear it, and somewhere in the rumor mill, it has been assumed that I do as well. I think I have been removed from the governing of our people for too long, and my absence was perceived as apathy, but hopefully my actions tonight will change that. I have been alone for three millennia, and that isolation is not something I would wish on anyone."

His mouth set in a thin line, and he paused. "I do not fear that you have joined as bloodmates… I envy it."

Emperor Zhao bowed. Doug and Olivia did the same. Moments later the club's house lights went out, and the strobes and lighting flickered to life.

Through the flashing lights, Doug saw a sly smile on Zhao's face. "I will expect the two of you to meet me at the Presidium offices at sundown so we can discuss your new stations." He winked. "But for now, I leave you to enjoy the day."

Then in a shimmer of red smoke, Emperor Zhao vanished into the air, leaving Doug and Olivia alone. Doug turned to Olivia and found her looking at him with a wide smile, which prompted him to do the only thing that came to mind.

Kiss her.

He captured her lips with his, tenderly at first. He intended to kiss her sweetly and cherish the fact they hadn't lost one another. However, when her soft, plump lips melded with his, and her cinnamon tongue explored eagerly, there was no holding back the flood of need that consumed him.

Lust. Relief. Passion. Love. Desire.

Olivia.

His mind touched hers as he tangled his hands in her red curls and kissed her greedily. This woman, the woman he dreamt of and longed for, was here in his arms, and no one would take her from him.

They shed their clothing, frantic to get closer and feel skin pressed against skin. Weapons clattered to the floor as their coats and ammo belts were cast aside. Olivia broke the kiss and pushed him away as she peeled her catsuit and boots from her beautiful body. She watched through heavily lidded eyes as he did the same and threw his clothes on top of hers.

She moved toward him, her pale skin glowing as the lights flickered, revealing her body in rapid-fire bursts. He reached out and took her hands in his, pulling her nakedness against his own. Her breasts crushed against his chest as she kissed him in a rush of lips, teeth, and tongues. He groaned and ran his hands down the beautiful curve of her waist as his erection pressed against her belly, and all he could think about was being inside of her.

He picked her up in one swift motion as she wrapped her legs around his waist, clinging to him and kissing him desperately. As Doug walked her to the VIP tables, his hands cupped the smooth skin of her ass, and his fingers pressed into the tender flesh. Olivia suckled his bottom lip and broke the kiss as she wiggled against him temptingly.

"I want to taste you," he murmured against her lips as he placed her on the edge of the table. "Lie back."

Olivia complied and lay with her arms stretched out over her head. Doug dropped to his knees as he wrapped his arms around her thighs and dragged her to him, trailing butterfly kisses along the quivering flesh of her inner thigh. She squirmed, eager for more, as the pounding music surrounded them.

Her musky scent filled his head as he kissed the soft flesh of her thigh and worked his way up to her hidden treasures. She bucked as his mouth found the sweet spot, and his tongue dove deep, tasting every bit that she gave. Doug groaned as her juices flowed into his mouth, and she cried out as his tongue worked the tiny bundle of nerves mercilessly. Sensing she was close to the precipice, he pulled back and kissed his way up the curve of her hip and along her rib cage.

"You have to fuck me now." Impatient, she sat up, grabbed him by the hair, and kissed him, her fangs scraping his lip and severing the last bit of resolve he had.

He lifted her knee, and she opened wider as he thrust his hips and entered her. The pleasure built, and she cried his name as he pumped into her furiously. Ecstasy flashed over him, coiling deep inside, and he knew what she needed—what *they* needed. At the peak of climax, they bared their fangs and sank into one another as the orgasm burst, and they fell into the exquisite abyss together.

Olivia walked the club surveying the dancing patrons, finally feeling as though life was back to normal. It had been over a month since the rogue attacks, and only now was she beginning to feel as though her family had recovered.

Sadie was spinning records like she always had. Holding the headphones to one ear, she beckoned Olivia with a wave.

"What's up?" Olivia said as she climbed the steps to the platform.

The only downside of being bloodmates with Doug was the inability to telepath with her coven. It made her feel as though they were vulnerable. However, since they could still telepath with each other, it gave her some peace.

"You look good." Sadie gave her a look of approval. "I told you that you just needed to get laid."

"Right," Olivia said through a laugh.

"Seriously," Sadie continued. "You look really good. I can't explain it, but ever since you hooked up with Doug…"

"Yeah, yeah. I know. You were right." Olivia gave her friend a pat on the back. "I'm going to head down to the floor and check on the VIP table. Don't forget to play that song they requested, okay?"

"You got it, boss."

Olivia descended the steps and turned her attention to the bar. Trixie and Maya were serving drinks, and their newest regular was hanging out at the bar, as he had been most Friday nights since the shit-show.

Olivia nodded to Shane, who as usual, didn't smile. The guy had only one night off a week as a sentry, and he spent it sitting at a bar, not drinking. She had a pretty good idea that he was there for Maya, but so far the guy had not made a move. Maya, of course, didn't seem to mind.

Her two newest coven members were adjusting quite

well to their new lives. Damien moved into Olivia's old apartment, and Suzie was rooming with Sadie while she adapted. Although, her transformation came with an added bonus no one expected. Suzie had a sixth sense and could see hidden traits in people sometimes. It scared her at first, but she slowly got used to it, although she wasn't great at sharing the information. She turned into a blurter and spilled info at inopportune moments.

When Olivia and Doug took over as czars, the first thing they did was turn the Presidium's main chambers into living quarters and a more traditional office setup. Their lives had taken a bizarre turn, and since they were already vampires, that was really saying something.

As Olivia checked on the folks in the VIP booths, who were nicer than Moriarty and his crew, she noticed Suzie standing off to the side of the club, by the entrance to the bathrooms. She was waving Olivia over frantically and not exactly subtly.

Olivia excused herself from the guests and went directly to Suzie. The girl's pale blue eyes were wide with wonder and a touch of fear. Her whitish blond hair fell over her forehead as she looked Olivia up and down in absolute shock.

"What's going on, Suzie?" Olivia tried not to sound annoyed, but the place was slammed, and she hated making her customers wait for drinks. "You're acting weird."

Suzie grabbed Olivia's arm and pulled her toward the office. Olivia rolled her eyes and let out an exasperated sigh through a smile as Suzie dragged her through the mass of writhing dancers. Suzie bumped the office door open with her hip and yanked Olivia inside. Hands on her hips and her patience at the breaking point, Olivia arched one eyebrow at the latest addition to the coven.

"This better be good." Van Helsing, now fully recovered, came directly to her feet and sat down with Oreo at his heels. Olivia scratched his head but kept her eyes on Suzie. "We've got a club full of people. What gives?"

Suzie pointed at Olivia's belly, and her doe-like eyes filled with wonder. "You're pregnant, Olivia."

"What?" Olivia said through a laugh. "That's ridiculous. There's no way that I could be pregnant. Vampires can't have babies."

Suzie put the empty drink tray on the desk and grabbed Olivia's hands before placing them on her belly. "Close your eyes." When Olivia didn't initially comply, Suzie stomped her foot. "Now."

"This is silly, Suzie." Olivia let out a dramatic sigh and complied. "Vampires don't get—"

White light flashed through Olivia's mind, and the image of a little girl with bright red curls and big blue eyes, eyes just like Doug's, flickered vividly. The girl was running through Washington Square Park in the bright sunshine and laughing loudly as she looked over shoulder, calling Olivia… *Mommy*.

Suzie dropped her hands as the vision faded and the room spun into focus, but Olivia, dizzy from the vision, had to sit in her chair and regain her bearings. She looked at Suzie, but before she could say anything, Suzie grabbed the tray and ran out of the office yelling, "Congratulations, boss lady."

Tears fell freely down Olivia's smiling face as she sat in the chair with her hands on her lower belly. She had been feeling strange. She felt like she was operating in a fog since the attacks at the club, but she chalked it up to recovery. Van whined and immediately placed his head in her lap, and Oreo hopped up in one swift leap.

Seconds later the door to the tunnels slid open, and Doug whisked into the room, fangs bared and gun drawn as he looked around the room wildly.

He looked so fiercely protective, she didn't know whether to kiss him or smack him. He still hadn't, and probably wouldn't ever, get past his macho nature, so she shouldn't have been surprised that he showed up. They learned early on in their mating that when one experienced strong emotions, the other was equally affected. Apparently, this little experience was no different.

"What the fuck is going on?" he said as he holstered his gun. His look quickly went from furious to concerned as he knelt at her side, squeezed Van out of the way, and brushed her hair off her tearstained face. "Olivia?" he asked quietly. "What's wrong?"

"Remember how I told you there could be other side effects of being bloodmates?" Olivia sniffled and rubbed Oreo's soft head.

"Yeah." He leaned in and kissed her lips warmly. Oreo meowed, and Doug scooped the kitten up and plopped her on the floor. "Sorry. I get first dibs on the girl." He kissed her again. "So far, I like 'em all. Hot sex. Daywalking. You and me, for eternity..."

Olivia took his hands and placed them on her belly as she held his curious gaze.

"Make that... you and me plus baby makes three."

Doug stared at her blankly and blinked as if he didn't hear what she said, and for a split second, Olivia thought he was unhappy. However, as that charming smile cracked his handsome face and his blue eyes twinkled at her, her fears were put to rest.

He captured her lips with his and gently rubbed her belly. Olivia could barely remember how lonely she was before they found each other. *I love you, Doug. For eternity.*

"Eternity," he murmured against her lips before resting his forehead on hers. "Damn, baby. It just doesn't seem long enough."

Acknowledgments

Thank you so much to everyone at Sourcebooks, but especially Deb Werksman and Cat Clyne for their editorial awesomesauce, Danielle Jackson for her publicity with pop, and the art department for beautiful, standout covers.

Thank you to my agent, Jeanne Dube, and to my beta-readers, Sheila and Jennifer. You rock!

Thank you to my husband and children for their unconditional love and support.

A shout out to my street team—Sara's Angels. I don't know if I can ever thank you all enough for the support, enthusiasm, and dedication. I appreciate you all, and this one's for you!

Last, but definitely not least, thank you to my readers. Thank you for coming along on this crazy journey.

Dream on…

Sara

In case you missed it, read on for
an excerpt from *Undone*, part of the Amoveo Legend
series by Sara Humphreys

"Humphreys's skillful storytelling is so intriguing, you'll have a hard time putting this book down."

—*RT Book Reviews* Top Pick of the Month

White light pulsed and flickered through the club in time with the gritty dance music. The crowd of writhing bodies throbbed with the unmistakable energy of lust as they clamored for a connection—any connection. Hands wandered, looks were cast, and figures melded together, almost becoming one.

Maybe living like a human wouldn't be that bad.

Marianna leaned back in the horseshoe-shaped VIP booth and watched the humans as they danced. The scene before her flickered rapidly between darkness to blinding, artificial light as the strobes flared. She observed couples as they disappeared into the crowd, losing themselves in the music, the sex in the air, and in the moment.

No conversations. Eyes closed.

No past. Bodies touching.

No future. Hips swaying.

No consequences.

Just now.

She sipped her champagne and crossed her bare legs as she witnessed the mating rituals that they participated in with relentless energy. They spent their lives looking for someone to ease the loneliness, with no idea who or what they were looking for. No predestined mate. No clan. No telepathy. No shapeshifting. No powers of visualization. Aging and eventually dying.

On second thought, living like a human was going to suck.

Marianna shuddered and took a swig of her champagne. As a pure-blooded Amoveo female from the Bear Clan, she should have found her mate by now, or he should've found her, but he hadn't. Having past her thirtieth birthday, she could already feel her Amoveo abilities waning, and if she didn't find her mate soon, they would disappear altogether, and she would have to live, for all intents and purposes, as a human.

Mateless. Powerless. Alone.

Yup, she thought, sighing heavily, it was going to suck.

The bass beat vibrated the tabletop beneath her fingers. Hayden sat next to her with his arm draped behind her, wearing his usual air of irritating arrogance. She wanted to tell him where he could stick it, but instead, opted for ignoring him as much as possible.

He hated this place—most Amoveo did because it was owned and operated by vampires—but of course, that's exactly why she came here. Up until tonight, hanging out at The Coven had been a surefire way to keep Hayden and the rest of the Amoveo out of her hair. Apparently, his desire to try and get her to mate with him overrode his innate disgust of vampires.

"I have to admit, Hayden," she said over the music. "I'm more than a little surprised that you came to The Coven tonight."

Marianna glanced at him over the rim of her glass and offered him a tight smile. She could still connect with any Amoveo telepathically, but didn't necessarily want to. She didn't care for being next to him in the booth, so the last thing she wanted to do was invite him into her head.

"You practically live here now." He drained the rest of his scotch. "Although I can't fathom why."

He didn't look at her, but leveled his dark eyes at the humans who passed by their table. Marianna noticed how hard and unforgiving his features were. Hatred and contempt oozed off him like bad cologne and stuck in her throat. She knew most women found him handsome, but she thought he was far too much of an asshole to be attractive.

Hayden was a self-entitled tool who rode his father's coattails with obnoxious ease and made no secret that he wanted her for himself. He wasn't her predestined mate, and he knew it as well as she did, but that didn't stop him from trying. Unfortunately.

"Olivia is my friend, Hayden. If I'm going to go clubbing in the city, then I may as well go someplace where I'm friends with the owner." She narrowed her eyes and struggled to keep her voice even. She didn't want to fight with him. She just wanted him to go away. "I like sitting at the VIP booth and doing a bit of people-watching."

"Your *friend*? She's a vampire," he said with contempt. "Vampires are dirty, disgusting creatures. They drink the blood of humans, which makes them no better than humans. In fact, it makes them worse and puts them far below us on the evolutionary chain. If it weren't for you, I would never step foot in a place like this."

At that moment, a young human girl with dark, heavy eye makeup sauntered by the table and gave Hayden what was surely her most seductive look. Clad in a tiny black dress, fishnets, and several tattoos, she looked like a regular here at The Coven. She ran one hand through her long dark hair and winked at Hayden as she swayed to the music.

Hayden promptly looked away and inched closer to Marianna. The girl shot him a dirty look and turned her attentions to another clubgoer who had almost as many tattoos as she did. Moments later, they were absorbed into the dancing mob.

"As for your *people-watching*," he sneered, "I could do without it. I may as well be at a farm watching pigs wallow in mud."

Your friend looks a tad uncomfortable. Olivia's voice touched her mind gently, and Marianna suppressed a grin. She scanned the club and found Olivia behind the bar with her two bartenders—both vamps. Her bright red hair made her easy to spot in the sea of black. Olivia was the owner of the club, the head of this all-female vampire coven, and one of Marianna's best friends.

He's not my friend, and you know it, but I'm thrilled that he's squirming, Marianna thought back with a smirk. *You have to come over here soon. It will annoy him and hopefully get him to leave.*

He's not bad looking, but you obviously loathe him, and you already told me he's not your mate, so why even bother? Olivia continued to make drinks and tend customers without missing a beat. *Tell him to fuck off.*

Let's just say it's politics. She gripped her champagne flute and gave a slanted glance toward Hayden. *I have no interest in picking sides in this stupid civil war that my people started. However, I'm getting tired of playing nice. Now be a good friend. Get your ass over here, and flash him your fangs.*

Olivia's laughter jingled along her mind. *Now, come on. If any of my human customers got wind of my wiles, we'd have a serious problem on our hands. I don't feel like fending off silver, crosses, garlic, and wooden stakes—that's so last millennium.*

I thought that garlic couldn't hurt vampires?

It can't, but Hollywood keeps perpetuating the myth. I really don't care for garlic, and it takes forever to get rid of the stench. She threw a wink from behind the bar. *I'll be over in a second.*

Another song erupted loudly, and the startled look on Hayden's face made Marianna want to bust out laughing. If he insisted on chasing her, then she was going to make it as uncomfortable for him as possible.

"I love this freaking song!" Marianna raised her arms in the air. "I think it's just about time to dance."

"I don't think so." He grabbed her arm and yanked her toward him, preventing her from leaving. "Aren't you almost finished with your champagne?" He shouted over the music and looked at his watch for the tenth time in as many minutes.

"Oh dear, I hope you're not leaving yet." Olivia's voice cut into their conversation, and Marianna smothered a giggle when she saw the look of surprise flicker briefly over Hayden's face.

"Hey, Olivia," Marianna said with a big smile as

she tugged her arm free of Hayden's grasp. "The club is packed tonight, so thanks again for hooking me up with the VIP booth. I would tell you that you don't always have to give me VIP status, but I'd be lying. However, as much as I adore it, I don't want to wear out my welcome."

"Anything for you, Marianna. You know that," she replied without taking her emerald green eyes off of Hayden. Olivia folded her arms over her chest, and her lips lifted at the corners. "I don't believe I've had the pleasure."

"Hayden," he bit out. He kept a neutral expression on his face, but his energy signature—the spiritual fingerprint that all Amoveo had—pulsed with nerves and fear in the air around her.

Holy shit. Marianna arched one eyebrow and touched her mind to Olivia's. *I think he's afraid of you.*

Marianna had expected him to be uncomfortable. To climb up on his high-horse of superiority and look down his nose at Olivia, but never, in a million years, did she think he was *afraid* of vampires.

Slap my ass, and call me Sally. A smile spread across Olivia's face. *This is going to be more fun than I'd hoped.*

I thought you didn't want to do anything to draw attention to yourself. Marianna rubbed her thumb along the edge of the champagne flute as she surveyed the humans who brushed by the table. Clad in her Armani suit, Olivia may as well have been wearing a sign that said, "I own this place and could buy you free drinks if I wanted to."

Don't worry. I'm just going to see how easily his

buttons are pushed. Her voice dropped low as it wafted along Marianna's mind. *Besides, I don't like the way he put his hands on you. This guy isn't just a dick; he's violent. I can see it in him as clearly as I can see his hideous taste in clothing. No man—Amoveo or otherwise—should be caught dead wearing a T-shirt like that. He looks like a* Jersey Shore *reject*.

Marianna almost spit out her mouthful of champagne on the last comment.

"Where the hell is the waitress?" Hayden flicked his cold gaze back to Olivia and slid his glass across the table. "I need another Scotch."

In a blur of inhuman speed, Olivia leaned on the table with both hands and got right in Hayden's face. "I'm sorry," she said innocently. "I couldn't hear you over the music. What did you say?"

They all knew that was bullshit. Olivia's hearing was better than any Amoveo's. Members of the Fox Clan had extremely acute hearing—the best of all ten clans—but not better than a vampire. She was just messing with Hayden, and he knew it.

"A Scotch," he seethed. "On the rocks."

"Are you sure you wouldn't like something with a little more *bite*?" Olivia's green eyes flicked down to Hayden's throat, which worked as he swallowed. "Our signature drink is very popular." Her grin broadened. "The Bloody Mary."

Hayden's lip curled in disgust, and sweat broke out on his brow. "Scotch."

"Of course." Olivia sighed and pushed herself off the table, while keeping her attention on Hayden. "I suppose there's no accounting for taste, but who am I to argue with the customer?" She flashed her fangs so quickly that Marianna almost missed it. However, based on Hayden's pasty complexion, he didn't. "I'll be right back," she said with a wink.

Hayden's energy signature calmed down as Olivia increased the distance between them and went behind the bar to collect his drink. Marianna studied him more closely and scolded herself for not seeing it before. She wondered how many other shifters were afraid of vampires like Hayden was. It made sense. Most prejudice was rooted in fear, wasn't it?

"It's time to go, Marianna." Hayden threw a wad of cash on the table. "This place is making me sick to my stomach."

"You're welcome to leave anytime you like, but I'm not going anywhere." He tried telepathy again, but she held up a mental barrier to prevent it and was certain that bothered him more than the ear-shattering music. "Besides, Olivia will be back soon with your Scotch."

"I ordered another just to get her the hell away from me. I can't abide the stench of vampires." He looked at his watch again, and she suppressed a smirk. Vampires didn't smell bad. Maybe he was smelling his own fear? "It's well after midnight, and we still haven't discussed the subject at hand."

"There's nothing left to discuss." She sighed without looking at him. "You aren't my mate, and I'm not yours, so I don't know what else there is to talk about."

"Marianna," he growled. "This isn't just about us."

She let out a short laugh and shook her head. "There is no *us*."

"You still haven't declared your allegiance to the Purists," he said, ignoring her last comment. "My father is losing patience. You are a high-ranking member of the Bear Clan and served on the Council before it dissolved. I don't understand what the holdup is." He waved at Susie, the only human waitress at the club, but she failed to see it, which increased his level of aggravation. "Since you're obviously not siding with your brother and the rest of those human-loving traitors—"

"Don't," she ground out. Marianna leveled a deadly glare at him. The space suddenly felt too small, and if she didn't get control over her emotions, she was going to shift into her Kodiak bear form and tear off his head off right there in the middle of the club. "Don't you dare say a bad word about Dante. He is *not* a traitor, and you can tell your father that I said as much." Her dark eyes narrowed. "We may be part of the same clan, Hayden, but that doesn't mean much these days, now does it?"

"Really?" Hayden let out a harsh laugh. "Your brother is mated to a half-breed freak. He and the others like him are breeding human weakness into our race." He grabbed her upper arm, pulled her close, and growled into her ear. "Your father knew this and tried to wipe them out. He's dead because of the hybrids and the other Amoveo who have the nerve to call themselves Loyalists. How can you consider soiling the Coltari name any further?"

"Stop it." Marianna squeezed her eyes shut and flinched as his fingers dug into her bicep. He was as strong as he looked. She struggled to keep from letting him know how much he was hurting her. Causing her pain would only get him off. His Scotch-tainted breath puffed along her cheek and made her want to puke. "Get your hands off me," she hissed.

"Is there a problem?" Pete's voice washed over her, providing instant relief.

Marianna opened her eyes to find him standing at their table with a lethal stare locked on Hayden. His intense eyes, the ones that made her stomach flutter every time she looked into them, were fixed on Hayden, and he looked ready to pounce. His broad-shouldered frame cut an imposing figure and towered over them with surprising authority, especially since he was only a human.

Even if he weren't dressed in that dark gray suit, he still would've stuck out like a sore thumb at the nightclub. Pete Castro was strikingly handsome in a wholesome, Midwestern way and lacked the piercings and tattoos that covered most of the patrons. At the moment, he looked just like a cop, which wasn't all that surprising, because up until a couple of years ago, that's exactly what he had been.

"Ms. Coltari?" His lips barely moved, and if it weren't for her acute hearing, she wouldn't have heard him above the pulsing music. His eyes didn't move from Hayden's face. "I think it's time to leave."

"We'll leave whenever Marianna wants to," Hayden bit out as he met Pete's stony stare. He released Marianna from his grip and slipped his arm over her shoulders with unwarranted possessiveness. "Now, why don't you be a good boy, and go back and wait in the car like you're supposed to. You're her chauffeur, so run along, and she'll let you know when *we're* ready to go." He leaned back in the booth, picked up his empty glass, and waved it at Pete. "I requested another Scotch, but that *woman* seems to have gotten lost. Find out where my drink is on your way out, would you?"

"I'm fine, Pete." Marianna mustered up a smile, but Pete continued to stare down Hayden. She rubbed her arm as she glanced back and forth between the two men. Pete didn't flinch, but his energy waves, which were remarkably thick for a human, fluttered violently around them. He was one hundred percent tuned into Hayden. One of the girls at the club could've run past him stark naked, and the guy wouldn't have flinched.

"I think we should go." He turned those piercing blue eyes on her, and her stomach did that odd fluttery thing again. He must've sensed her apprehension because his features softened, and his energy waves shifted subtly. "I'm ready to take you home whenever you've had enough." He glanced at the empty champagne bottle on the table and then back at her.

The fluttering in her stomach was swiftly replaced by a knot of anger as he gave her a scolding look. What the hell? Yet another man who felt he had the right to judge her, tell her what to do, and monitor her choices? Apparently, Amoveo men hadn't cornered the market on being bossy and butting their noses into what doesn't concern them. Pete may be human, but he could be as alpha male and overbearing as all of the men in her clan put together.

She wondered whether he'd be this bold if he knew she could shapeshift into a bear and tear him a new one. She smirked. He was just a human, and if he knew what she was, he'd probably piss his pants.

"Really?" Marianna's eyes narrowed. She placed the

champagne flute on the table and held his gaze as she slid to the edge of her seat. She smiled as she noticed his attention instantly went to her bare legs and admittedly short hemline. "Well, I'll be the judge of that—not you. My brother hired you to be my driver… not my babysitter."

"Yeah?" he scoffed harshly. "You could've fooled me."

She rose slowly from the table and stood to meet his challenging gaze. She kept her eyes fixed firmly on his as she moved her body close, but he remained motionless. In her stilettos, she was just a few inches shorter than he was, and she noted that his heart beat faster as she closed the distance between them.

Her intent was to intimidate him and unnerve him, but something far more surprising happened.

Heat wafted from his muscular body and flowed over her erotically, which sent her heightened senses into overdrive. She took a deep breath to steady herself, but the instant his distinctly male scent filled her head—it had the exact opposite effect. Her eyes tingled, and she struggled to keep them from shifting into those of her Bear Clan. It was common for an Amoveo's eyes to shift into the eyes of their clan animal during moments of extreme emotion. Like lust. Red-hot, fuck-me-blind kind of lust.

Right now, Marianna was more turned on than she had ever been before. It was as though he was tuned directly into her energy, her soul, and her body. Suddenly and inexplicably, she was connected to this man—*this human*—more than she had been to any other creature she'd encountered.

For a second, she forgot where she was—where they were—and she had the ridiculous urge to kiss him.

Forget that Hayden was sitting right next to them and would flip his lid—nothing mattered but the man standing in front of her and how he made her feel.

Her eyes wandered over the hard planes and angles of his face, his strong jawline with late-night stubble, the high cheekbones, and strong dark brows that framed those ice-blue eyes flawlessly. It seemed for a moment as if they were the only two people in the entire place.

All she could see was him.

Her body moved to the music, subtly at first, and willed her toward him almost imperceptibly. She inched nearer, until their lips were just a breath apart… and then she heard him.

What in the hell is this woman doing to me?

Marianna blinked, breaking the spell as the rest of the club and the crowd came roaring into focus. She stepped back as if he'd slapped her—and in a way he had. She'd heard his voice in her mind, which made absolutely no sense. Not only had she been actively shielding her mind to keep Hayden out of it—but Pete was human, and there was *no way* she should've heard him like that.

"I—I want to dance." Her confused eyes searched his equally befuddled ones as she backed away toward the dancing mob. "This is a nightclub after all," she shouted. Marianna strutted into the writhing crowd, hoping that neither Pete nor Hayden was aware of how rattled she was.

She threw her hands up and swayed to the beat amid the sea of bodies, but kept her sights fixed on Pete. A handsome, young human male sidled up behind her and began to bump and grind to the pulsating tune. Marianna danced with him as though she didn't have a care in the world, a facade she prayed that both Hayden and Pete would buy.

Pete glowered from his spot by the table as she dirty-danced with the stranger. Then he said something to Hayden, and he stalked out. Marianna watched him go and wondered if he even knew what he'd done. She'd heard his deep, gravelly voice in her mind, and he'd touched her in a way that only one person on the planet could… her mate.

Unleashed

by Sara Humphreys

What if you suddenly discovered your own powers were beyond anything you'd ever imagined…

Samantha Logan's childhood home had always been a haven, but everything changed while she was away. She has a gorgeous new neighbor, Malcolm, who introduces her to the amazing world of the dream-walking, shapeshifting Amoveo clans…but what leaves her reeling with disbelief is when he tells her she's one of them…

And shock turns to terror as Samantha falls prey to the deadly enemy determined to destroy the Amoveo, and the only chance she has to come into her true powers is to trust in Malcolm to show her the way…

Get swept away into Sara Humphreys's glorious world and breathtaking love story…

For more Sara Humphreys, visit:

www.sourcebooks.com

Untouched

by Sara Humphreys

She may appear to have it all, but inside she harbors a crippling secret…

Kerry Smithson's modeling career ensures that she will be admired from afar—which is what she wants, for human touch sparks blinding pain and mind-numbing visions.

Dante is a dream-walking shapeshifter—an Amoveo, who must find his destined mate or lose his power forever. Now that he has found Kerry, nothing could have prepared him for the challenge of keeping her safe. And it may be altogether impossible for Dante to protect his own heart when Kerry touches his soul…

Praise for the Amoveo Legend series:

"Sizzling sexual chemistry that is sure to please." —*Yankee Romance Reviewers*

"A moving tale that captures both the sweetness and passion of romance." —*Romance Junkies*, 5 blue ribbons

"A well-written, action-packed love story featuring two very strong characters." —*Romance Book Scene*, 5 hearts

For more of the Amoveo Legend series, visit:

Untamed

by Sara Humphreys

An ancient race of shapeshifters has lived secretly among humans for thousands of years… they are… the *Amoveo*

Her worst nightmare is coming true…

Layla Nickelsen has spent years hiding from her Amoveo mate and guarding a devastating secret. But Layla's worst fear is realized when the man who haunts her dreams shows up in person…

He has finally found her…

William Fleury is as stoic as they come, until he finds Layla and his feelings overwhelm him. She won't let him get close, but then an unknown enemy erupts in violence and threatens everything Layla holds dear…

"Compelling… Deft world-building and sensuous love scenes make this paranormal romantic thriller an enjoyable journey."—*Publishers Weekly*

"Humphreys's spectacular talent is on full display… You will feel as if you are entirely immersed in her world… This series is getting better with each book." —*RT Books Reviews*, 4.5

For more Sara Humphreys, visit:

www.sourcebooks.com

Flirting Under a Full Moon

by Ashlyn Chase

Never Cry Werewolf

Brandee has been dumped in every way possible, but by text is the last straw. That's it—she's officially done with men. Unfortunately, she's just been told her "soul mate" is the drool-worthy hottie all her friends call One-Night Nick.

Nick has been searching for true love for one hundred years. After all, werewolves mate for life, and he does not want to mess this up. As soon as he kisses Brandee, he knows she's the one. But how will he convince a woman who knows nothing of paranormals that she's about to be bound to a werewolf forever?

"Hot sex scenes and a breezy tone with a nice, happily-ever-after ending makes Chase's story a fun read."—*Booklist*

"It made me laugh, crafted a mystery that had me guessing, and the romance was sweet, steamy, and paranormal."—*The Romance Reviews*

For more Ashlyn Chase, visit:

www.sourcebooks.com

If you're interested in joining Sara's street team, Sara's Angels, email Sara at sara@novelromance.net, and put Sara's Angels in the subject line.

About the Author

Sara Humphreys is a graduate of Marist College, with a bachelor's degree in English literature and theater. Her initial career path after college was as a professional actress. Some of her television credits include, *A&E Biography*, *Guiding Light*, *Another World*, *As the World Turns*, and *Rescue Me*.

Sara is the president of Taney Speaker Training, which specializes in public speaking, presentation development, and communication skills. She has trained executives at Verizon, Bristol-Meyer Squibb, Westchester County, and the United States Navy. Her speaking career began with Monster's Making It Count programs, speaking in high schools and colleges around the United States to thousands of students.

Sara has been a lover of both paranormal and romance novels for years. Her sci-fi/fantasy/romance obsession began years ago with the TV series *Star Trek* and an enormous crush on Captain Kirk. That sci-fi obsession soon evolved into the love of all types of fantasy/paranormal: vampires, ghosts, werewolves, and, of course, shapeshifters. Sara is married to her college sweetheart, Will. They live just outside New York City with their four boys and two loud dogs. Life is busy but never dull.

You can find Sara online at www.sarahumphreys.com, @authorsara on Twitter, or www.facebook.com/pages/Author-Sara-Humphreys/